RIBBON OF DREAMS

Randy O'Brien

RIBBON OF DREAMS

Histria Fiction

Las Vegas ◊ London ◊ New York ◊ Palm Beach

Published in the United States of America by
Histria Books
7181 N. Hualapai Way, Ste. 130-86
Las Vegas, NV 89166 USA
HistriaBooks.com

Histria Fiction is an imprint of Histria Books. Titles published under the imprints of Histria Books are distributed in the United States and Canada by Simon & Schuster and worldwide through Unified Book Distribution. We appreciate your support of copyright by purchasing an authorized edition of this book and for respecting intellectual property laws by not reproducing, scanning, or otherwise distributing any part of it by any means without permission. You are supporting authors and enabling Histria Books to continue publishing books for everyone.

All rights reserved. No part of this book may be reprinted or reproduced or utilized in any form or by any electronic, mechanical or other means, now known or hereafter invented, including photocopying and recording, or in any information storage or retrieval system, without the permission in writing from the Publisher. No part of this book may be used or reproduced in any manner for the purpose of training artificial intelligence technologies or systems.

Certain characters in this work are historical figures, and certain events portrayed did take place. However, this is a work of fiction. Names, characters, places, and incidents are either the product of the author's imagination or are used fictitiously. Any resemblance to actual persons, living or dead, is entirely coincidental.

First Edition

Library of Congress Control Number: 2025944110

ISBN 978-1-59211-677-5 (softbound)
ISBN 978-1-59211-701-7 (eBook)

Copyright © 2026 by Randy O'Brien

Thanks to the team at Histria, Diana Livesay, Amna Majid, and the editors and designers for their support and professionalism. Thank you to my classmates from the 1972 Central High class. Go Tigers! Thanks to the Nashville Writers Alliance. Thanks to the crew at WMOT-FM —Shawn Jacobs, Gary Brown, Greg Lee Hunt, John Egly, Laura McComb, and Station Director John High — who took a big chance on me way back when. Thanks to my mother and father for their belief in me and to my sister Cindy for her continued support and love. Thanks to my daughter, Molly, for bringing light and happiness, and to my darling wife, Beth, who brings joy and laughter into my life.

Since it was in Time that he was to have met his fate, so it was in Time that his fate was to have acted; and as he waked up to the sense of no longer being young...

From *The Beast in the Jungle* by Henry James

Chapter 1

January 2, 1975

"You ain't worth killin'."

Clarence wondered if saying something like this in front of the school guidance counselor would get him in trouble. But it slipped out before he had a chance to edit himself. And it was, after all, a direct quote from Rod.

"I'm not sure what you mean," Miss Black said. She wore a thin, braided, leather headband around her hair. It could have been seen as a statement, or maybe she just wanted to look like a hippie. Clarence didn't know which and didn't feel comfortable asking her.

He looked up from staring at a smudge on the toe of his tennis shoes. His right knee bounced as he said, "My stepfather says that sometimes when somethin' happens."

Her training kicked in. "Does your stepfather hit you? Have you ever felt threatened?"

Clarence shook his head. While her words were soft and imploring, Rod's voice was more forceful. Besides, he'd heard his stepfather's words for much longer.

"Have you ever had thoughts of hurting yourself?" She asked.

Of course, he had, but he knew that saying so would start some serious shit he didn't want to fool with. "No, of course not," he lied.

And then the framed diplomas caught his eye. He read the names "Belmont College," "Vanderbilt University," a certificate of membership in "Phi Beta Kappa," and something that wasn't a diploma, "Licensed Clinical Social Worker." Her name was printed somewhere on all the pieces of paper, "Roberta Black."

As you would expect from a therapist who also doubled as the "health" teacher, the school counselor dressed conservatively, except for the headband. Her black knit dress had a high collar, and her mascara and lipstick were understated.

The "health" classes included personal hygiene and sex education, but nothing too specific. The principal wanted to keep those classes under the radar as much as possible. The counselor played her part well, believing teenagers needed information about their bodies to make decisions that could impact the rest of their lives. She didn't use film strips, language, or pictures that would draw an uptight parent's attention.

"Clarence," she continued.

"Skid, please. Everyone calls me Skid."

"All right, *Skid*."

"It's a nickname my friends gave me." He said with a smile, "Maybe I'll tell you the story someday."

"Oh, okay," the counselor said. "It has nothing to do with gym class and underwear, does it?"

"Surprisingly," Skid said. "No."

She nodded and looked up from the form she'd filled out as they talked. "I'm new here, but I want you to know I've met all the other teachers and most of the students who will need my help," she stopped, and then added, "My help with college applica..."

"I haven't made up my mind about college," he interrupted.

She tried again. "It's just that since you'll be graduating soo…"

"All right, Miss Black. I said I'll think about it," Skid interrupted again, changing his tone so the words sounded more like he was flirting. He couldn't help himself. She looked like a young Ingrid Bergman in his favorite film, *Casablanca*. Of course, she was too old for him now. She looked twenty-five, maybe even twenty-six. "Ancient" in *his* mind.

"Good," she said. "Thinking is good."

"One thing's for sure, I'm gettin' the hell out of here."

Bookcases lined the north wall of her office, but the shelves were mostly empty. Several framed pictures of whom Skid could only guess might be family members sat on an eye-level shelf. She didn't wear a wedding ring, so he assumed she wasn't married.

"I'll need a hall p..."

She had already removed a small pad and pulled a pen from behind her ear. She wrote with an exaggerated flourish at the end of the sentence as if she were conducting a symphony and had signaled to the musicians the last note.

"Here, just give it to your homeroom teach..."

"Mr. Salman," Skid interrupted.

"Yes, Mr. Salman," she said as she tore off the slip of paper and slid it across the desk.

Skid stood and picked up the note.

"My grandmother was Japanese, and when something bad happened, she always said, 'Nana korobi ya oki.'"

"And what does that mean?"

"Literally: seven falls, eight getting up," she said, smiling.

Skid thought, "So, I *am* worth killin'." But he knew that was the one thing he couldn't tell her.

The bell signaling it was time to change classrooms rang. Skid glanced up at the clock and nodded in agreement. In life, he'd found, timing was everything.

Skid stepped through the open door. He glanced at the piece of plastic with the former counselor's name still embossed in white on black.

"I hope you get a new nameplate here," he said, pointing to the door.

She nodded and pulled a notebook from under a pile of papers. "I'm workin' on it."

***

Skid shifted his books and notebook from his left arm to his right. He nodded at friends who passed him in the hallway. The floors were black linoleum tiles, and just the past summer, painters had painted the cinderblock walls above the gray lockers white. A faint smell of drying paint and disinfectant was in the air as he moved from the west end of the two-story building to the east. He smelled dust in the air. As he passed the physical science lab, he got a whiff of ozone from what he could assume was an electrical experiment.

The students dressed in the fashion of the day. It was high-waisted bell-bottom jeans with matching, long-sleeved, colorful tops for most girls. The boys wore long-sleeved shirts, some buttoned to the top, and bell-bottoms. Jackets and sweaters were deposited in lockers, indicating their rank in different sports teams. Skid didn't play sports, and while he and his mother had conferred on most of his fashion choices, now he was on his own. So matching colors and textures took on a more casual theme.

There were three competing fragrances in the air as the students passed Skid. Many boys wore English Leather or Aramis aftershave, though most were not shaving regularly. And the girl's popular choice was Jean Naté.

Skid stopped in front of his assigned locker, stuck his hand into his jeans pocket, and pulled out a ring with two keys. One was for the house, and the other was for the silver padlock guarding his books and papers.

The swirl of students surrounding him bore evidence of how overcrowded the school had become over the past decade. Battleboro grew, with dozens of new families moving into the city daily. As a result, subdivisions with hundreds of houses were popping up on the outskirts of town like weeds. The school capacity was set at one thousand students twenty years ago. Currently, over twenty-five hundred attended. The city had commissioned two new high schools to serve those subdivisions.

Politicians debated the future use of the current high school, demolishing the decades-old building or finding a new service for it. That decision would happen next semester, and Skid's concern focused on the next few months and not much else. Today. The crowd jostling you like a leaf in the wind was just part of the education experience for the last graduating class at Mid-Town High.

Skid slid his books into the locker and reached for the biology book on the top shelf. It was his favorite subject, followed by English, with Algebra coming in dead last. Nevertheless, his grades were above average, except for a "D" in math. While he managed most of his subjects easily, he was most interested in English. He loved reading and had read most of the classic novels in the library. Mr. Salman led that class, and Skid was one of his most attentive students.

He turned and bumped into Dee Dee's shoulder. She was tall with long hair parted in the middle, bell-bottom jeans, and a knit top that showed her belly when she reached up. The school dress code outlawed this kind of shirt, but Dee Dee figured out how to make it look longer around teachers.

She was in Skid's English class, and he sat one row over. They'd met in first grade and bonded like a brother and sister. Skid swore there were times when they could read each other's minds. She was a lifelong friend, and he needed all the friends he could get.

"Watch it, Skid," she said. She had "ping-ponged" into him by the rush of students passing by them.

"*You* better watch it," Skid said. He smiled, hoping his joke would land and not be an insult.

Dee Dee giggled. "*You're* the one who better watch it," she said as she playfully punched his shoulder.

"Goin' to Biology?"

"Yep, let's scoot, Skid."

They peeled off from the flow of students still trying to navigate the crowded hall and ended up next to each other in the biology lab. Frog dissection day was next week. Skid hated the thought of cutting into the tiny carcass, but he had no choice. And the smell, yikes.

Mrs. Jenkins entered the lab in a long, white cotton coat and placed her briefcase on the desk. She was Skid's second Black teacher in his twelve years of education. She stood around five feet tall and sported an upswept hairstyle. She wore little makeup, but her eyes, her best feature, emitted warmth and kindness. She understood when he turned in papers and assignments late and always gave him extra time. "You've got a lot on your plate now, Skid. I want you to know that I'll work with you. I want you to do well."

The lab had ten black marble-topped tables with two students assigned to each one. Mrs. Jenkins glanced around the room, nodded to both the left and right, and picked up a stick of chalk.

"D-N-A," she said as she wrote. "First discovered by Swiss researcher Friedrich Miescher in 1869. Recently described by James Watson and Francis Crick as a double helix. Can anyone tell me what that is?"

Dee Dee didn't raise her hand, and neither did Skid. He'd failed to read the assignment. It was one of those nights, but I didn't know why she would shy away from answering. Dee Dee was the smartest kid in the class.

Jacob French, thin and Black with a puff of an Afro, answered without Mrs. Jenkins calling on him. "Deoxyribonucleic acid presents itself as a spiral of information that determines living beings' character and physical traits."

"That sounds like the definition in the book, Jacob," Mrs. Jenkins said, "break it down for me a bit more."

"Well," Jacob began, "all molecules have different information, and that's what makes my eyes brown and your eyes green."

"True. What else does D-N-A determine? Skid?"

His mind had wandered a bit during the discussion. He finally put together the scientific fact that people's skin color was determined by their genetic makeup. "I'm not sure what you're going after."

"Can D-N-A determine more than just physical traits?" The teacher asked.

Skid paused and said, "I think it can be seen in physical *and* mental traits."

"And what makes you say that?" Mrs. Jenkins asked.

Because, he thought for a moment, my mother had green eyes, and so do I. Also, my mother was right-handed, and I am too. Before he had a chance to speak.

"Can you roll your tongue?" The teacher asked. She stuck out her tongue and rolled it into a red tube.

Skid stuck out his tongue and mimicked the teacher. "Yep, sure can," came out weird and juicy.

"That ability is just one kind of character trait passed down from generation to generation."

Skid nodded and said, "I get it."

Mrs. Jenkins turned back to the chalkboard and drew the DNA double helix.

Skid glanced at Jacob as he took notes. He'd never noticed just how pale his hands' palms were compared to his dark arms and face.

Dee Dee put her pencil behind her ear and whispered, "Hey, do you think the frog we're going to cut up could roll his tongue?"

Skid took a deep breath and looked down at his notebook to avoid laughing. He considered thinking about something sad, like his mother's death. But instead, he just scraped his thumb's cuticle with his forefinger.

Chapter 2

Both girls wore bell-bottom jeans and tank tops, but the taller one had a ring of daisies in her hair. They walked up the gravel road and failed to look up as Clarence, not called Skid yet, let off the brake and turned the handlebars.

"Look out," he yelled as he pushed the girl with the daisies out of the way, saving her from falling and suffering cuts and bruises on the rocky road.

But, immediately, because of the steep road angle, he took off like a rocket.

"Oh, Lord," he muttered.

Clarence wondered what his good deed might cost him. He realized he had two choices. Hit the brakes and possibly flip the bike or ride it all the way down, hoping he'd make it to the bottom of Tiger Hill without crashing.

It wasn't a mountain but the highest elevation in the county. It was impossible to ride a bike up the hill. Everyone had to walk their bikes up the road, mostly two hardened strips of gray gravel. Some cars couldn't do the climb. No one in their right mind would ride down on a bicycle without brakes.

Clarence, still not Skid, saw the driveway entrance to the rustic cottage where the only people who lived full-time on the hill were. A fleeting thought, *what would it be like to drive up and down this hill every day? What would you do if the road were iced over?*

And then the notion slipped from his mind, and he focused on the narrow ribbon of dust leading down the hillside. He was riding a simple, gold and white Roadmaster. And there were no hand brakes, only a rear-wheel brake that engaged when you stepped back on the pedals.

The thought, *this is how I'll die. Oh, Lord. I don't want to die,* slid into the back of his mind. "No, I need to focus," he muttered to no one who could hear him.

Somehow, time slowed, but he continued racing down the hill. It was a paradox that he hoped he'd have an opportunity to think about one day if he lived.

There were four adventurers that day, three boys and Dee Dee. Clarence had decided this was the day they'd walk their bikes up the hill and explore the fire tower. They'd talked about it for weeks, and this bright, sunny Spring Day with a clear blue sky seemed the perfect opportunity to see how far they could see. Forest Rangers manned the post when the mountain's trees and brush became dry and combustible. But today, Clarence believed no one would be in the little cabin on top of the metal structure. As a result, the group would have access to the best viewpoint.

It was Friday afternoon, and this was their first taste of freedom each weekend brought. They were rising Seniors and knew the subjects would get harder until they eventually graduated. Then, they would have all the freedom anyone could want.

They walked their bikes up the hill and down the small valley leading to the tower two-by-two, with Dee Dee slightly behind Eddie, bringing up the rear. She was always welcome to join the rowdy group. Still, she rarely added to the conversations or observations of the budding men. Instead, she saved most of her comments for Clarence. They shared more common interests and the same warped sense of humor.

As their mother used to say, Eddie and Monte were Irish twins only ten months apart. They looked nearly identical when they smiled. Both had dark blond hair, freckles, and high cheekbones.

"How much further?" Eddie asked.

With his chin, Clarence pointed to the top of the mountain and said, "It's right up there. You'll see it in a second."

They turned a corner and saw the parking pad and short sidewalk at the bottom of the fire tower. Clarence smiled and jumped on his bike, coasting the last hundred yards.

The climb to the top, or at least to just below the observation deck floor, took two minutes, what with the yelling and jostling on every landing. The boys ignored Dee Dee's scolding.

Clarence tapped the trap door on the top step, hoping someone would answer. After waiting a moment, he pushed against the flap, which didn't budge. "Dang it."

Dee Dee pointed to a lock embedded in the wood panel. "Not gonna happen."

"Maybe we could pick it," Eddie said.

"Go ahead," Monte said.

"I don't know how," The younger brother muttered.

"And there it is," Eddie said, smiling.

"Maybe they'll be a Ranger up here later this summer during the dry season," Dee Dee said. She scanned the vista and pointed out the local airport. "I can see my daddy's plane." Her father had flown jets in Vietnam and now worked as a flight instructor and pilot at the Battleboro Municipal Airfield.

Eddie pushed close to Dee Dee and shielded his eyes with his hand. "Oh, yeah, I see it, too."

Monte looked down at the concrete parking pad. "Do ya' think the bikes are okay down there?"

Clarence said, "Nobody's gonna bother them."

"Oh, okay," Monte said. "It's just that my momma gave it to me for my birthday."

"We were all at the party," Skid said.

"I know. It's just that if somebody takes it, there goes my freedom."

"That's a bit dramatic," Dee Dee observed.

It only took a few minutes of the boredom of looking at the scenery for the group to begin their way back down the steps. Dee Dee led this time, and Clarence brought up the rear.

They mounted their wheeled steeds and coasted down the hill. Clarence shot his long legs to each side and laughed. "I'm flyin'," he shouted.

They had to walk their bikes up the less steep side of the hill before reaching the pinnacle and looking down the almost vertical road. Clarence led this time. He set his cap and clutched his handlebar grips. He saw the girls with their handfuls of picked flowers and considered trying to talk to them. He needed a date for the upcoming dance, and the tall one was cute. He liked the ring of flowers she'd fashioned into a headband. He smiled and doffed the edge of his cap. Then he realized he was headed right for her and that she'd fall and probably tumble down the hill if he didn't push her out of the way. He immediately lost control of the bike and reached optimum velocity in seconds.

In his mind, everything slowed. He glanced to his left and saw the cedar and pine trees become an undifferentiated blur. The branches and needles became mere suggestions of green. He took a deep breath, believing it might be his last, and opened his eyes wide. He looked to his right and saw two huge boulders. He wondered why they were there and how they hadn't rolled down such a steep hill long ago. What stopped them, and what was keeping them there?

He knew a slip, a slide, or any application of the brakes might cause him to lose control and suffer injury or even death. So, he prayed, "Oh, Lord. I need your help."

He looked down and realized he couldn't see the bottom of the road. The steep angle was so vertical that a small portion of the hill jutted out even farther before dropping the last three hundred feet. He said another little prayer as he approached, "Oh, Lord, forgive me."

The bike's front wheel spun so fast the silver spokes were invisible as he glanced down, approached the cliff's edge, and felt cooler air on his face. There was an updraft, and he considered putting his arms out for a second so he could fly. But instead, he kept his hands on the handlebar grips and guided the front wheel down the gray, sandy pathway.

Clarence glanced up for a moment and noticed the bright, blue sky. He considered how it might be the last sky he would ever see. He wondered what death would feel like. Would he land on his head and die from the concussion? Would he land on his back and die slowly from internal bleeding? Would he land on his side and feel the bones in his arms and legs bend and break from the fall?

Suddenly, without thinking, he yelled, "Wha whoooooo!"

He felt free.

He yelled again, only this time even louder, "Wha whooooooo!"

Clarence had no idea how fast he was going, but he knew it was fast because he reached the bottom of the hill in what seemed only seconds. He tapped the brake and laid the bike down. He left a dusty trail and felt the heat build on the back of his jeans. He lay there for a moment and looked up at the sky. He realized he'd been holding his breath for the final plunge, and the air felt cool and fresh in his nose.

The rest of the group walked their bikes down the steepest part of the hill and rode the last fifty feet or so to meet him.

"Why did you do that?" Dee Dee yelled.

"I didn't do it on purpose," Clarence muttered. He stood up and brushed the back of his jeans. Gray dust floated around his butt, and he noticed a small hole at his left knee in the cloth.

"That was so cool," Monte said. He brushed a sprig of hair back from his forehead. It was a blond lock that curled and, at times, embarrassed him because he believed it made him look too feminine. It didn't. In fact, he was the most handsome of all the boys in the group.

Dee Dee pulled her bike next to Clarence's. She smacked him hard on the shoulder. "What were you thinking?"

"Ouch," Clarence said, rubbing his shoulder. "I was thinking that if I hit the brakes, I'd flip over, and that would be all she wrote."

Eddie skidded to a stop. "That was the coolest thing I've ever seen."

"And if he'd gotten hurt?" Dee Dee asked.

"Not as cool," Eddie said, his gaze dipped to his bike pedals, "but still....."

She turned to Clarence and said, "If you'd flipped, there wouldn't be nothin' left of you but a hundred-foot skid mark."

"Skid," Eddie said and laughed. "Yeah." He would make sure the nickname stuck.

The group turned right and headed back to Clarence's house. Then, finally, it was time for dinner, and Rod had promised the gang burgers and hot dogs from his recently purchased Weber grill.

Chapter 3

Skid was White, and no one had clued him in on the plan for the protest.

It began as just another day in American History class. But, when all the Black students stood up as if on cue and marched out of the room, he knew something was happening.

The bell alerting everyone it was time to change classes hadn't rung. So, a curious hush fell over the room when this group of students left.

Skid looked at his friend Eddie, who sat before him, and mouthed, "What's goin' on?"

He shook his head, letting Skid know he was also clueless.

The bell rang, but no one in history class moved.

Skid assumed the White students in other classrooms must have picked up their books and gone to their next class. He could hear the squeaking and scraping of their shoes in the hallway as they passed the open door.

Skid took a deep breath. Should he join them? He supported voting rights and equal opportunity. He'd read about the lunch counter protests in Nashville and how Selma, Alabama, marchers had been beaten on the Edmund Pettus Bridge. He remembered the coverage on television and how horrified he and his mother were. Rod wasn't in the picture then, so there was no way of knowing his opinion.

He knew a walk-out would get attention from the local media. But, on the other hand, did Skid want to be one of the few Whites joining them?

He wasn't sure of the protester's grievance. Deep down, he didn't feel he could justify joining when he knew his skin color might detract from the effectiveness of the protest. But what must it be like for people to judge you because of how you looked when you were born, your DNA? Skid had never felt those stares or heard the racist words each demonstrator had heard at some time in their young lives.

The classroom windows folded in, and Skid and the students left behind could hear movement outside. They rushed to the window, joined by the teacher. Hundreds of protesters were sitting on the grass in front of the school.

"History in the making," Mr. Lewis whispered.

"How so?" Skid asked.

"I marched in downtown Nashville when the lunch counter protests started." Mr. Lewis said, pulling back a dangling part of his near-shoulder-length hair. There was a small, circular scar on his scalp. "I caught a Billy club to the head. I was out for six hours."

"Dang. Does anybody know what they want?" Skid asked.

Chris sat behind Skid in class, confusing the instructor and one student teacher. They both had black, slicked-down, parted on the left hair, and wore similar clothes, bell-bottom jeans, and white, long-sleeved shirts. They would sometimes switch seats just to mess with the adults.

Skid and Chris had become friends and bonded over a shared fandom of the TV show *Kung Fu* starring David Carradine. They would call each other "grasshopper," like the kick-ass priest in the show.

Chris put his hand on the handle that locked the folding window. "I heard they want a Black speaker at commencement and more Black majorettes."

"Do you mean we replace the White ones we have now or just add some more?" Skid asked.

"I'm not sure," Chris said.

The idea of non-violent protests had fascinated Skid since Mr. Lewis's talk about the March on Washington led by Dr. Martin Luther King, Jr. He'd related to the words of challenge and hope delivered on that day. But he knew some people felt threatened by the speech.

"Who's leading the protest?" Skid asked.

Chris pointed out the window, "Looks like Leon is talkin' with the principal."

A VW van pulled up across the street from the school, and a man wearing headphones and carrying a small, shining box strode across the sidewalk. He looked to be in his mid-twenties and was already losing his hair. The headphones cut a swath across the top of his head. He wore a white shirt, a green tie, black pants, and black sneakers. The remote transmitter's weight forced him to lean to the right.

The principal waved to the reporter, indicating he should leave the grounds, but the young man kept coming. He talked as he walked and stopped before Leon and the principal. The student continued to sit with his arms and legs crossed, looking up at the authority figure.

Skid couldn't make out what they were saying, but it was clear the principal was upset. Despite the moderate temperature, his face glowed red, and sweat circles were under his arms.

When the reporter finished talking with the principal, he pointed the microphone toward Leon. The principal pushed the microphone away from Leon, but the reporter moved it back.

The newsperson nodded along with Leon's statements and smiled as the student sat beside the other protesters. He spoke for a bit longer and flipped a switch on top of the silver box. Then, he turned and walked back to his van just as another car, this time with the local newspaper's logo on the side, slid to a stop.

The reporters approached each other but didn't stop walking. The newspaper reporter wore almost the same outfit as the radio reporter, a white shirt, black slacks, and black shoes. Still, unlike the radio reporter, she wore a yellow scarf. She'd pulled her black hair into a bun and carried a large purse. The young woman stepped around the seated protesters and found the principal. He raised his hands as if to say no comment but relented as the newspaper reporter kept talking.

Leon stood and looked over the reporter's shoulder as she took notes. She waved at him to sit, but he continued standing. Eventually, she turned from the principal to Leon. He briefly talked to her, but she didn't take notes. Instead, she frowned as Leon spoke and shifted her weight from one foot to the other.

The reporter whipped a small camera from her bag and motioned to the two men to stand closer together. Leon crossed his arms and scowled at the lens. The principal jutted out his chin and matched Leon's glare. The camera flashed despite plenty of light from the morning sky.

"She's wearing the school colors," Chris said.

"Why didn't I notice that?" Skid asked.

"Because you're an idiot."

"Hey," Skid took offense.

"Just kidding, grasshopper."

The reporter walked through the seated protesters and opened her car door. She slid under the steering wheel, took one last look at the students, and cranked the car engine.

Mr. Lewis let the metal window shades snap back into place. Then, he turned around and walked to his desk. He wore jeans, a blue work shirt, and sandals. Of course, it was still too cool in the morning for this footwear, but Skid admired the teacher's commitment to the belief spring was coming.

"And that's that," Mr. Lewis said. "Everyone, get to your next class."

***

The school intercom constantly interrupted classes for the next two hours. "Juliet Johns, come to the principal's office," the disembodied voice of the Vice-Principal echoed through the rooms and down the empty hallways.

One after another, announcements disrupted the school's quiet until, "Clarence Bekins, come to the principal's office."

Chris touched him on the shoulder, saying, "Call me later and let me know what's going on."

They were in Algebra class, and Skid was glad he didn't have to sit through another lecture. The teacher wasn't the problem. He had a hard time focusing on the numbers on the board; sometimes, when he'd write notes, the numbers would be backward.

Skid nodded to the teachers and gathered his books. He glanced over his shoulder as he left the room, somehow intuiting his world would be different when he returned.

Rod stood in the foyer of the main entrance next to the Vice-Principal. He wore greasy coveralls and a black baseball cap. His real name was Peter, but he'd picked up the nickname "Ramrod" while driving short-turn racetracks in his youth.

His blackened hands moved as he spoke, and he laughed and touched the Vice-Principal's shoulder as he finished what Skid would guess was a joke. Skid saw the V-P flinch as he felt Rod's dirty fingers smudge his shirt.

"Have you got all your stuff?" Rod asked Skid.

The boy nodded. "What's goin' on?"

"I'm bustin' you outta here. I promised your mother I'd keep you from gettin' killed."

Skid turned his head and smiled. He'd never told Rod about his near-death experience riding his bicycle down Tiger Hill with no brakes last fall. Instead, he wondered what Rod would have had to say.

The Vice-Principal saw Skid's smile and laughed along with the boy, but his voice had a nervous treble. Then, he waved at Skid as a cue to leave his office and the school.

"But don't I need to file the paperwork..." Skid said.

"It's been a crazy day," the V-P said. "Just go." And he waved at Skid and Rod as if to say, "I wish I could join you."

***

"Where'd you get this one?" Skid asked.

Rod shifted gears with the stick on the steering column. They drove out of town toward the small farm he'd co-owned with his wife. A big barn was on the property, and Rod had converted the space into a car restoration shop.

"I'm going to use it for parts," Rod said. He patted the ripped seat covers and looked through a windshield clouded by age and weather.

"It's a '42, isn't it?" Skid asked. He'd been around Rod and the business so long that he'd learned about everything there was to know about internal combustion engines, makes models, and options.

Collectors and hot rodders like the 1942 Chevrolet for its solid lines and high-performance engines. Rod restored, chopped, and channeled dozens over the years. He liked American cars but became known in the car enthusiast community as the "go-to" mechanic and body man for any American or Foreign collectible.

"Right. You're really gettin' it. You'll be a fine mechanic someday. You could join the Army like I did and learn on the motor pool, transport, and armored vehicles, or work with me," Rod said and eased up on the accelerator as they approached a curve in the two-lane.

"Yeah, sure." It was sometimes easier to agree with Rod instead of arguing constantly. He liked the cars after being cleaned up and ready for service, but he didn't pick up the dirt and the oily grime of the vehicles that came into the shop. In truth, he didn't find the projects interesting. So, Skid had eliminated the possibility of working in the garage long ago.

"This one's got some problems," Skid said. He fingered the rusted window handle and scuffed his foot against the floorboard.

"Be careful there." Rod said, smiling, "Pull up that mat."

Skid listened and guessed the problem before lifting the rubber and carpet mat. The road surface, wet from the early morning rain, raced below the car. He lifted his feet and placed them on the part of the still intact floor. "I see now why it's not worth fixin'."

"Parts of the engine and tranny are still good."

"Say," Skid said. He raised his voice slightly over the sound of the road surface and the engine. "Why did you come get me?"

"I was afraid the local yokels were gonna bring in the National Guard to control those niggers, and I didn't want you to get hurt."

Skid nodded. He'd heard Rod's comments on how the country was out of control and the government needed to crack down on all the war protesters, bombers, and especially Civil Rights activists. "Thanks," Skid said, "I guess."

"Whataya mean? You don't think they'll go in there and crack some heads?"

"I didn't see it as a violent protest," Skid said over the failed exhaust system and ambient road noise.

"Whata *you* know. You're just a kid," Rod said as he shifted from second gear to third. "You don't know anything."

Chapter 4

After finishing his homework, Skid's job was to inventory all the parts and supplies delivered daily at Rod's shop. Many came from local junkyards, while some boxes had labels from France, England, and Italy. Rod's clientele not only included drag racers but there were also several restoration projects he'd taken on for collectors. Skid checked on a note from a customer named Larry Cox about dropping off a Mercedes. He put the message on Rod's desk. Business as usual.

When he left school early because of the protest, he found two boxes marked Ferrari and one with a return address in Iowa. He opened the boxes and noted where they were from, their use in which car, and the date on the inventory book. He and Rod had learned long ago that collectors and race car enthusiasts were impatient. Keeping good records of each car's progress was essential for their happiness.

"You logged in all the boxes?" Rod asked. He'd just walked into the small office at the north corner of the enormous building.

"Don't I always," Skid said. He was chewing the end of a pencil and didn't appreciate Rod asking him if he was doing his job.

"You've forgotten in the past. You're only human. Besides, with all that goin' on today, it would have been easy to make a mistake."

"Thanks for your concern," Skid said in a snarky tone.

"I'm gonna let that one by. But, hey, you're a smart kid. It's good to know you wouldn't get involved in anything like that."

Skid considered this. He'd been against the Vietnam War and was glad the draft had ended. He didn't believe himself Army material like Rod was. He didn't have to go to Southeast Asia. Still, Rod's tour included Italy and Germany, hence his expertise in repairing and restoring vintage European cars.

"You'd be a good soldier," Rod said, anticipating the younger man's thinking.

Skid looked down at the parts and shipping log and realized he'd doodled a US flag in a margin. But he hadn't connected serving in the military with the flag.

Instead, he thought about all the people who'd marched and died for their Civil Rights. And his classmates, who organized a sit-in to air their grievances.

"The protest today. Chris said it was about Black people being represented in the school graduation and the band."

"Whining crybabies," Rod said as he picked up a Ferrari carburetor. He turned the device over in his hands, looking for flaws. "They don't realize just how good they got it."

"I'm glad they protested. If you don't stand up for yourself, you'll fall for anything."

Rod fingered the fuel lever and watched the chamber covers flash in the afternoon sunlight slashing through the window.

"That's a good one. Did you come up with that?" Rod asked.

"I heard it in English class."

"I guess that's true," Rod said, mustering up as much authority and wisdom in his voice as possible. "But you gotta pick your battles."

Rod tucked the carburetor under his arm and patted the back of Skid's head. This wasn't the first time this had happened. In fact, the gesture was something he'd done since he and Skid's mom first began dating. Skid had a cowlick back then in the swirl of hair at the top of his head. Initially, the pat was an attempt to bring order to the stray sprigs of black hair, but Rod had changed the act into a show of dominance and control. Skid shook his head in protest, but Rod changed the pat into a slap.

"Hey," Skid said, surprise edging into his voice.

"Know your place. That's all I'm sayin'."

Skid sighed, nodded, and returned to his parts log. "I'll finish up here and start dinner."

"Nothin' too elaborate."

He was surprised by Rod's use of the word 'elaborate.' He considered how many vocabulary choices his stepfather might have made, but he chose this one. Skid knew he loved his mother from the way he treated her. Still, he always seemed uncomfortable and over the top when choosing methods and practices when dealing with him. Was there something in the older man's mind besides engines, bodywork, and electrical wiring?

"No problem. I'm a simple cook," Skid said.

Chapter 5

When Skid returned to school the Monday after the walk-out, he sat silently in Mr. Salman's homeroom, waiting for the day to begin. He stacked his books on the desk and looked at row upon row of sad, taut faces.

The protest was big news. The story had already played on the radio several times and even made the state-wide radio network. Moreover, the newspaper article featured a black-and-white photo of Leon standing next to the principal. They looked as if they had been interrupted during a heated discussion. Still, the article made it seem the issues raised were legitimate and addressed without repercussions.

The bespectacled teacher stood at a thin podium and shuffled through class announcements. Mr. Salman hailed from Chicago and appeared to be of Asian descent. He slicked his hair with Brylcreem and always wore a white shirt and a thin black tie. His slacks had a sharp crease, and his shoes shone from what Skid believed could only come from daily attention.

There was a time when Skid used Brylcreem to help control the cowlick at the crown of his head, but as he matured, the need to use hair products daily other than shampoo lessened. However, he did remember how much he liked the smell but not the feel of it on his head. He shook his head, already sleepy and daydreaming.

The brown loudspeaker box over Mr. Salman's left shoulder crackled to life. It was routine to hear the principal read the announcements of the day's happenings, and most students had tuned out the noise months ago.

"The following students will make their way from homeroom and congregate in the auditorium." He read an alphabetized list, and Skid's ears perked up when he heard his name.

He looked over his shoulder and mouthed the words to Chris. "Did he say my name?"

Chris nodded and took a deep breath. It was never good to hear your name announced during the morning update.

Skid sorted his books and slid them off the edge of his desk. He left the room without looking back. There was an ominous tone to the principal's reading of the names. This was the second time Skid had heard the principal call him out of class. The first time was when Rod found his mother's body in the kitchen next to the refrigerator. She was so weak from cancer that she'd fallen. It was determined later that she'd had a heart attack from what the doctor guessed was her exertion from trying to get up.

***

Skid sat and put his books at his feet. He searched the room for familiar faces. The auditorium sat five hundred with a hardwood stage and a red curtain. Today, there were probably twenty students in the audience. The principal stood at the edge of the curved proscenium.

"Have a seat, everyone," he said, directing students closer to the stage. "I don't want to have to shout."

The house PA was off, but Skid believed he was close enough to hear every word the principal would say. The school nurse tested the students every few years, and he'd never complained of pain or hearing loss. He'd attended several loud rock concerts since the last time he'd been tested but believed his hearing was still good.

The final students on the list seated themselves and stared at the stage. Skid coughed and rubbed the back of his head. His cowlick was fighting his comb this morning. He'd used hair oil to tame it.

"Last week, we had a walk-out and a sit-in with students showing their need for change in several areas of the school's policies. Those concerns are now being addressed, and the matter will soon be settled to everyone's satisfaction."

Skid had read the newspaper article detailing the protest's reason. He agreed the issues in question needed to be addressed.

"During the protests, you people took advantage of the chaos and confusion and decided to cut class." The principal said with a mix of animation and banality.

Skid knew this wasn't the case. Rod had picked him up, and glad-handing with the Vice-Principal led to what Skid could only perceive as approval for him to go.

"We have a clearly stated policy for leaving campus, and none of you followed that. So instead, you cut school, and now you're all suspended for three days. See you on Thursday."

The murmuring in the crowd grew louder. The students' faces registered shock and confusion. Wasn't there a crisis? Aren't the protest issues more critical than a petty exercise of the rules? Was this a way for the principal to reclaim the challenge to his authority?

Skid joined the chorus. "Hey, I had permission. I just didn't get the paper signed."

A student sitting in front of Skid stood and turned. He was a basketball player and a point guard and grew a neat, small mustache and goatee. "What's done is done, and there's nothing else to do."

"But it's not fair," Skid grumbled.

The principal waved his hands to quieten the students protesting their expulsion. "Your parents have been called and are waiting for you in the front parking lot." Then, he reiterated, "See you on Thursday." Then, finally, he turned and strode off the stage.

Skid gathered his books and glared at the other students in the same predicament. He'd left legally, but the principal had lumped him into the same group as the cheaters and rule-breakers.

"I'm not a-," Skid started.

"Looks like you are," the basketball team leader said.

***

Skid walked past the Vice-Principal as the young man stood in the doorway to his office. It was next door to the school counselor's room, and Skid saw Miss Black stand up from behind her desk as he walked past. The Vice-Principal stared at the boy and frowned. Then, Skid could hear him close and lock his office door.

Rod waited in the parking lot in a chopped and lowered '55 Chevy. He'd finished the first coat of paint on the top half of the car, and there were bits of tape and newspaper still stuck to the pillar around the back window.

Skid walked up to the car, opened the back door, and tossed his books into the seat. He stomped around the vehicle's front as Rod turned the key and started the engine. He was still revving the motor when Skid closed the passenger side door.

"It's not fair. You were there. How is this fair?" Skid asked. "Can't you do anything?"

"You gotta play by the rules. Whatya gonna do?" But it wasn't a question. Rod had decided he'd have three days of uninterrupted help around the shop, which was good. "We'll get a lot of work done."

"That's not the point. What about justice and respect? How is this teaching kids they should play by the rules?"

"I don't know," Rod said. He pulled up to the red light leading to the downtown square. The engine chugged and stopped. Rod turned the key and pumped the gas.

"Didn't you talk to the Vice-Principal?"

"I did," Rod said. He sucked in his bottom lip as the engine turned over. He held the gas pedal down so the motor would idle a bit higher. He would adjust it at the shop, but he'd have to get there first.

"And what did he say?"

"He said there was confusion, and when the principal asked him, he had to say you left without permission. He made it sound like it might cost him his job if he stood up to the principal on this."

"That's weak," Skid groused.

"You could protest," Rod joked, hoping to lower the temperature of Skid's anger.

"That's not funny." Didn't work.

Skid looked at his right thumb. He'd thinned the cuticle by his earlier routine of scratching at it, and now he realized he'd bitten a part of the skin around the nail, and it was bleeding.

"Do your time, no matter how unfair, and let it go," Rod said as he tickled the accelerator, and the car pulled away from the light.

Skid stopped sucking his bloody thumb and said, "Bullshit." He didn't like cursing around Rod. He knew the old man didn't appreciate it, and he'd have to pay the price by missing dessert or something.

Rod changed the gears from first to second, slapped Skid on the back of the head, and dodged a pothole.

"Ouch, hey, what's that..."

"Just keep talkin' if you want another."

Skid reached into the back seat, pulled out his spiral notebook, and turned to a blank page. He pulled a pen from his pocket and put the point on the first line. He could feel the anger, no rage, build from the back of his head, and he pressed down on the pen.

Dear Editor.

He would write a letter to the editor. But he'd write a letter to the school paper first and then to the city's newspaper.

Unfair, he wrote. *Injustice* was the next word, and the rest poured out of his pen and soul.

The pen's point scratched, flowed, bit into, and pierced the paper. Skid stuck out his tongue as he wrote, and once bit so hard he paused and looked at Rod. The stepfather stared straight ahead. The man's jaw worked on a stick of gum, and his high forehead wrinkled. Then, finally, he glanced over at Skid.

"I'll go pick up your homework tomorrow if that's what you're working on there."

"No, I mean, yeah, sure. I'm writing a letter to the editor at the Journal," Skid said. He tucked his tongue into the corner of his mouth again and finished a sentence.

"That's not a good idea."

"And why not?"

"One thing I learned in the Army was that if you break a rule, you do your time and move on."

"I'm not a soldier."

"And you're not a mechanic yet either, but when you work long enough with me, you will. But, look, I get it. There was confusion. There was chaos. You got caught up in the riptide of the thing, and there's nothin' I can do about it."

"I could make a list about all the things you can't do anythin' about," Skid said. He regretted the words as he said them and wished he could take them back.

Rod weighed at least fifty pounds more than Skid, much of which was solid muscle. Skid would drink milkshakes his mother would make to help fatten him up, but it was to no avail. A real fight between the two would be one-sided.

"I see." Rod tapped the steering wheel. A vein throbbed on the side of his forehead. "Why don't you just cool down a bit now, write your little letter, and then trash it. Believe me, you don't want to bring that kind of heat down on yourself."

They were approaching the turn to take them to the farm and Rod's shop. Skid knew when Rod was working on a car, that's where his attention would be. So, he would keep the letter going but save whatever discussion about school and homework until later. He didn't want to say anything else he might regret.

"I'll get lunch started when I get back."

Rod said, smiling, "Good boy. Of course, you could also hit the floors with that new vacuum if you get a chance. You'll have time before your TV show."

"Yes, sir," Skid garbled a bit as he chewed the end of his pen.

Chapter 6

Skid believed he had three seconds until the song's end, but he only had two. He was standing on his chair, a rickety, metal, folding variety that was easily five years older than he. The auditorium roof was shaking, or at least it felt like it, as he looked up and saw the super trooper lights sweep over the crowd.

Constance had agreed to go with him after he showed her the tickets. He knew it was her favorite band, and there might be some reciprocal affection in repayment for admission. He'd stared at her from afar for so long, finally working up the courage to talk to her and ask.

Now, Skid saw the guitarist looking at the drummer and nodding. He knew this was his chance. He grabbed her hand and pulled her toward him. She glanced at him, frowned, and put her other hand on his chest. He continued his move and closed his eyes. He was going to kiss her, and she would be his girl.

Constance shook her head. The crowd and the music were so loud he couldn't hear what she'd said. She pushed him back and looked at the stage.

The Allman Brothers Band had Nashville ties. Skid bragged he knew Greg and Duane's grandmother. He lied that she lived in his neighborhood. He would have said anything to get a chance to be close to her. He was so in love with Constance. Or maybe it was just lust. It was so hard to tell the difference at this age.

She challenged him. "How do I not know her? It's a small town."

"She keeps to herself. She's on their mother's side of the family." Again, a lie. How far would he go to gain her affection?

Skid wouldn't let his disappointment show about not getting his kiss. He'd been rebuffed and was slowly beginning to accept he and Constance would just be friends like he was with Dee Dee.

He started clapping along with the music and watched as row after row of fans sat down in their chairs. It would be a long night. The band was infamous for their hours-long shows and featured solos that could last fifteen or twenty minutes.

They'd talked in the car on the way to the show about the Allman's music. They'd listened to a cassette of "Brothers and Sisters" and found they'd both loved songs like "Ramblin' Man," "Jessica," and "Southbound." They talked about Duane, sometimes called "Skydog" and his tragic death, and how the band continued without him and still sounded like the Allman's. But losing the best lead slide guitar player in history shifted the emphasis toward Gregg and his keyboards. Dickey Betts had stepped up, but it was impossible to fill Duane's soulful playing.

Skid had taken one of Rod's shiny modified cars with his permission. While he had offered to take Constance to dinner, she declined. She was too excited.

He knew this would wear off as the night wore on, and they'd likely do a "Krystal" drive-through run back home. The tiny, square hamburgers with the steamed buns were the favorite of stoners, drunks, and music lovers late at night.

"Are you sure I can't get you anything?" Skid yelled over the rumbling bass guitar and double drum arpeggios.

She shook her head again, just like when he had tried to kiss her. He thought she didn't like him and was just using him to see her favorite band in concert.

He returned his attention to the stage, slapped his thigh, stamped his feet, and let the music inside his mind. He needed the distraction, given his recent expulsion from school. They'd discussed the situation. She believed him when he said his suspension was unjust. He didn't mention his protest letter to the paper's editor because he was still composing it. But the writing made him feel better, which was significant at this point in his life.

Skid glanced at Constance and saw that she was smiling and tapping her foot to the thundering beat. She was as tall as Skid with long legs, a flat stomach, and still-developing breasts. Her nose was a bit too big for her face, and a small bump was on the bridge. Her father had the same bump. The genetic trait made her self-conscious, but it didn't bother Skid.

She wore jeans, sneakers, a "hippie" top with long sleeves, flared cuffs, and a V-neck. A red ribbon gathered her shoulder-length hair and fashioned it into a ponytail.

Skid wore one of his three pairs of jeans, a long-sleeved T-shirt, and Converse All-Stars like most other young men at school. He'd tried out for basketball in middle school but was terrible, slow, stumbling, and couldn't shoot worth a darn.

Skid did like the spectacle of the game, though. The idea hundreds of supporters would cheer at your successes and sympathize with your losses would be a great ego builder. He understood the appeal, much like the professional musicians stalking the stage before them. And not to mention the feeling of winning. *That must really be something*, he thought.

Somewhere, deep down, he believed he would do something someday that would bring an audience to their feet. Right now, though, he just couldn't imagine what that might be.

The band was nearing the crescendo of their signature song, "Statesboro Blues," as a tiny, old woman shuffled onto the stage. Skid saw her first and pointed her out to Constance.

"That's Gregg's grandmother," he shouted with his mouth as close to her ear as possible, "I thought she might show up." But, of course, he was guessing since he'd lied about knowing the old woman. So, he crossed his fingers, hoping that his story would work.

Constance smiled at him. Her dark brown eyes crinkled at the corners, and her nose twitched. He loved that about her.

The woman wore a floral dress with a white collar and black shoes. She wobbled as she made her way through the cables and amplifiers behind Dickie and Butch and put her hand on Gregg's B-3 organ. Then, she scooted behind the organ's cabinet and touched Gregg on the shoulder. He smiled at her, and she kissed him on the cheek. She looked out over the screaming fans and waved and smiled. Then, she turned and left the stage the way she came.

"That's gotta be a once-in-a-lifetime kind of happening," Skid shouted, but not as close to Constance's ear this time.

She nodded and patted him on the shoulder, much like Grandma Allman had Gregg. Then, she stood and cheered at the old woman waving to the crowd.

"She likes the stage," Constance yelled. Skid couldn't hear clearly what she said, but he could guess.

The song ended, and the crowd went wild. They chanted "more" and "encore," knowing the band hadn't played their most requested and the ultimate rock-blues song, "Whippin' Post." The band left the stage, but the houselights remained off as the crowd cheered for more.

"This is the best," Constance said. She looked at Skid and smiled. She put her hand on the back of his neck and pulled him to her for a kiss. He closed his eyes. He felt her lips on his and smelled her Jean Naté perfume.

"No," he said, opening his eyes and smiling, "that was the best."

The Allman Brothers Band returned to the stage, and shortly after, the rumbling bass notes of "Whippin' Post" shook the roof and everyone inside.

Chapter 7

Skid didn't drive by Tiger Hill every day, but there were occasions when he would sit at the bottom and look up at the gravel road and the steep incline. "What the hell was I thinkin'?" he asked himself. "Tryin' to be a hero."

He revved the engine and considered taking the '55 Chevy that Rod had almost completed up the hill. He realized how much trouble he'd be in if he chipped the paint, broke something in the engine, or, God forbid, wrecked it. No, he'd conquer that hill again someday, but not today.

This was the day he'd decided he was ready to publish his letter in the local newspaper. He stopped by the mailbox as he pulled into the driveway.

"There, that'll set things right," he said as he closed the lid.

Skid had picked up a box of pamphlets and flyers from the printers next door to the Post Office for Preacher Jake. That's what he liked the kids to call him. Skid thought it was his attempt to "relate to the teens," so he played along, though he had a tough time bonding with someone who believed in the church and God.

Skid wanted to believe, but the Bible was confusing and contradicting from one book to the next. However, he attended because his mother had insisted, and it had become a habit. And sometimes, sitting in the pews and listening made him feel better.

Rod didn't attend, though, and thought it was a waste of time. He worshiped at St. Serta and only took time off from his work to watch pro football on Sunday. He was a Pittsburgh fan and had plenty to root for. They were the best in the business, and while the stadium was almost six hundred miles from Battleboro, it was his home team. He spent most of his tour of duty at Letterkenny Army base in Pennsylvania before being sent to Europe for the rest of his time in the service. In Rod's mind, that made him a Steelers fan.

Rod told Skid how he'd tested well and already had basic mechanic knowledge. Keeping the cars and trucks running at a base is essential for a smooth-running facility. Skid remembered he'd told him all this on their second meeting to impress him. The boy couldn't care less but tolerated the new man in his mother's life because Skid knew she was lonely after his father's death.

All this change provoked Skid to visit the parsonage to talk with Preacher Jake. However, after their session, he was still confused and depressed. Skid and his mother had fallen into a routine that served them both well. The boy wasn't sure a new man would benefit him or his mother.

Preacher Jake crossed his bell-bottom jeans and leaned forward in his office chair. He affected a kind and understanding expression and said, "I'm sure you can make a small sacrifice to your everyday habits for your mother's happiness."

Skid nodded slowly, and the preacher mirrored his gesture. He'd specialized in classes focusing on confused teenagers in his seminary. His instructors believed he had a very young-looking face and would do nicely. He'd been an associate pastor in a huge church and now independently led the local Southern Baptist church.

So much had happened so quickly, Skid explained to Preacher Jake. The school had suspended him unjustly, he'd gone to an epic concert, and a girl kissed him instead of him kissing a girl. His mind spun.

After the counseling session, Skid opened the back door and put his books on the kitchen table. His reading assignment for the night was Hamlet. Of course, he was aware of the characters and plot. Still, his English teacher's enthusiasm about the play motivated his curiosity. A young, indecisive prince weighs the decision to get revenge against his uncle, who murdered the king, Hamlet's father, to gain the throne and his brother's wife. Who wouldn't enjoy that kind of complicated plot and tortured characters?

Miss Wilson's tenure at Central High neared thirty years. She was short and wore reading glasses on the end of her nose. She dressed exclusively in black dresses and shoes. Gray shocks now streaked her once jet-black hair. She was Skid's favorite teacher, and he hung on every word.

The day's lecture involved fate versus free will. But unfortunately, while Skid listened, he failed to put together how many people in his life stood for those two philosophies.

Rod certainly believed in free will, while Skid believed Preacher Jake taught God controlled everyone and everything. Mrs. Wilson seemed to sit somewhere in the middle. Her choices for their reading assignments also took both points of view.

After reading the play that night, Skid realized Hamlet seemed fated to kill his stepfather. But what other choice did he have? He had to avenge his father's murder. It was the right thing to do. And yet, as Skid lay awake that night, he considered how Hamlet could have let the king live and found revenge in another way. Skid nodded slightly as he drifted off to sleep. But his last thought was, *wow, that Shakespeare guy, man, he was good.*

Chapter 8

Skid's first day back from suspension began with a few of his fellow students giving him the stink-eye. In contrast, others agreed with his choice to leave school illegally. No one was interested in his explanation of what happened.

He reached his locker and put two books in the bottom compartment. Then, he closed the door and turned to face Leon, the protest leader.

"That was pretty low, man."

Skid stepped back, fully expecting to be punched or slapped because of his seeming lack of support for the Black students' walk-out.

"No, no, no, it was all a mistake. My stupid stepfather got me without doing the paperwork. When they took the roll that afternoon, they put my name on the list. I support the cause."

"'Cause?" Leon said. He crossed his arms and looked down at Skid. He was at least six inches taller and forty pounds heavier. Skid knew coaches tried to recruit Leon to play football, but instead, he focused on basketball. He wasn't a violent person, but Skid wasn't sure. Who could read another man's mind?

"Yeah," Skid said as he closed his locker door. A wave of students passed behind them. Some boys looked like they were hoping for a fight and could join in or at least urge them on. The girls walked past with expressions of indifference and boredom. "I believe in equality for everyone."

"You got a funny way of showing it."

Suddenly, the idea came to Skid. "I wrote a letter to the editor explaining what happened and how I'd been wronged."

"And you think people are gonna buy that?" Leon said. The corner of his mouth twisted into a sarcastic grin. "You think you've been mistreated?"

"No, not like Black people," Skid said. "But I've been abused."

This amused Leon even more, and he put his hand over his mouth to keep the other students from seeing him laughing at Skid. When he finished, Leon said, "We've all got our crosses to bear, brother."

Leon slapped Skid on the shoulder, hiked his books under his arm, and walked down the hallway. He had the walk of a conqueror. He looked like a man who had won a battle and was on his way to winning the war.

How did he do that? Skid turned in the opposite direction and asked himself. Why can't I do that was an even more important question. Was it an athlete thing that Skid would never have because of the physical traits his parents, grandparents, and even further back had given him? Or was it something Leon had developed over his seventeen years of life?

Skid frowned and committed himself to finding out how Leon was the way he was. There had to be a book on self-confidence he could check out of the library. Miss Cardwell could help him.

"Leon, check the paper," Skid said, quickly realizing he was shouting. Several students glared at him as he nodded and smiled. "Have a good day."

Skid could see Chris and Monte as they approached him. They stepped from the stream of students. They were both smiling and pointing at him.

"Hey, hey, big man on campus," Monte said.

"I can't believe you did that. But, holy cow, that took balls, man," Chris joined in.

"No," Skid said, "it was all a mistake. I..."

"You let people know where you stood," Chris said.

"Rod came and got me. He didn't. I mean, I'm in favor of..."

Monte sidled up to Skid and whispered, "We gotta teach them, troublemakers, to stay in their place."

"That's not what happened," Skid began, but Monte cut him off.

He looked at Chris as if to say all the white students were on Skid's side. "We're proud of you."

He punched Skid on the shoulder and turned before the conversation could continue. The class bell rang, encouraging a new urgency in the student's steps.

Skid slammed his locker door and turned into the onrushing students. A clump of Black students passed, and Skid raised his fist in support. "Right on," he said, smiling and pumping his arm.

The group giggled at him as they passed.

"Dammit. There has to be some way to fix this," Skid muttered.

Chapter 9

Skid sat in the slant of light he favored in the school library. He "tromboned" the newspaper farther away, then up close. Did he need glasses?

He'd already conferred with Miss Cardwell on a self-help title and checked out *How to Win Friends and Influence People.* The librarian assured Skid it was a classic and had sold millions of copies. He put it in the middle of the textbooks in front of him.

Dee Dee sat across from him at the big, wooden table. She was working on an essay for English class. Her subject was the effect of the Vietnam War on American society.

"How do you spell 'corrosive'?"

"We're in a library. A dictionary too big to pick up is right over there," Skid said. He cut his eyes to the podium to the left of them. He snapped the newspaper to smooth out the copy as if to say, 'You're bothering me'.

Skid had already scanned the front page and the sports page. Then, finally, he stopped at the headline in the national wire story that read "State Department Bombed in Protest."

"Holy Moley," he whispered.

When Dee Dee returned from the dictionary, she carried a slip of paper and set it down next to her notebook. "Asshole," she whispered.

"C-o-r-r-o-s-i-v-e," Skid said.

"Sometimes you beat everythin'? You know that?" Dee Dee asked. It was a quote from one of their favorite TV shows, the reruns of *The Andy Griffith Show.*

"Trying to gain favor by quoting Andy won't win you any points. Besides, I won't be around forever. You're gonna need to learn to do for yourself."

"And you," she said as she gave him her middle finger, "need to screw off."

"Shhhhh," Miss Cardwell spewed at them. "You two know better."

"And the fight with *'the man'* continues," Dee Dee whispered.

"Check this," Skid began. He held the newspaper close to Dee Dee so she could see what he was about to expound on.

"What's the Weather Underground?" She asked.

"They're a protest group. They used to be called the 'Weathermen' after the Bob Dylan song, but they changed the name. I guess they didn't want Bob mad at them." He returned to the article. "It says the bomb caused extensive damage to the building, but no one was injured."

"It sounds like they got lucky," Dee Dee observed.

"Says here the bomb took out twenty offices on three different floors. So that must've been one big bomb. And another was found at a military induction office in Oakland, California."

"How much damage did *that* bomb do?"

"It was defused. Wow, that sounds like a dangerous job," Skid leaned back and looked at Miss Cardwell. She was stamping books for a freshman checking out what looked like enough reading for the rest of the year. But, in the empty air of the library, it sounded like she was setting off small firecrackers.

"All that folderol about politics. It seems a waste of time and money," Dee Dee said. She returned to her notebook and inserted the word she'd looked up in the dictionary.

"' Folderol,' nice one. I think the protesters were trying to make a point," Skid said. "I don't condone violence, but I understand people who believe the system isn't listening to them."

"You're not gonna set off any bombs, are you?" Dee Dee muttered loud enough for Skid to hear but not for Miss Cardwell.

"Naw, of course not. There are other ways of getting your point across. The walk-out the other day. That was peaceful and effective," Skid said.

"Seems like small potatoes when you compare it to bombing a building."

"It is, no doubt, but just because the stakes seem small to you and me, it's still valid if you try and walk in another person's shoes. At least, that's what my momma always said."

"Your momma was a wise woman," Dee Dee said.

Skid returned to the newspaper account. "The FBI has labeled the group a terrorist organization and is offering to work with local law enforcement agencies to apprehend the bombers."

"It sounds like they won't be walkin' about free much longer," she said.

"Once the FBI gets on the case, it's pretty much over."

He read on. "They have a manifesto calling for ending the war, racism, and other left-wing causes. 'Our intention is to disrupt the empire…to incapacitate it, to put pressure on the cracks'." That's from Prairie Fire, the group's stated purpose.' They work in small, unconnected cells to protect others in the movement."

"That's smart. If they're not in touch with other people in the group," Dee Dee surmised, "they can't tell the authorities what the others are up to. You're not thinkin' about joinin' up, are you?"

"No," he answered quickly, "but I get it. I don't wanna go to Vietnam."

"I don't know. Sometimes you look at some of them protesters and think," Dee Dee recalled another Andy-ism, "their cornbread ain't done in the middle."

"You may be right." He snapped the newspaper and folded it. He'd return it to the stand and let the next reader become informed.

"But you'd go if you got called up? The Army, I mean," Dee Dee asked.

Skid took a deep breath and frowned. "I'm not sure."

"Doubt. You know what I always say. You gotta nip it. Nip it in the bud," Dee Dee said, laughing at her performance of Barney Fife's most famous line.

Chapter 10

"We gotta live in this town, and I have a bidness," Rod said.

Skid knew better than to correct Rod's pronunciations. He'd once caught a backhand across the cheek for saying, "You mean Chicago, not Chicargo." But, for some reason, Rod always added the 'r' in the middle.

"I can do as I please," Skid shot back.

"You live under my house and my rules," Rod said without looking up from the malfunctioning engine he was repairing. "I said no," Rod looked up.

"I'm almost eighteen," Skid said. He stood at the shop door and held the envelope in his left hand. He didn't know if he would need his right to block a blow.

"I said no. And that's that."

It had been a week since Skid had mailed his letter to the editor, and it still hadn't run in the newspaper. He felt pride in his explanation of how, while it was necessary to file the proper paperwork to leave school early, extenuating circumstances that day made it difficult, if not impossible, for that to happen. He enjoyed the feeling of putting the words on paper and organizing his thoughts into a coherent and, he believed, convincing argument. If people read it, he was convinced they'd see his point of view.

Skid flipped open the paper, and scanned the editorial page. A small-town newspaper focused on significant local issues like crime, the city budget, sewage treatment, street signage, and potholes. All required attention and spotlighted the problem in hopes of bringing about change.

Of course, the protest at the high school had generated several days of letters to the editor. The published missives split fifty-fifty. But Skid had no way of knowing the breakdown of people, young or old, rich or poor, Black or White, who'd taken the time to set pen to paper and either support or denounce the civil action.

Five days after the protest, an article reported the school board and the administration would meet both main concessions to the students who'd walked out. It seemed to Skid a hollow victory because the stakes were so low, but Leon was quoted saying he was pleased with the outcome. Then, of course, he didn't say it, but he implied there might be more protests on other issues.

Skid considered writing a follow-up letter but believed the more time passed, the less newsworthy his complaint about the injustice of his suspension might be. So instead, he decided to visit the paper's downtown office and ask some questions.

The newspaper office sat on a single-story corner lot two blocks from the town square. It could have used a coat of paint, and one of the loading dock doors had graffiti on it reading, "Javelins Rule." This was a jab from a rival high school's football team and their appearance in an upcoming game. Unfortunately, this expression of support had become a tradition between the two schools, with both hometown papers experiencing the same kind of vandalism.

Skid parked one of Rod's rehabs in the parking lot and strode toward the office like a man on a mission. He turned and grabbed the doorknob. A middle-aged man pushed the door open and stood in front of Skid.

"Is there something I can do for you?" The man asked. He wore a white shirt, a red tie, and black slacks. He wore basketball shoes but didn't look like he was headed for a game.

"Mr. James," Skid said, genuinely surprised that the editor was heading out early in the day. He'd once heard the wordsmith speak to his English class and felt inspired and patriotic.

"Yes, can I help you?"

"I'm Skid Bekins, ah, Clarence," he said as he stuck out his hand. The editor took it and grasped the fingers a bit too tight.

"Okay, what's goin' on?"

"I wrote a letter to you about something that happened at school, and I was hoping you'd run it," Skid said. He glanced down at his shoes and realized they were the same make and model as the editors.

"Refresh my memory, if you could please."

"I was suspended from school because I didn't, ah, my stepfather didn't do the paperwork to get me out."

"Ah, yes, a grievance. An injustice, but not of the highest order." The editor wagged his finger under Skid's nose. "I won't publish that because I believe people should take personal responsibility. If you needed to leave school, you and your stepfather should have followed proper procedures. You didn't, and you paid the consequences."

"But..." Skid began and then stopped.

"Our society operates on an agreed-upon set of rules, laws, and moral obligations. When we do not follow those rules, even if we don't know what the rules are or might entail, we must pay the consequences. That would be my response to your letter if I were to publish it. Is that something you would want?"

Skid thought for a moment. How would he appear if they published the letter and the editor's response made him look foolish and immature? How would that play with Constance and the rest of his friends and associates?

"No, that's okay. You've got a good point. I've already done my time. Why drag this along for no good reason?"

The editor clapped the boy on the shoulder and smiled. "I think you've made the right decision. It was a good letter, though."

A young woman burst through the door and said, "Someone's taken a shot at President Ford."

The editor paused for a moment and put his finger to his chin. "I've got to go back." He turned and walked back toward the door. "Thanks for coming by, Skid."

The door snapped shut, leaving Skid standing on the landing. He looked at the graffiti on the metal door and said, "Go Tigers," as if just saying the phrase would offset "Javelins Rule."

Chapter 11

Skid never let go of his dream of appealing and winning his argument that he'd been unjustly suspended during the sit-in. He realized he could control his anger and hurt and channel that energy into something else. Someday, he could express other grievances to the editor in another letter or try and draft articles for the school paper. He liked the notion of using words to express his feelings. It made him feel heard.

So, he'd file all that in the back of his mind and remember what happened at the concert on the weekend where he'd been suspended. And he'd remember Constance's kiss. But, of course, she wouldn't have done that if he had appeared angry and bitter. But, instead, she looked at him and, in Skid's mind, thought, here's a boy who needs a kiss. Did any of his silly letters or articles really matter compared to that?

It was near the end of September, and a second woman had taken a shot at assassinating President Ford. The journal ran stories from the wire services describing the events before and after the attempts. Both women appeared wild-eyed and dangerous in their arrest photos.

The first was Lynette "Squeaky" Frome. She was a member of the cult that grew up around Charles Manson. She wasn't involved in the murder of Sharon Tate and the others, but she was clearly unbalanced.

The second attempt on President Ford's life involved Sarah Jane Moore, a young woman with left-leaning political ties. Her try at killing the president was thwarted by a young bystander. He stood next to her in a crowd of well-wishers across the street from the president in San Francisco and wrestled with her as she fired. Moore's shot missed, and he became a hero.

Skid decided these attempts at violent protests mattered more than the slight injustice he'd suffered. In his mind, they were brutal and ineffective. He knew anyone who felt anger and injustice might choose bloodshed over peaceful protest. Still, he didn't see himself in that role.

He decided to take a nice long ride in the country to take his mind off his troubles. So, he took the tarp off the '55 Chevy Bel Air Nomad with the famous small block V-8 engine. Rod had bought the car as his first anniversary present for Skid's mother. He'd tuned up the motor by replacing the standard carburetor and added mag chrome racing wheels and wider tires. It was a classic, and Rod's refurbishment of the motor, interior, and body was a gift to Skid's mother. She wasn't interested in drag racing, but if she ever changed her mind, her husband assured her, the car would be "hot as fire."

Skid searched a coat pocket for the key. He opened the door and yanked the hood release handle. He'd check the oil, a routine that was a show of affection for his mother on a subconscious level.

It was his mother's car; he always felt strange driving it. It had been sitting for several months, and he wasn't sure the battery would turn the engine over. So today, he just sat behind the wheel and tried to imagine what he looked like sitting across from him as she drove.

He liked to watch her hands on the steering wheel. Her long, red nails swept over the chrome horn button and grasped the pearl-white knob on the end of the gear shift. The Hot Rodders didn't like the shifter on the column. Instead, they wanted "four on the floor" with a chrome stalk and black plastic knob. Skid knew there were chrome shifter grips that looked like a skull. Absent the floor shifter, Skid liked the fact this made for more legroom in the front seat.

Donna's shoulder-length sandy hair swept around her head like a halo with the windows rolled down and doing about forty. Skid could see her natural red highlights when the sun slanted just the right way. She wore red lipstick and mascara, accentuating her deep, brown eyes. She usually wore a knee-length dress, even when vacuuming or washing dishes. However, there was a time when he caught her changing a light bulb on the porch, standing on an aluminum ladder wearing high heels.

As he sat there, so many memories flooded his mind. When Rod entered the garage, Skid did not notice as he stood next to the back fender. He was rubbing his hands with a white cloth and smiling. Skid finally saw him standing there through the driver's side rearview mirror.

"I put a new battery in her yesterday."

"I thought I saw something different, but I couldn't place it," Skid said. He brushed a single tear away from the corner of his eye before Rod could make his way to the driver's side door.

"I thought it was something more serious, but that's all it needed." Rod said, standing in steel-toed boots, dirty coveralls, and a Steelers cap.

"Let me," Skid put the key in the ignition and turned the key.

"I'll put the hood down," Rod said. He circled the passenger side fender, opened the door, and sat beside Skid.

"A lot of the Hot Rodders wouldn't have a stick shift on the column like that," he said, adding an air of authenticity and professionalism to the tone of his voice.

"I know, but I like it that way," Skid said, touching the smooth steering wheel. It was as if he could still feel his mother's fingers on the wheel.

"Let's take her for a spin," Rod said.

Skid nodded and checked the garage door. Tools and a lawn mower crowded the left side of the garage, while the right side held a flat spare tire and a floor jack. The garage was a "catch-all" with several garbage cans, dutifully emptied each week by Skid.

The teen checked the mirror and turned the key. The engine sprang to life and purred like a kitten. Rod had taught him how to drive after Donna's death, and he'd passed his test after the first try. Rod was a great driving teacher, patient and encouraging. And he didn't freak out when Skid made a mistake. "Slow and steady wins the race," he'd said.

Skid rolled down the window to adjust the outside mirror, and the draft allowed him to catch that smell. He'd noticed it before around Rod, but now, he'd begun smelling it during the day instead of only at night. It was bourbon and not the expensive kind.

He'd heard Rod call it "rotgut." Skid believed the phrase captured the taste, smell, and eventual outcome of drinking it. He was driving, so what did it matter if Rod had a "refreshment" while working?

Skid muttered. "What harm could that do?"

"What," Rod asked, "what did you say?"

"Nothin'," as he revved the engine.

Skid moved the gear shift stick into first and let off the clutch. The tires crunched on the gravel driveway, and as he turned onto the neighborhood street, he heard a "bump" in the front.

"Is that a flat tire?"

"Don't worry, it'll be fine," Rod said as he touched the boy's shoulder. "Hit it. Let's see what she'll do."

Skid pushed down on the accelerator, and the car lurched to life. He shifted from first to second gear and then, with the engine whining, into third. He glanced down at the speedometer and noticed it had passed fifty miles per hour.

They neared a two-lane, and Skid slowed as he approached the intersection.

"Ain't nobody coming," Rod said, waving Skid through the stop sign.

"But..."

"Just go," Rod said, "don't be a pussy."

The car's back end spun out slightly as Skid pointed the nose toward town. They passed the blacktop leading to Tiger Hill with no acknowledgment from Skid. He hadn't told Rod about his brush with death on the hill and felt no need to. He might tell him someday, but not today. And Rod hadn't asked Skid about the origin of the nickname. Instead, he added it without question, remembering how he'd gotten *his* tag so many years before.

The intersection to the four-lane approached, and Skid slowed. Rod sat up and checked in both directions. "I think you can make it."

Skid slowed and put on his turn signal. He glanced in both directions and saw the lanes were clear.

He slowed but didn't stop and shifted from third gear into second.

"That's the way," Rod said, smiling.

Skid pointed the car away from town and stepped on it. The engine gasped and caught fire, pressing them both into the upholstery. Skid glanced at the speedometer as it approached sixty.

"Wooooo Whooooo!" Rod screamed, slapping the side of the car through the open window.

"She's not a horse," Skid said over the roar of the air passing through the open windows.

"The hell she ain't," Rod said. He patted the metal dashboard and smiled. "She's a Detroit thoroughbred. Get on it!"

Skid glanced at the speedometer again. The needle approached sixty-five and kept moving. "I think that's enough. Remember that tire," the boy said.

"Don't worry so much," Rod said. He placed his foot over Skid's and pressed the gas pedal to the floor.

They were on Highway 99. While most of the asphalt ribbon was straight and true, several mounds in the low-bid, defective construction had caused accidents in the past. Drivers pushed their cars to the limit, and several paid the price.

The engine roared as if in pain, and the car pulled to the left, where Skid had first heard the tire whining. "I think that's enough," he screamed.

"Boy, you ain't no fun at all," Rod said. He let his foot linger on Skid's for three more seconds and then moved it. Skid let off the gas, and the car was soon cruising at fifty.

"Yeah, this old car's seen better days," Rod said. He put his forearm on the door's armrest and smiled. "But she's still got some life left in her."

"What about if we had an accident? That tire..."

"You worry too much. Be young and don't care about nothin'. That'ssh your job from now on," Rod slurred.

"But you were worried about me when they had the sit-in, weren't you?" Skid asked.

"That's what grown-ups do. Children shouldn't have to."

"And when they kicked me out?"

"Pick your battles, Skid," the older man said. "You gotta pick which hill you're willin' to die on."

Skid felt his cheeks flush, and he gripped the wheel tighter. He knew if his mother were still alive, she'd have stood up to that Vice-Principal. But instead, Rod was willing to let it go. Is that what all "real" men do?

Chapter 12

Skid remembered when his English teacher, Mrs. Wilson, said, "Conflict is the key to good drama."

He sat at a table in the back of the library. It was quiet, and the stacks and bookcases let him escape detection by most teachers, librarians, and administrators. This was where he'd written the first draft of his letter to the editor explaining the injustice of his expulsion. After finishing his letter, he kept a journal and wrote down his observations and ideas. Writing made him feel better. He liked confirming the day's events and how he could look back and see where patterns had appeared.

Both hardback and paperback books filled the bookcases, each carefully labeled. A large wooden cabinet sat at the end of one row. Cardboard labels sat in slots at the end of small drawers. The last names of alphabetized fiction writers sat on raised tabs. At the same time, librarians arranged the non-fiction books by subject alphabetically. The Dewey decimal system worked well for students, teachers, librarians, and school administrators.

A bank of windows to the south let light and heat into the room. In the winter, it warmed the students sitting at long tables. A radiator cracked and popped as hot water rumbled up from the boiler room. In the summer, the librarian would pull large curtains blocking the light, and the open windows would stir much-needed cooler air.

Skid looked through the card catalog, found a book on writing stage plays, and wondered if trying something like that might be fun. But then, he remembered how much he'd enjoyed reading *Hamlet* and the film version by Laurence Olivier that the teacher had played on the school projector. There sure was plenty of conflict in that one.

He smoothed the lined notebook paper and set his pen at the top of the page. He began the story in a typical American high school with a cast of lively and happy students. The topic was getting a date for the prom. Of course, he didn't have to worry about that since he had a steady girl, but Skid believed it would be a good story with ideas he could explore.

His favorite television show at the time was *The Waltons*. It was about a young man living with a large family during the Depression. The father and mother were exemplary, and a grumpy grandfather and loving grandmother also lived in the two-story house. The stories focused on the eldest son, a junior nicknamed "John-Boy." The main problem for the family was economics. They struggled to keep their children fed and clothed by operating a sawmill. In addition, the parents had to deal with issues presented each week by different children. John Boy's ambition to be a writer was often a featured topic.

Skid decided that since he was a show fan, he'd write a play for them about John-boy getting a date to the prom. But unfortunately, he didn't know how to do this. So, he asked the librarian if there were any books she could recommend that might give him an idea of what it would take to scratch this itch.

According to the school gossip string, Miss Cardwell had never married, and there was speculation about why that didn't happen. However, Skid always liked how she would smile at him as she pounded the date stamp onto the lined label in the back without looking where the ink-smeared device was. She was remarkably exact, and Skid surmised the act must have taken years to perfect.

She sat behind the desk at the front door and read as the students entered and exited. She was tall and thin, and today, she wore a long-sleeved white blouse with a frilly collar, a black skirt, and a light red sweater.

"Miss Cardwell," Skid said as he approached her desk. "I looked through the card catalog for a book on writing for television. But, unfortunately, there doesn't seem to be any. Can you help me?"

"Not much call for that kind of book here. I am not a fan of television or movies, Clarence," she began. He'd tried repeatedly to get her to use his nickname, but she refused.

"That's okay." He turned and headed for the exit.

"Wait, please," she said. She spun in her office chair and picked up a form from a tray on her desk. "Fill this out, and I'll see if I can get a trade from another library."

"What do I ask for?"

"A how-to book, maybe something like how to write for television." She said. She handed him the form, and he put it on the books he carried.

"We have the complete works of William Shakespeare, and I know there are several other collections of other playwrights. Have you looked at them?"

"A few. I know the writing is probably similar, but I'd like to try something for television."

"What brought this on?" She asked.

Skid considered talking about the horrible injustice of his suspension from school after the sit-in. But instead, he thought about maybe someday letting the librarian read a copy of his letter to the editor so she would better understand how he felt following the incident.

"I've just been thinkin' about it. I like that TV show, *The Waltons*. I may have a story they could use."

She put her finger to her bottom lip and thought for a second. Then, finally, she nodded and said, "You might get some ideas from reading one of the scripts they've already used." After that, she said, "I'll look up the production company and write a letter." Then, she smiled for the first time since they'd started talking. "Let me know of any other way I might help."

"Sure," Skid said. "Much obliged."

Chapter 13

May 1, 1975

Why would Constance be in his mom's Chevy Nomad with Rod?

Skid couldn't stop wondering about this while watching filmed footage of the evacuation of the American embassy in Saigon. The line of people trying to climb over the fence and others who waited for the Marines to helicopter them from the roof distracted him. Newspaper articles and photos had already told the story a few days before. However, seeing the evacuation film on television created a more visceral response. He knew this was an extraordinary time, and these images would be in the history books.

And Skid knew his involvement in the war was likely over. His draft number was in the mid-two-hundreds, and enlisting still didn't appeal to him.

The evacuation had occurred earlier, but the television newscasters said it had taken a few days to get the film to show what happened. So that's how the news business worked.

There were two kinds of news. Something you know will happen, and you have someone there to record the event. Or, two, the correspondent covers the aftermath of something earlier.

Skid had never thought about this, never considered what it took to be a news reporter, but suddenly it dawned on him the nature of the job. He had watched the journalists from the radio station, and the newspaper cover the student sit-in. He realized they had reported on the result of the event since no one had called them before the walk-out.

After the protest and his expulsion, he considered writing for the school newspaper. But, of course, his first story would have been about the aftermath of the walkout and his unjust punishment. Still, time had passed, and he was beginning to release his anger and disappointment. Now, the idea of writing news intrigued him. Could he correct other injustices by writing stories about them?

He believed writing news stories exposing under-reported issues and societal problems might be exciting and fun. Skid didn't know what those issues or concerns might be, but he realized that reporting the news could be a full-time job.

Instead, earlier today, he had another job. He stood in the church's front yard wearing a big-brimmed hat, a white T-shirt, and shorts. Even though the temperature was still cool, he knew he'd soon be working up a sweat. It was his Saturday job to mow the grass. He liked staying busy, which was one way to make pocket money. In addition, he wanted to take Constance to more concerts, and this undertaking was one way to make that happen. So he stood next to the push lawnmower and fiddled with the throttle.

He looked up, recognizing the exhaust sound from his mother's car. He'd ridden his bike to the church, not wanting to disturb Rod from sleeping late on a Saturday. A flash of light bounced off the hood, and he squinted as the car drifted some hundred feet away.

It looked like Constance in the passenger seat, but he couldn't be sure, given the distance and the light hitting the car. It was a woman with her hair color, but she had turned her face. Maybe Rod had a girlfriend? Perhaps he was just picking up a part for a car? He'd have to find out at dinner.

Skid pulled the starter rope on the mower, and the engine turned over. He pulled again, and the tiny two-stroke roared to life. He pushed the John Deere mower to the sidewalk. He began the mindless effort he needed to make the lawn look presentable for the minister.

Preacher Jake was the one who paid him, and he knew he could be something of a tyrant from last year. Was he feeling stressed about the services on Sunday? Skid liked to speculate, but he knew hard facts were more important.

Pushing the mower allowed his mind to drift from the film of the final evacuation of Saigon to his unjust expulsion to seeing Constance and Rod in his mother's car. Can someone's eyes deceive them? Finally, he looked up at the church spire and thought, *people believe in things they can't or won't see every day.*

He turned a corner and glimpsed the minister standing on the front doorstep. He was holding a glass of ice water and smiling. He motioned to Skid.

Preacher Jake instructed Skid on how he wanted the lawn to look, and the boy feared this would be another lecture. But there seemed to be something different about Jake, and Skid couldn't read his expression.

Here was a man who'd anticipated Skid might get thirsty from working on the yard. Jake stood there, a slight smile on his lips, waiting to hand one of his parishioners something that might ease a minor pain.

Skid hadn't evolved into a "go to church every Sunday" kind of believer, but he liked to sing in the congregation and hear what this young minister had to say. So, he killed the mower's engine and walked over to the man only slightly older than himself.

"You've really got it all together, don't you, Rev?"

The minister handed the glass to Skid and watched him drink. "It's always from one moment to the next. Can't live life any other way."

After drinking, Skid said, "I get it."

"Say amen," Jake said.

Skid noticed the change in Jake's attitude from last year. He'd relaxed and now seemed mature and thoughtful. Maybe the preacher was settling into the job.

He considered the withdrawal of troops and personnel from the roof of the Saigon embassy. Skid could see how desperate the refugees appeared. How would he react in a similar situation? Sure, it was rough when his mother died, but he'd found a way through. And Jake had been helpful.

"Thanks," he said as he handed the glass back to the minister.

"Take a break if you feel like you're gettin' too hot."

Skid nodded, grabbed the starter rope for the mower, and yanked. The engine chugged to life, and he walked behind it as quickly as possible. He needed to return home soon before that movie he'd seen in the TV guide started. Something about the 'War of the Worlds' panic following the Orson Welles broadcast on Halloween in the 1930s.

Skid loved that people would believe an alien invasion just because it was on the radio. Now a television network would broadcast a movie decades later about the production and airing of the radio play. Viewers could see the end of a war ten thousand miles overseas and feel sick to their stomachs as he had.

It's a weird, wonderful world, the boy thought.

Chapter 14

Graduation was weeks away, but the students involved in the sit-in had a letter in hand that the school would meet their demands. In addition, a local Black minister would deliver the commencement address. Next season, the school would expand the pep squads for the two new high schools, and Black cheerleaders would fill those positions. They didn't get one hundred percent of what they asked, and there were no majorettes in the band yet, but the protest succeeded.

Skid occasionally played pick-up basketball on Friday nights at the community center. While he was tall, he wasn't particularly good. So, it was an extraordinary occurrence when Leon dropped by and joined the skins squad against the shirts. The game rules applied, but you could call your own fouls.

Leon played power forward on the school's team, and Skid's job was to try and guard him. It did not go well. Leon had moves and could hit the fall-away jumper, a shot that Skid couldn't stop. Meanwhile, Skid scrubbed past the center when Shirts had the ball and found himself open in the corner of the court. He glanced at the basket and turned loose his best jumper. Leon appeared out of nowhere and slapped the ball out of mid-air. He kept the ball on the court so his team could perform a fast break. Skid found himself trailing the play and bumped Leon on the way back to his end of the court.

"Hey, man, watch it," Leon said.

"Sweet block, Leon. Why don't you pull somethin' like that during the school games?"

Leon wiped his forehead with the back of his hand and took Skid's swipe at his play for the school's team in stride.

"I got nothin' to prove to you."

"You got somethin' to prove to college scouts if you think you're gonna play with the big boys," Skid said as he pulled up the end of his T-shirt and wiped the sweat from his forehead.

"I'm not sure that's for me," Leon said.

Skid backpedaled, and circled the back of the key. Leon followed.

The point guard surveyed the court and pointed to the corner with his chin. Skid read the assignment and dashed to his spot. Leon followed.

The guard raced to the open lane and tossed in a lay-up. He grinned and pointed to Leon. "Broke your ankles tryin' to get to that one, didn't I?"

"That's twenty," Skid said.

They decided the game was the first team to twenty-two. Leon took the ball and dribbled from one end of the court. He posted up Skid, faked right, turned left, and took the jumper.

"Winner," he said and pointed to the basket before it cleared the net.

"Good game," Skid said, winded and humiliated by letting the last shot go uncontested.

"Yeah, man," Leon said, offering his hand.

"You're good. You should get serious about playing in college," Skid said. He had a new respect for the leader of the sit-in. "You got skills."

"I ain't got the grades, though," Leon said. He bounced the ball all the way back to the rack.

"You can get the grades. That's easy. But, makin' that jumper is what's hard," Skid said, smiling.

"Well," Leon began and then let his voice trail off.

"Look, I'm in an algebra study group. We meet on Saturdays. I'm sure there's a group for whatever subject you're havin' trouble in."

"I'll think about it," Leon said. He has the same smile he had when he blocked Skid's shot. "Thanks."

The gym grew quiet as the teams exited the cavernous space. Skid stood by the exit door and held it for Leon.

"Thanks," Leon said. He smiled at the shorter man as he passed.

"Don't even think about bringin' that jumper with you next time. I got that one covered," Skid said, laughing.

"Like a blanket, man," Leon said, "like a blanket."

Chapter 15

Skid wrote a condensed story of his *The Waltons* episode on the back pages of his notebook. He wanted to make sure no one would happen upon his doodling if they flipped the sheets.

Of course, his story involved John Boy, but he changed his mind about the young writer trying to find a prom date. So instead, Skid wanted to explore how John Boy came up with an idea for a short story. It would be about someone coming to town and inspiring the budding writer. Skid was sure they hadn't had an episode like that, so he began with what the visiting character might need if they came to the mountain. Peace, solitude, a job, or something harder to find.

Skid sat at one of the long tables near the back of the library and looked out the window. It had become his favorite spot, and he felt this was where he did his best thinking. He liked watching the elementary school students playing and hanging out on the school's back lawn. Their energy and enthusiasm inspired him.

The Easter break gave him time to consider what the Waltons' story would need to be to get the attention of the producers and writers on the show. And then the horrible news came out of Hamilton, Ohio, of a young man who shot and killed eleven family members. Skid scanned the AP story from the newspaper on his right. He wondered what James Ruppert was thinking when he was killing his family.

Skid read the horrific headline in the Battleboro Journal first and waited for the information to sink into his mind for a second. "Father Kills Eleven Members of Family Easter Sunday."

He looked across the table at the library and asked Dee Dee, "Can you believe somebody would do something like this?"

She was sneaking a breath mint from her bag and looked up as Skid tapped the tabletop.

"People suck, man," she said around the tablet. "What more can I say?"

Sunlight slanted through the east windows. It was Skid's favorite time of day in the library. Dee Dee had her head down, and her new haircut covered her face. She had to pull it to one side to talk.

Skid nodded and returned to the article above the fold. "It says here the guy went to his mother's house for Easter and shot eleven family members. The police report says James Union Ruppert of Hamilton, Ohio called the police and was waiting on the front step. Five bodies were found in the living room when they showed up, one of them a small child still holding a chocolate easter egg. He was only four years old."

"God," Dee Dee said. "That's twisted."

"The Easter dinner was still on the stove." Then, Skid read on, "He shot each of his relatives twice, once in the head and once in the chest. Why didn't they fight back or run?"

"Maybe he was so fast they didn't have time to react," she said.

"Maybe they were just so shocked they couldn't move. He shot everyone in under five minutes and changed his bloody clothes before calling the police."

She smirked and said, "They'll never know what really happened."

Skid considered this. While it wouldn't make a good subject for "The Waltons," he could write another story based on what happened. "The story says Ruppert was bullied by his father and older brother. His brother married an ex-girlfriend, and they had eight children. He will be evaluated for mental defects and tried for murder."

Dee Dee's face darkened. "You're not thinkin' about doin' somethin' like this, are you?"

"No," Skid said, "of course not." He paused momentarily, allowing his mind to wander into what must have been the very dark place that Ruppert must have experienced. "But I think I can imagine what it must have been like for him."

"He's crazy," Dee Dee said. She opened her book. "And now you're crazy too."

Skid nodded and returned to the newspaper. He said, "I hope he lives a long, horrible life in prison and wakes up every morning remembering what he did."

"So, that's worse than executing him?" Dee Dee asked, her voice attracted the attention of Miss Cardwell. She gave Dee Dee a stern look but refrained from putting her finger to the lips and shushing. This was her usual reaction to loud students.

"Oh, yeah," Skid whispered. "It is to me anyway."

"I hear you, but if it was up to me, I'd let him fry."

"Good to know," Skid said.

He finished the front page and moved to the comics.

"How's *Peanuts* today?"

"Okay, Snoopy and the Red Baron are at it again."

Dee Dee nodded. She turned a page on *Wuthering Heights* and clicked her mint with her front teeth.

"I think I could see Rod doing somethin' like that," Skid said, not really understanding why he said it.

"Take on the Red Baron?" Dee Dee asked.

"No, be violent. I'm not sure, but if Rod was drinking, I think he could do somethin' crazy."

"Has he," Dee Dee asked slowly, "done anything to make you think that?"

"No, of course not, I'm just thinkin' out loud," Skid said. "Rod is a trained killer, though."

"Rod was a mechanic in the Army, not a killer," Dee Dee said.

"He took basic training. Rod once told me he was a crack shot."

"If you think you're in troub…"

"No," Skid cut her off, "I'm fine. We're fine. It was just a fleeting thought."

"I see." Dee Dee said, "Call me if you think you're in danger. Promise me."

"I promise," Skid said. He looked at her and could see she was deadly serious.

"I mean it," she emphasized.

"Okay," Skid said, laughing now to try and ease the tension. "I was just thinkin' about that man in Ohio. What was going through his mind?"

"Crazy people do crazy shit," Dee Dee said, closing her book. Then, she said, "Gotta bounce." She collected her things and left.

Miss Cardwell pushed a book cart past Skid and tried to glimpse his writing. "I found you a book on writing for television and movies at a university library."

"Great," Skid said, genuine appreciation in his voice.

"I also contacted the production company that produces 'The Waltons.' They said if I sent them a self-addressed stamped envelope, they would send me a script for one of the earlier episodes."

"So cool," he said. "I can't wait to read it."

"I'll let you know when the mailman delivers it."

He asked her as she sorted books. "What makes the Waltons a good family?"

She rubbed her chin with her index finger. "They love each other, number one." She pulled one book from the row and placed it at the end of the cart.

"But they don't always get along," Skid said. He closed the notebook cover and put his pen on the table.

"Conflict is needed for drama. But, come to think of it, you need conflict for comedy, too." Miss Cardwell continued, "You can love someone and not agree with everything they say or do."

Skid asked, "The conflict in my script should be between family members?"

"You need to ask your English teacher about all this. I wouldn't want to send you in the wrong direction. I'll just say there's plenty of drama in every family, just as there is comedy. The grandpa gets most of the comedy in the show, while the rest of the cast deals with the drama."

"Thanks," Skid said and flipped open the cover of his notebook. He knew she might be able to read what he'd written, but the text would be upside down and difficult to make out.

"The script should be here any day. I'll ensure you get it as soon as it arrives."

"Thanks for all the trouble," genuinely thankful.

"No problem," Miss Cardwell said, "just be sure to mention me when you accept your Emmy award."

Skid smiled and felt his cheeks redden. *Should he even consider dreaming of something like that?*

He remembered how the Ohio shooter explained how his mother mistreated him. He could fake being insane, spend a few years in a mental hospital, and then inherit the family's money, just over three-hundred-thousand dollars. While Skid could see some twisted logic in Ruppert's plan, he was obviously insane. Would this be the plot of a story?

The Waltons and the Rupperts are clearly opposites but still families. Skid marveled at how differently the two families dealt with problems. Was there a story there for the show? He asked himself.

He knew from watching the show 'The Waltons' had never depicted a murder. Most of the conflict came from characters with different points of view. How would the older generation judge the younger generation's choices? Finally, some family members would solve the problem. The last dialogue you always heard was the family saying good night to each other at bedtime.

Skid turned the notebook page and scribbled the phrase, "all that we leave behind." It was bizarre to write about the show, but he'd been thinking about it for a while. He would graduate soon, and he believed his future was anywhere but here.

Chapter 16

"I thought I saw you with Rod the other day," Skid said. He dipped his French fries into a puddle of ketchup oozing over a corner of the paper placemat on the rubber tray.

Constance didn't look up as she asked, "Where?"

"It was on Saturday. I was mowing the grass at the church, and I could have sworn I saw you in my mom's car with Rod driving."

"Oh, yeah, right," she said. She took a bite of her hamburger and washed it down with a swig of milkshake.

The new McDonald's on Church Street had become "the" place to be in town. Everyone went on about the fries, but Skid favored the shakes. They were milk, not ice cream, and strawberry was his favorite.

This was Constance's first trip to the new restaurant. There were plenty of others in town, but a fast-food eatery with a drive-through was something new. They'd considered ordering there, but the line was long, and it was too cold to sit in the car and eat tonight.

"Well?" Skid asked.

Constance snatched more fries from the stack in the middle of her placemat and stuffed them into her mouth.

"My car wouldn't start," she said as best she could around the potatoes. A drop of catsup ran down her chin. She swallowed and tucked her hair behind her right ear. "So, I called your house, and he answered. He said it was probably just a dead battery. So, he came over to the house, checked it, and we went to the parts store."

"And he fixed it?" Skid asked.

"Yep, runnin' like a sewing machine," she said, again around her food and sipping her milkshake.

"Oh, okay. You know you could have called me," Skid said.

"I said I did call you." She squinted her eyes as if the food didn't agree with her. "Rod said you were busy, and I didn't know the number there at the church. Besides, it had just happened, and Rod wanted to help." She stuffed more fries into her mouth and said, "He's a great guy. He wouldn't take a dime for his time."

"I know," Skid said. He tried to keep his sarcastic tone out of the answer, but it oozed right in, just like the catsup on his tray.

There was something off about Connie's story. He'd started calling her "Connie" since they'd passed the one-month anniversary of the Allman Brothers concert. He knew she was serious and when she was just having fun. But he wasn't sure how to read this new expression.

Skid watched the line of cars inch toward the outside menu and ordering speaker. The line stretched around the restaurant parking lot and backed into the street. A police officer had his cruiser in the corner with his blue light flashing to keep people from running over each other trying to get in.

"I sure didn't see this place catchin' on. The Shoney's is almost next door," Skid said.

"This place is cheap, fast, and the food tastes good. The Shoney's cost more; you have to sit in your car, and the servers are old and slow. So, this place makes sense."

"It does for some people," Skid concluded.

"How's the script coming?" Connie asked. This time she glanced out the big picture window at the front of the restaurant. She nodded at a red Mustang as it passed by.

"I'm still at the thinkin' stage. I read the script Miss Cardwell got from the producers. It's different."

"How do you mean different?" Connie tucked a sprig of black hair behind her ear and sighed.

"It just looks weird. Everything the actors say and do is on the page. I've gotta lot to think about."

"Well, maybe it's not for you," she said.

"No, I'm not giving up," Skid said, defensive. "I just have to think about what I'm tryin' to say."

"And what are you tryin' to say?"

Skid remembered the feeling down in his gut when the principal had unjustly expelled him and how that hurt, still ached, and he didn't know why. Writing that letter to the Editor made him feel better, but was that the sum he wanted to express?

"It's got to be more than just complaining. It has to be personal, a story with a point-of-view that might mean something to someone else." He sipped a milkshake as if it might make his sentence even more meaningful.

"What's really on your mind?" Connie asked. She glanced out the window as a car with a loud muffler rumbled.

"My mother, I guess. I'm still thinkin' about that. How she died."

"And what can you say about that?" She asked.

A worker walked by the table for two and glanced over the surface. It was crazy busy, and it seemed odd the management would send someone out in the lobby at a time like this. Then, finally, the young man in the blue polyester shirt and jeans said, "Are you done with your tray?"

Connie glanced up. "Don't I know you?"

"I'm a freshman in your typing class. Tommy."

"Right," she said and smiled. "How are you doin'?"

"Twenty-two words a minute with three typos. How about you?"

"Pretty much the same. It's hard, isn't it?"

"Yeah, ah, they sent me out to get some trays. Are you guys done with yours?"

Skid pushed the black plastic tray across the table. "Take it. That's a hell of a job you've got."

Tommy had bobby-pinned his paper hat to his big afro as best he could, given the size and physics of the outfit. Finally, he puffed his chest out and said, "Three dollars an hour. So, if I stay six months, I get a raise to four."

Skid nodded. He worked several small jobs, but nothing would generate that much cash flow. "Maybe I ought to get a job here."

"They're hiring. At least you wouldn't have to drive to Nashville for training."

"Oh, right," Connie said, "this is the first one in town."

"They have a specific way of doin' just about everything."

"I bet they do," Skid said. "Hot, fresh, and tastes good. Can't beat that with a dead squirrel."

Another car with straight pipes drove by. The rumble shook the window with the McDonald's logo painted inside.

"Pretty damn loud," Skid complained. He knew Rod specialized in tuning big engines and making cars that sounded like that.

"Pretty damn loud," Connie said, smiling. She picked up her milkshake and stared at the Mustang as it swept through the parking lot.

"I hope they don't break the glass," Tommy said.

"No chance of that," Skid said, trying to add a tone of authority to his voice when he had no idea if it were possible to break a window with engine noise.

"And you know this?" Connie asked.

"Science," Skid said as he pointed to his temple. "Got it all right up here."

All three laughed as the Mustang parked and the engine shut off. The conversations in the room returned to normal as the driver opened his door.

"Why would someone drive a car like that?" Tommy asked. He picked up the black tray and put it under his arm. He held a white cloth and touched it to the closest side of the table as if he might clean some dust.

"Probably overcompensating," Connie said and put her pinky up. She waved the finger around and laughed.

"Somethin' else to think about," Skid said.

"Too much thinkin'," Connie said. "It's time to get to work."

Skid nodded and watched the Mustang driver saunter into the restaurant. "Why would he drive a car like that?" He asked himself. Somewhere in his mind, he was already making a list of answers.

Chapter 17

Skid changed his mind about the script. Instead, he wrote a short story version of what he had in mind. His story would have no dialogue and be written in the present tense, just like the script he'd received from Miss Cardwell.

The screenplay was from a past season. Skid was fortunate when the episode played as a rerun on the Thursday after Easter. He was lucky the script arrived just in time to follow along with the produced episode. He remembered his mother saying, "Sometimes, it's better to be lucky than smart."

In the script, a two-page scene at the beginning would set up who in the family had the problem and who would solve it. Skid would read the script and look up to see the produced scene on the screen.

The following Act 1, labeled at the top of the page, included a line in all caps describing the scene's setting and whether it was day or night. Again, Skid noticed much of what was happening on the screen followed the script.

Maybe this won't be as hard as I thought, he concluded.

The next day, he sat in front of one of the typewriters in typing class and rolled a sheet of paper into the platen. He checked his notes and the story he'd written earlier. He was glad he'd printed the words. Unfortunately, his handwriting was becoming illegible.

He typed "Teaser" at the center of the top of the page and hit the return bar.

Next, "INT. WALTON'S LIVING ROOM" with a dash, and then "DAY." He hit the return bar twice and typed a description of what was in the room that he thought he might need for the characters to interact and every character in the scene. They sang a song while Jason played the guitar. Grandpa was the loudest, but Grandma gave him a run for his money. John Boy sat reading while the Hootenanny continued. He pulled a pencil from his shirt pocket and wrote on the paper.

The song ended, and there was laughter and smiles all around. Grandpa saw John Boy making notes. Skid decided that Grandpa was annoyed that John Boy didn't join in and made notes of the family singalong. How could he show this on screen?

Skid wanted Grandpa to talk. So, he pulled a ruler from his notebook and measured the produced script to figure out where Grandpa's name should be on the page.

"Three tabs ought to do it," Skid muttered to himself. He glanced around the room, suddenly aware of the quiet. The rows of small desks, each with its own typewriter, filled the room. An imposing tan teacher's desk sat at the front with a wooden office chair behind it.

Skid, hit the tab button three times, and typed "GRANDPA" in all caps just as it appeared in the script.

He'd imagined what Grandpa would say in the scene. He could hear the old man's pauses and emphasis on certain words and phrases. But he'd have to mimic that for it to sound in character. So, he ran the lines in his mind and eventually came up with something that might work.

He measured the script and decided the dialogue would mirror the produced script if he hit the tab button twice. Is this how they do it? It seemed too simple.

He typed, "Come on and join us for the next one, John Boy."

Skid liked what he'd written and how it looked on the page. And then, he glanced at the produced script. It looked the same as what he'd typed.

"This might work," he whispered.

He hit the return bar and laced his fingers behind his head. He looked at the ceiling. *What would John Boy say?* He asked himself.

His revised story about what would be in his episode featured a talent show at the town square. There would be a prize for the best performance, and the money would be handy for the family. In Skid's story, John Boy didn't believe he would help the family band, so he declined to sing along. Grandpa would insist he join in, but John Boy would refuse. Finally, he'd change his mind, and the family would get second place in the competition, a songbook.

John Boy's refusal to participate in the group would have to begin in the first scene, so Skid had to decide why he didn't want to sing. His voice, lack of rhythm, and stage fright seemed obvious, so Skid had to produce something else.

John Boy would be interested in a girl, and appearing on stage with his extended family, how they dressed and sang might be embarrassing. But, of course, he'd have to withhold that information until the end of the episode, so in the beginning, he'd just say he couldn't sing.

Skid hit the tab button three times, and typed "JOHN BOY" in all caps.

He hit the tab button twice and wrote, "You know I can't sing."

Skid wanted the actor to pause before answering but didn't know how to put that in the script.

He typed a line describing how John Boy would drop his pencil and bend over to pick it up. Skid knew the viewer would see this and sense that John Boy was stalling.

"Well, guess I'd better start over," Skid said. He pulled the paper from the roller and inserted another in the typewriter. He typed "FADE IN" in all caps.

"Maybe this isn't gonna be that easy after all," he said. He pulled the paper from the typewriter and tucked it into his notebook. He paused for a moment and looked at the script. It was forty-eight pages long, and while there was a good deal of white space on the page, Skid realized writing a script would take time and effort. Did he have it in him to finish it?

"Stop or keep going?" He asked himself.

He looked out the window and saw several fellow students playing volleyball in the sun. It seemed so much fun. But he hadn't had any "real" fun for a long time.

Skid found himself sitting on a bench as the volleyball game continued. The boy's voices were loud, boisterous, and distracting. He pulled his notebook from his stack of books, opened it to a blank, lined page, and wrote at the top.

"FADE IN."

"I'll write it out in longhand and then type it," he said. "It'll have to be twice as long as the script, but it'll work."

Skid smiled at the solution to his problem. He nodded as if saying, I can do this, and closed the cover of his notebook.

Chapter 18

The question wasn't "when" but "if."

Skid drove past Tiger Hill once a week. He would go up to the start of the nearly vertical road and veer off, knowing how difficult it might be to climb in his mother's car. The car was in good condition now, but he wondered what might happen if it stalled.

He could park the car, walk, take in all the views, and climb the fire tower. He might even take a few snapshots. He likely had his new camera but was still figuring out how to take good pictures.

But not today.

"What kind of student are you?" The Assistant Manager asked.

Skid saw the "Help Wanted" ad in the local newspaper and asked the first person he saw at the front of the Rose's store where he could pick up an application. He filled out the form in his car and held it in his left hand as he opened the two glass and metal doors leading into the store. The little box creating an "air foyer" kept cold or warm air from entering the store.

"I'm good, mostly Bs and Cs," Skid answered the man who didn't appear much older than himself.

The Assistant Manager's name tag read "Bobby." He flipped through the two pages and settled on the section asking why the applicant wanted to work there. It was a "corporate question" likely thought up by someone in the home office in North Carolina. What would the answer say about the person filling out the boxes? What was the reason for the question?

"And you want to work here because…" The Assistant Manager let the question trail off.

"I need the money for school and think I can do a good job."

"Money's important but not as important as your education."

Skid looked at the young man in the white shirt and brown striped tie. He glanced around the small office and saw family pictures and a couple of framed, printed slogans hoping to encourage the workers. "When you set a goal, you make the invisible into the visible."

"I'd like to be a store manager someday," Skid said with as much energy and enthusiasm as he felt might be right.

"Really," Bobby said. It wasn't a question, but something like wonder.

"I mean, maybe, someday," Skid said.

"You'll be fine. Start on Saturday. You're a Stock Boy now. You'll be making three-ninety-five an hour. Is that okay?"

"Good," Skid said, standing and offering his hand to the Assistant Manager for the shaking. The Boss appeared in the doorway. It seemed he'd been listening from the other room. He shook Skid's hand.

"Welcome aboard," The Boss said.

Skid noticed a couple of pictures of yachts and a fishing boat with the Boss sitting next to an older man. They were both holding fishing poles and two strings of fish.

"Aye, aye," Skid said, smiling.

On Saturday, Skid drove to his new job at the department store. His assignment was to fill a bin with stuffed animals. After finishing, he was told to sweep the aisles but not disturb the shoppers. It was a big store, so cleaning with the big, shaggy mop took a long time.

When he finished sweeping, it was time for a break, and he soon found himself in a small room with other workers. It was an odd assortment, some happier looking than others.

Bobby popped his head in and asked how Skid was doing on his first day. The Stock Boy nodded and smiled.

"And someone showed you where the time clock was?"

Skid shook his head no, so the Boss took him to the room next to the office and showed his card to him.

"This is money," the Boss said. "Take care, and don't clock in early or late."

"Got it," Skid said.

The Boss took a pen from his pocket and wrote Skid's start time. Then, he initialed the correction and put it in the metal holder next to the clock.

"Money," Skid said.

He was assigned to put together a bicycle after his break. He'd never done that before, and the instructions were impossible to understand. He did his best but knew it was a mess when he finished.

The Boss looked at Skid's work. He put his finger to his bottom lip and shook his head. "I'll have Huskey look at it. Maybe he can fix it."

Huskey was the head Stock Boy with over ten months of experience. After the store closed, he was the one who took Skid to the back loading dock and showed him the truck that needed to be unloaded.

After clocking out that night, Skid walked to his mother's car with his chest out just a bit more than usual. He smiled at the successful completion of his first day.

The job would mean less time with Connie, but she understood his need for cash. He'd have to pay for tuition and books if he wanted to attend college. That could run into hundreds of dollars. He thought about living in a dorm but decided, for now, commuting the thirty miles and living at home with Rod was the best thing to do.

A week later, Skid stood in line with the other workers and received his first trim, tan envelope with his pay, forty-two dollars, and sixteen cents, after taxes. He went to the electronics department on break and picked out a camera. He used his employee discount at check out and put the purchase in his car trunk.

Monday afternoon, he drove to Tiger Hill and parked the car at the bottom of the incline. Then, he walked up the gravel road and the ladder to the fire tower. He focused the camera lens on the surrounding landscape and clicked away, using all twelve frames on the roll.

Now, he had a record of where he'd cheated death.

Chapter 19

"It'd take too long for me to tell you all that I seen there," Rod began. It was after dinner, and it was time for his first beer.

"You can't, or you *won't*?" Skid asked. He pushed the dirty dishes to the side and pulled out a ledger. It was time to organize the most recent orders and deliveries.

He was curious about Rod's experience in the Army since he was getting ready to fill out his draft card. At that time, it was the law, and while his chances of being drafted ended, it was still the law. But, of course, he didn't want to.

Rod stood and began clearing the table. He carried the dirty dishes to the sink and turned on the water. He ran his hand under the faucet and smiled as the water warmed.

The empty can of Pabst Blue Ribbon sat beside the sink, and Rod opened the refrigerator door to get another one. He wiggled the tab from the can and slotted it into the empty can on the counter.

"I was only there for a few weeks before I got sent to Germany. Some kinda paper snafu." Rod pulled a toothpick from his shirt pocket and dug between an incisor and a molar. "Anyway, I met my cousin over there, and he was the one who had all the stories. He was in intelligence, and he served three tours. So, Joseph called the other night when you were out and said he might come by for a visit."

Rod drained the beer can on the counter and pulled another from the refrigerator. He cleared the rest of the dishes and picked up a dishcloth. He shifted the toothpick from one side of his mouth to the other as he worked.

"He's a wild man. There was never any tellin' what he was goin' to do."

"What ya think he wants?" Skid asked.

"He just got out, so I think he's just drivin' around seein' the country. He said a funny sound comin' out of the front right side of his car, so he wants me to check it out."

"That sounds kinda dangerous, drivin' around like that, I mean," Skid said, not looking up from his ledger book.

"It's probably nothin'," Rod said. He shook a plate and propped it up in the sink.

"Probably," Skid said as he closed the ledger's cover. "I'm gonna watch some TV."

It was almost time for *The Waltons*. Skid picked up a notepad and walked into the dining room. He turned on the set and settled down to try and figure out a way to finish the script he'd begun last week. It wasn't going well, and he hoped the new episode would inspire and guide him on what to do next.

"Whatcha watchin' that for?" Rod asked as he flopped down in his recliner. He sat his half-empty beer can on an end table and picked up the newspaper. He clicked on a floor lamp. The light shone across Skid's view of the television, but he knew it was futile to complain. He'd just have to adjust.

"I'm studyin' the show for my script," Skid said, barely over the sound of a commercial.

"What'a ya think the odds are of a teenager writin' a script gettin' to the show?" Rod asked without lowering his newspaper.

"Million to one," Skid said. "Maybe more."

"So why do it?"

"I like it," Skid said. He pointed his pen at the notepad and waited for the show to begin. There was a short scene with narration like he'd already written, following the theme song.

"You're settin' yourself up for failure," Rod said again without lowering his newspaper.

"It's my failure," Skid said, a bit lower in tone this time, hoping the sound from the television might cover his comment.

Skid knew the narration from the show's creator set up the rest of the story, and he struggled to encapsulate what he wanted to say in the short speech. He knew the narrator was also the show's creator, Earl Hamner Jr. Many of the episodes were based on experiences of his growing up in the Blue Ridge Mountains of Virginia. Hamner had set the show during the Depression. Even after the show was a hit for years, most of the family's woes still involved making enough money to support a large, extended family living under one roof.

Rod rocked his recliner, and Skid noticed the paper slowly lowered to Rod's lap. Physical labor takes a toll, and there were few nights Rod didn't fall asleep in the big, brown chair. The recliner was a last gift from Donna. Skid knew it wasn't his chair and rarely sat in it.

The episode progressed. Skid timed the placement of the commercials and checked their appearance against the page numbers on his script. Act one began with the narration, followed by three scenes introducing the featured characters in the show, and a final showdown about the show's theme, followed by the conclusion.

Skid looked over his notes and tried to make sense of the scribblings. But first, he would have to check it against the script Mrs. Cardwell had gotten for him.

Rod snored softly. His now cleaner hands still clutched the edge of the newspaper. He'd washed them before doing the dishes and even used a cleaner he kept in a tin can in the barn, but some of the stains persisted. They were strong hands, and the older man awakened as Skid glanced at his sleeping guardian.

"Don't," he said. "It ain't right!" He was loud enough that Skid could hear the sound of the last few commercials but still quiet enough that Rod wouldn't wake himself.

Skid couldn't imagine what Rod was dreaming that would elicit such a response. Was it a customer complaint or the remnants of some argument he'd had with Skid's mother?

Rod startled awake and looked at the screen. "Is that shit still on?"

"Yep, almost over." Skid acknowledged the odds against his selling a script to the show was near zero. Still, even that million-to-one shot gave him hope. He believed he had something to say and convinced himself this was how to express it.

Ma and Pa Walton sometimes argued but always settled disputes before the following program. Their fights were unlike what Skid had seen with his mother and Rod. *Is that what families are really like?* Skid asked himself.

Chapter 20

His part-time job at Rose's, writing his *Waltons* script, and working with Rod kept Skid busier than a one-armed paper hanger. But he still found time to see Connie when she was available. But, of course, she was working, too. She was a sales associate at Goldstein's, a men's and women's clothing shop on the square. Mr. Goldstein was one of the few Jewish merchants in town, and while he was curt with some of the customers and his workers, he always came down on the side of what was fair.

Goldstein's was among dozens of small businesses surrounding the county courthouse. The goods and services supplied ranged from a pharmacy, a dry goods store, and attorney offices. Two rival banks sat on opposite sides of the government building that had suffered mini-ball damage during the Civil War. The holes were left unrepaired, but Skid never found out why.

Skid knew Connie was outgoing, but until he saw her working with a customer, he didn't know how attentive and influential she was in helping customers.

"So, what's Mr. Goldstein like?" Skid asked. He sipped his strawberry milkshake and picked up his double cheeseburger. They were eating at McDonald's again. The restaurant's proximity to the downtown square made it easy for Skid to pick up Connie, eat, and return to work during her lunch hour. She could have taken her lunch to work but wanted to spend time with Skid.

"He's okay. He's loud sometimes and has some weird expressions, but he's good." She picked up her milkshake and drained the last remnants. Yes, it made a loud sucking noise that embarrassed Skid.

"Expressions? Like what?" Skid said. He glanced out the front window at the large logo on the glass.

"Mazal tov, that means good luck. Meshugaah means crazy. He uses that one a lot. He says I have chutzpah, which means ambition, I think. I like him."

"He doesn't get fresh with you or anything, does he?" Skid asked. He knew lots of men found Connie attractive, even ones old enough to be her father.

"Oh, no, nothin' like that. He's happily married. He joked with me the other day that he can't afford a divorce, so he's got to stay married. I thought that was funny."

Skid took a bite of his burger and said, "That *is* kinda funny."

"Skid, don't talk with your mouth full," Connie said.

He nodded and swallowed. "Sorry, manners aren't all that important when two men live together."

"Are you guys gettin' along all right now?"

So, he thought, she remembered his complaints after his mother had died. "I guess he drinks a lot more now, but that's probably to be expected."

"And how about you? How are you doin'?"

It was lunchtime in the restaurant, and a large crowd lined up in the lobby waiting to give their orders. He saw a couple of people from school and noticed Leon was taking orders behind the counter. He wondered how he was doing, getting his grades up.

"Hey," Connie said and placed her hand on his. She looked at him, and he could see she was concerned.

"I have trouble getting to sleep sometimes. Other times, I can't keep my eyes open."

"That doesn't seem unusual. Did you talk to Miss Black?"

"I did, some, a while back. She was worried about my grades, but they're goin' back up."

"Good," Connie said. She pulled off her sweater and draped it over the back of her chair. The bodies pressed together in the lobby generated so much heat the window with the decal was fogging.

"Are y'all doin' okay?" Leon stood beside the table with a black plastic garbage bag and a white cloth in one hand. He smiled at Skid first and then at Connie.

"I thought I saw you back there. How's this workin' out?" Skid asked. Without slurping, he finished his milkshake and put the cup on the tray.

"Money's good. Only trouble is with the customers," Leon said. He pushed his paper hat back from his forehead a bit. His afro was getting big, and he'd have to get a trim soon for his job.

"I know," Connie said, "work would be great without customers."

"But then it wouldn't be work," Skid joked. "It would be a vacation."

"That's weak," Leon said and smiled. "Gotta get after it."

Leon turned, and when he'd gotten out of earshot, Connie said, "He was brave to lead that walk out. Could you have done anything like that?"

Skid thought for a second. "I'm not sure. We played basketball, and he's really good. He's a nice guy, but that doesn't always mean you're gonna get what you want."

"Ain't that the truth." Connie checked her watch. "You can take that with you. We've gotta go."

Skid nodded, put his leftovers in the bag, shoved the paper cups and napkins in the trash, and put the tray on top of the garbage can next to the front door. Then, from the corner of his eye, he noticed Leon clearing the table in front of an elderly couple. The old man sneered as Leon picked up their trays and trash. Then, he turned his face away as if to say, you're getting too close.

Skid saw that Connie noticed the same reaction. They looked at each other, and she sighed. "That's a crazy old man," he said.

Connie smiled and said, "He's meshugaah."

"Can you imagine summin' up Leon like that just by lookin' at him?" Skid asked as he opened the door for Connie. A brisk breeze met them, and Connie hugged herself. "My sweater."

Skid turned and picked up her sweater from the back of the chair. He caught Leon's eye and nodded as if to say goodbye. Leon smiled back and continued clearing tables and picking up trays.

Outside, Skid said. "It's not fair."

Connie said as she got into Skid's car. "Life isn't fair."

Skid knew the last part of the expression she usually said but hadn't since his mother's death. "And then you die," he finished the sentence as he closed her door. Connie looked at him through the glass and gave him a small smile.

Chapter 21

The Black Cat cave's mouth looked dank, and Skid could smell the damp soil as they approached. Connie protested the adventure and said the place had a "creepy" vibe.

They had driven past the Alvin C. York Veterans Administration hospital as Skid explained the background of its namesake. "York was a World War One hero who killed twenty-five German soldiers and captured 132 others while his troop cleared machine gun nests in France."

"Are you tryin' to impress me with this info?" Connie asked.

"No, just makin' conversation. I did a report on him in the eighth grade. York was born in East Tennessee and joined the Army after declaring himself a conscientious objector."

The rain from earlier made the roadway shimmer with reflected light from signs for small businesses and gas stations. Mist hovered around the streetlights, creating glowing orbs of yellow along the highway.

Connie asked, "So, he had religious grounds for not serving?"

"But he changed his mind. A movie starring Gary Cooper, *Sergeant York* was a big hit, and the actor won the best Oscar award for 1941."

Skid guided his mother's car as they drove past the huge hospital complex. The Nomad had a broad back seat that flipped down and had become a place where Skid and Connie had begun exploring each other's bodies. Skid's mother had told him to make sure his first love-making experience was someone he cared deeply for, and he had taken the advice to heart. However, the relationship was still too new, and sex would have to wait.

"And the movies comin' out when Hollywood was trying to convince America it needed to get involved in World War Two."

"You're like a genius," Connie said as she squinted through the rain at the collection of buildings. "I didn't say you were a genius," she said, smiling at her joke. "You're *like* a genius."

"Okay," Skid said, accepting her ribbing because she looked particularly attractive that night. "I get it."

The rain stopped, and a mist began to fall. Skid clicked the windshield wipers to a faster speed. The headlights cut a wide swath as they moved along the glossy blacktop.

"Am I supposed to be impressed with this knowledge?" She asked. She twirled a lock of hair in her fingertips as she stared out the window.

"I like history and thought you might like to hear about the man," Skid said. He squinted, looking through the falling rain for the gravel road where they would park.

"So, this is the romantic place we're going to make out?"

"There it is," he said as he pointed the Chevy's nose toward the gravel road. The rock parking area led to a trail in the grass where other explorers had hiked. Then, finally, the rain stopped, and they got out of the car.

"Black Cat Cave," Skid said. There was a lilt of wonder and awe in his voice.

"Looks horrible," Connie said. She watched Skid click on his flashlight and angle the beam toward a black hole in a mound of earth.

"This was a speakeasy in the 1930s. That's where people went to drink…"

"I know what a speakeasy is, Professor. Are you goin' to lecture me all night?" Connie asked. She swept a branch from the entrance as Skid led her into the cave.

The dank air smelled of mud and animal droppings. Some critters made this area their home but weren't there tonight. Maybe the rain had forced them into other, drier quarters.

"I wonder why they call it Black Cat?" Connie asked. As Skid pushed a rock with his tennis shoe, she put her hand over her nose.

"Unlucky to go into, I'm guessin'."

"So, why are we here?"

"It'll be fun," Skid said, smiling at her as he put the light under his chin. "Woooooooo."

"Not funny at all, young man," Connie said.

Skid's shoes squeaked on the damp concrete. Connie wore slippers with leather soles, so she was quieter. As a result, she didn't attract possible attention from any animals who might still be in the cave.

"We could dance," Skid said, "They put the concrete floor in here so people could drink and dance."

"Battery-powered radio?"

"Probably," Skid said, moving the flashlight around the cave walls, "not enough room for a band."

He pulled two PBRs from his coat pocket and cracked the tabs. He handed one to Connie and started in on the other one. It wasn't the best beer but cheap and would do in a pinch. They were free when Skid could sneak them out of the house. He hoped Rod wouldn't notice.

"So, we're here to dance and drink?"

He took her free hand and started doing a "White boy" dance where he closed his eyes and shuffled his feet. She had seen this before and wasn't impressed. The boy had no rhythm or talent as a dancer. But Connie did. She swung her hips back and forth and drank her beer.

"And maybe smooch a little bit," Skid said. He smiled at her, puckered up, and moved his face close to hers. She giggled and pushed him away.

"I'm not closin' my eyes in here. There's gotta be bugs, snakes, squirrels, just about anythin' you could think of."

Skid nodded. "You're right. Maybe this wasn't a good idea after all."

They emerged from the cave as a cloud moved across the moon. Moonlight filled the small field, and in the distance, a fawn stood so still it appeared as if trying to make itself invisible.

"Look at him," Skid whispered.

"At what? Oh," she said.

The fawn's ears perked up at her voice, and his right knee quivered. A cloud moved across the moon, and the light dimmed. When it passed, the fawn was gone.

"What do you make of that?" Connie asked.

"Nature's weird."

They walked through the grass, and Skid took Connie's hand. He told himself he was merely trying to make sure she didn't slip in the wet grass and as a guide around mud puddles, but he knew it was more than that. Was it time to go public at school and tell everyone they were a couple?

"Just how brave are you?" Skid mumbled.

"What," Connie said as they approached the car. She opened the door and clamored into the back seat. Skid followed.

"Oh, nothin'."

The damp air in the cave had made him shiver. Now, he was in the car, but he was still trembling.

"What's goin' on?" Connie asked.

He pulled the edges of his coat closer and scooted next to her. He'd spread a gray blanket across the back of the car. She scooted next to him and rubbed his shoulder.

"Let me warm you up," she said, smiling.

He looked through the windshield, and the fawn stood before the car.

"I'll get rid of him," he said, moving toward the steering column. When she tugged his shoulder, he was moving toward the headlight switch and was about to pull the knob.

"Leave it," she said. She turned him toward her and kissed him. He could taste the remnants of her cherry-flavored lipstick. Her warm breath held the whiff of hops and wheat.

"He's brave to just stand there," Skid said after the clinch ended.

"Brave or stupid."

"It's a thin line," he said. He moved toward her for another kiss, and she touched his chest.

"Why are we here?" She asked.

"Ah, I've been thinkin'."

"Oh, that never turns out well, Professor," she said, chuckling at her joke.

"Maybe it's time," he said. His gaze dropped to the floor, and his cheeks reddened.

She looked at him and raised his chin with her forefinger. "Really?"

"Maybe. What'a, you think?"

"Maybe," she said. "It's kinda cold to be thinkin' about, you know."

"I could turn on the motor." He said with just a bit too much enthusiasm in his voice.

"We've only been goin' together for a few months."

"Three months, three days, and two hours," he said, smiling.

"Oh, I see. So, you keep up with that kind of stuff."

"I started keeping a journal. It's private," he assured her. "Nobody else has access."

Connie smiled and nodded. "And our goin' together made it in?"

"It was the first entry."

"I see. Well, maybe not tonight. Let me think about it a bit more."

Skid was always a gentleman, and he knew to push the issue now might not be the wisest thing to do. He knew how he felt about Connie. But he wasn't as sure how she felt about him.

"Yeah," he said and leaned back. "Let's think about it."

She climbed into his lap and touched his cheek. "You really are a good boy," she said. And she kissed him.

Chapter 22

Journal Entry
April 28, 1975

News reports out of South Vietnam show the people there in a panic. I always thought we would win and the two factions would make peace.

I wonder what the thousands of veterans thought as they watched the chaos. The families of the dead and injured must also wonder what their sacrifice meant. I worry about my own draft status. Will I be called up to help stabilize or win back the territory that's apparently being lost due to the North Vietnamese moves?

Rod seems particularly upset by the news. While he only served there briefly, he was a brother-in-arms and knew the cost of the violence. What would he say if I had said I wouldn't go? What would he do if I declared myself a conscientious objector? Would he have supported me? Would he have bought me a ticket to Canada? It's all a moot point now, but I'm unsure how he would have reacted.

What is bravery? What does it mean? When I think about the television show "The Waltons," I see John-Boy as brave. He had dreams and had to take a stand several times during the show's run. His courage seemed based on the examples of his father and grandfather. Both had strong opinions and weren't afraid to express them. Rod was like that.

I remember watching the movie *Patton* with Rod and Mom a few years ago. I was so impressed by that intro he made at the beginning. Wow, what a great speech. It set up the whole movie. He said nobody ever won any war by dying for their country. Instead, you won a war by making the other soldier die for *his* country. Genius.

But another line in the speech came back to me just now. "America has never lost a war, and it never will." What did that mean today to the people who served in Vietnam?

If we didn't win, I thought the solution to the conflict might be something like what happened in the Korean War. Both sides would agree that there should be a demilitarized zone between the armies and that they would exist in a state of cease-fire. That system had been in place for decades in Korea, and while there was never a declared end of the war, the signed treaty allowed both sides to claim and defend their territory.

In my mind, Vietnam was supposed to end similarly. The American-backed South would exist as a democracy, and the North would be a communist country like China. That didn't happen, and now, as the final Americans leave the country, do we admit we lost?

Chapter 23

Skid was never a Boy Scout, but he did trust their motto, "Be prepared."

He believed he and Connie would be intimate soon, and he wasn't ready to be a father. He could have gone to the drugstore on the square and bought them there. But, because it was such a small town, he knew gossip would travel from the north side of the town square, where the pharmacy was, to the west side of the courthouse, where Connie's workplace was, in about thirty seconds. He didn't want to embarrass her, and most importantly, he didn't want to embarrass himself.

He'd seen the machines on road trips with his mother and even asked her for a quarter so he could buy one for himself. Donna blushed when he asked and tried to think of a way she could explain their use without going into too much detail.

"It's a sheath that's placed over the man's penis to help prevent unwanted pregnancies," Donna said. It was as simple an explanation as she could come up with.

Skid looked at her driving and felt his ears turn red. He wished he hadn't asked.

That was years ago, but he still remembered the conversation. This would be the second time he'd seen a condom after use, and the thought made him a bit queasy, just like the first time he'd seen a used one.

The machines hung near the door of the gas station on Highway 99. It was painted in a dull, unobtrusive color and stickers touting the healthcare aspects of using condoms. He guessed even in gas station bathrooms, the topic of birth control was too hot to handle.

Now that he was a Senior, the price of the prophylactics had risen to two quarters. He'd heard the other guys talking about how they felt and how they worked, so he had some knowledge of how this latex sheath would keep Connie from getting pregnant. The notion the condom would hamper the transmission of sexual disease didn't occur to him. He had never been with anyone before, and he was sure neither had Connie.

"So, how are you sure this will work?" She asked.

They had just wrapped up a make-out session in the back of Skid's car. His pants were unzipped, and his T-shirt was wrinkled. She was also disheveled, with her skirt unzipped and her blouse unbuttoned. The kissing had smeared her lipstick. A mascara smudge swept from the corner of her eye to her cheek.

It was a warm night, and the field near the entrance to Black Cat Cave had become one of their favorite places to "talk." A large, yellow moon shone down with the light bouncing off the car's shiny hood. The talk about whether to take their relationship to the next level had been detailed and pragmatic.

"Did you try it?" She asked.

"Whata ya mean?"

"Did you test one of them to see if it works?"

"Yes, of course," he said, his cheeks reddening.

"How did it feel?" She asked. A sly smirk played around the edges of her lips.

"F-f-fine, it was okay." He stammered a bit on the word "fine," and she poked him in the ribs.

"Fine. I mean, are you sure you want to go with that word?" She asked as she pushed herself up and pulled her legs back over the big hump separating the back seat floor.

"Okay, it felt terrible."

"But you're okay with that?"

Skid looked through the windshield and saw the chrome strip at the bottom of the windows reflect the moonlight. He chuckled to himself. "You know me too well."

"I do, don't I," she said with an even bigger grin.

She put her hands behind her head and interlaced her fingers. Her blouse fell open, and he could see the outline of her breasts and how the flesh strained against the bra's elastic.

"I want you so much," he said. He reached for her and pulled her close. His hand swept inside her blouse and cupped her breast.

She kissed him, and her hand fell onto his lap. "I know you do, and I want you to, but is this the best place for us to do this?"

They lived at home and were too broke to afford a motel room. Besides, they'd have to get out of town so no one would recognize them and feed the grapevine of gossip.

"I don't know. I want to," he said.

"I do, too," she said as her hand slid inside his unbuckled trousers.

"Okay," he said, his breath becoming ragged and short.

"Get the thing," she said between kisses.

"Oh, what, oh, okay." He reached under the front seat and pulled out the plastic-wrapped condom.

"We'll make believe it's a science experiment," Connie said. She reached behind her and unsnapped her bra clasp. The fabric loosened, and he moved his hand over her engorged nipple.

"Okay, like in Miss Black's health class?"

"Sure," she whispered. She took the condom from him, ended the kiss, and opened the wrapper.

"Let me," Skid said as he pulled it from the wrapper. With condoms, the problem was always deciding the inside from the outside. He'd already ruined one he tested at home.

"Okay," she said. Then, she pulled up her bra so he could see her naked.

"Ah," he said. "Fingernails."

He'd always enjoyed how Connie kept her nails trimmed and painted a glossy red, but those same nails might cause problems tonight.

"Right," she said, still grinning. She kissed him as she slowly unrolled the condom, fingertips with no nails.

She pulled him back as she leaned against the door. She was on the driver's side, and her left hand fell inside his almost completely removed pants and underwear.

"Whoa," he said as he shifted his body so she could get a better angle.

Skid knew they liked each other but wondered if they loved each other. Would college split them up? Would a job somewhere keep them apart? Doing this tonight might change everything.

She moved her fingertip over the end of the condom and stroked him. He moaned and wriggled against her.

"You like this, don't you?" She asked.

He kissed her, slipping his tongue into her mouth and rubbing her nipples. Then, he opened her shirt and slowly kissed her breasts, first the right and then the left.

This time it was Connie moaning. She tipped her head back, licked her lips, and closed her eyes. Again, she felt him rock hard against her. She was about to slip her skirt down when there was a knock on the window.

"You two doin' all right back there?" The officer asked.

Even though the back window passenger side was fogged over from their heavy breathing, Connie saw him first. She pushed Skid's hand from her chest and pulled her blouse around her.

"We're fine," she said, just a bit louder than she intended.

"We're fine," Skid said, pulling his underwear and pants back on his hips.

"Ya'll need to step out," the officer said.

Connie spun around in the seat and rushed to button her shirt. "

"Just a second," Skid said, fastening his belt and sliding out the passenger side door.

"Give me a minute," Connie chimed in.

Once out of the car, Skid looked at the police officer across the sedan's top. The moonlight had turned yellow to white and seemed brighter than before they began their make-out session.

Connie opened the door, and the officer helped her out of the car. She adjusted her clothes and smiled at the young man.

"This isn't a park, but it is city property. So, you're kind of trespassing."

"I know," Skid said. "We're sorry."

"I get it," the young man said as he glanced at Skid and then Connie. He was tall and thin with a bushy, blond mustache. Skid found the lip hair oddly out of character. Here was a man who had the authority to pull his gun and shoot someone suspected of a crime or who was uncooperative and threatening to a police officer. "But I wouldn't be doin' my job if I didn't get you to move along."

"Right," Skid said, searching his pockets for his keys.

"You haven't been drinkin', have ya?"

"No, Sir," Skid lied. He believed the police officer wouldn't smell the beer on his breath because he was on the opposite side of the car.

The officer stood close to Connie and took a deep breath. "Okay, move along."

Connie nodded and walked around the back of the car as Skid circled the front. He held his keys before himself, hoping to hide his waning erection.

The police car lights flashed on as the officer cranked the motor. He pulled back into the field and waited.

"I think he wants to see us leave," Connie said, now sitting primly in the passenger seat.

"Right," Skid said as he turned over the motor. "What time is it?"

She checked her watch and said, "Eleven-thirty."

"We know when he checks the cave entrance now."

"You devil. By the way, do you still have the..."

"Yes, it's still kind of on."

"So, it *worked*?"

"I guess."

"Good. That's good." She said as she patted him on the shoulder.

Skid pulled out of the field. He watched as the police officer drove in the opposite direction in the rearview mirror. He took a deep breath and put the car in second gear.

"That's one science experiment that failed," Skid mumbled.

"No, it was a half-success. What would Miss Black say?" Connie asked.

Skid could only guess what the health teacher might say about this incident. Questions could involve physiological responses concerning human reproduction. But, on the other hand, he could believe there might be some questions about the mind's involvement in preparing the body for the sex act.

Still, he knew what Rod would have said if Skid had been caught half-naked in the back seat with a girl and arrested. "The phrase that came to mind was, 'You know what you are, boy? You ain't worth killin'.'"

Chapter 24

Skid saw Connie walking down the hallway with two girlfriends the next day in school. She glanced at him as he stood next to his locker. Eddie and Dee Dee stood to his left and right. He dipped his chin, and he could feel his cheeks redden.

"Are you guys doin' okay?" Dee Dee asked. She had a pimple on her chin she'd tried to cover with makeup but was unsuccessful.

"Yeah, sure, why wouldn't we be?" Skid replied with his own question.

Eddie asked, "Has she decided where she's gonna apply for college?"

"She's got a list."

Dee Dee said, "Nothin' local, I bet."

"Whata ya mean?" Skid asked.

"Well, she's been talkin' about leavin' this town since I've known her. I wouldn't be surprised if she wanted to go up North. She's got the grades, and if she does well on the S-A-T, she can probably go wherever she wants," Dee Dee said. She touched her chin and remembered the eruption there.

Skid slammed his locker door and turned toward the East end of the building. Dee Dee and Eddie followed.

"I wonder what it's like to be that smart," Eddie said.

Skid and Dee Dee both looked at him and laughed.

"You're plenty smart, Ed," Dee Dee said.

"It's just that you hide it so well," Skid joked.

Dee Dee and Skid chuckled again, but Eddie didn't.

"There's different kinds of smart," Eddie observed.

Dee Dee and Skid looked at each other again and nodded in unison.

"He's not wrong," Dee Dee said. "But none of us are 'Connie' smart."

Skid and Connie hadn't talked much about college. He assumed they would end up at the same school, but she was more intelligent than him, and this decision could set her on a different path. Skid didn't have the same grades, but he knew he might get to go with her if he did well on the SAT.

Skid was ready to leave this "nowhere" town. He thought about what adventures lay past the city limits. Still, he didn't feel Rod would support his seeking opportunity away from home and the shop. And why would he? Rod had cheap, maybe even free labor, right there in the house. Skid didn't believe he'd give that up easily.

"I'm gonna stay home and go to 'the college,'" Eddie said. "The college" was a former Normal school, or teacher's college, which had recently been accredited as a university. It was a short drive and was 'good enough' for most of Skid's graduating class.

Dee Dee had also mentioned living with her parents for a while longer and commuting thirty minutes daily to "the college." She knew living in an apartment or a dorm could cost a mint.

"I can't think about that now," Skid said. He felt the same pain in the bottom of his stomach when he'd been called to the office and told his mother had died. *Gotta move on*, he thought.

"What are you thinking about?" Dee Dee asked.

"The family tree assignment for English. I don't know anything about my father's family, and now that Mom's gone, I can't ask her about hers."

"You could check the library. They have newspapers on microfiche. I mean the college library," Dee Dee said, always helpful.

Skid had frequented the city library since he first started reading. His mother would take weekly trips to the downtown Piggly Wiggly and drop him off in front of the two-story limestone building. She'd find him on the sidewalk juggling a stack of books from his waist to his chin.

In fact, the library was one of the places where he felt most comfortable and satisfied. He liked the smell of the books and how he would wander around and touch the spines of volumes that had existed for decades. It was as close to immortal as most people would become.

He'd visited the college library five times. It was as big as the one in the city. *Even more aisles of wisdom and pleasure to wander,* he thought.

On Saturday, he skipped working for Rod and drove to the college library. It was quiet since most students commuted Monday through Friday and stayed home on weekends. So, he had the place almost to himself.

Skid asked the librarian how to operate the microfiche machine and pulled out his notebook. He had his mother's birthday in 1949 and his grandparents Frank and Mamie's birthdays in 1907. Still, he had no data on anything else in their lives. So, he began with his grandmother and found her in the 1920 census. She was listed with her aunt, another name he'd never heard, and her age, 13, but little else.

Why was Mamie listed as living with her aunt and not her parents? Skid scanned several newspaper articles from the time but found no mention of his ancestors. Finally, he checked the 1910 census and found his grandmother listed with her parents and five siblings. He'd heard his mother say her family had died tragically, but little else of the story. They'd once visited the graveyard, and he saw all six names etched into the headstone. He couldn't remember the exact date of their deaths, but he believed it was 1910.

This captured Skid's curiosity, and hours passed as he searched for the names of Ida and Boyd. Lastly, he found a front-page story explaining everything on March 12th, 1910.

It was tornado season in Tennessee, and many touched down, leaving behind acres of destruction and death. Skid's family lived on a farm distant from the city. The article said they were well-liked in the community, but there was no chance for escape when the twister came.

The tornado demolished the tiny, three-room cabin where the family lived. Authorities believed the father or mother had tied the children to a pot-bellied stove and a post in the center of the house. The winds and debris had pummeled their bodies into submission. There were no survivors in what was left of the house. The three-year-old Mamie was discovered, muddy and crying, wandering in a nearby field. Her wounds were superficial, and at the end of the story, she was called a "miracle baby."

Skid sat stunned and looked out the window as the sun slowly fell. He'd been there all day, and only now did he realize he hadn't moved from the machine in seven hours.

"Holy cow," he muttered. He would have to leave soon, but there was one more thing he needed to check before he left. Skid concluded his existence must have been a stroke of fate. He was alive. Then, he squinted at the line where his great-grandmother's name was listed. In class, he'd listened to Mrs. Jenkins lecture about genetics and the miracle of life. Something he'd only heard of in passing caught his attention. He rubbed his eyes. He'd stared at the screen for so long that his eyes felt watery and sore. Finally, he put his finger on the screen.

Next to his great-grandfather's name was a large "W." Next to his great-grandmother's name was an "M." He sat back in his chair and puffed out his cheeks.

"What the hell does that mean?" he asked. He was loud enough for the librarian near him to glance over and "shush" him. He waggled his finger at her, and she politely came over.

Skid pointed to the screen and whispered, "This is a census from 1890. This 'M' here next to my great-grandmother's name. What does…"

"That means she was a mulatto."

He'd heard the word before but wanted confirmation.

"Mulatto?" Skid asked.

"Yes," the young woman said. She was short and wore glasses. She held a book in each hand. "The woman was of mixed race, Black and White."

"I see, thank you," Skid said.

"We're closing. You need to get your stuff and go," she said. She must have noticed the shock on Skid's face when she said, "It's not that unusual. Many slaveholders would breed with their slaves, believing the offspring would be smarter and more compliant."

"Like livestock," Skid said. A tear formed in the corner of his eye as he imagined what life would be like if you were considered little more than chattel.

"Yes," the librarian said. She noticed Skid wiping his cheek. "It's very sad."

Skid nodded and closed his notebook. Now, he would have to decide what to put in his report and what to leave out.

Chapter 25

Rod had forgotten to tell Skid when Joseph would be visiting. It wasn't deliberate. It wasn't a diss to his stepson. The chore of ensuring anything needed to comfort a guest would be on Skid. The visit had just slipped Rod's mind. That happened when he was busy with his projects, and a deadline neared.

Skid swept the porch and vacuumed the house after dusting most of the furniture. He didn't always venture into Rod's and his mother's bedroom because seeing some of her stuff still in there brought back too many memories.

He cleaned and rearranged the guest room and put fresh towels in the upstairs bathroom. Skid had only met Joseph once before, but he liked him.

The older man bragged that some of the missions he'd been on in Vietnam were classified, and if he told Skid about them, he'd have to kill him. Skid laughed, but he wondered if the threat might be true.

Joseph's Jaguar slid through the front gate and crunched to a stop on the gravel in front of the newly swept porch. He leaped over the driver's side door like Batman getting out of the Batmobile.

He was tall and thin, just like Rod. Skid guessed a genetic disposition ran through the men on that side of Rod's family. As a result, they sported balding spots on the back of their heads and large hands and feet.

Joseph also sported a shiner under his left eye and a long scratch on his right cheek. Both injuries looked new and were on the way to healing.

"Little Skid man," Joseph said as he bounded toward the porch. He had his hand stuck out, and Skid grabbed and shook it. According to Rod, handshakes were significant, and they'd practiced a few times to ensure Skid was doing it right.

"You've grown up since the last time I saw you."

Joseph pinched Skid's cheek and brushed the back of his hand near the boy's upper lip. A thin mustache would soon need daily shaving instead of the weekly chore.

"What happened with your eye?" Skid asked.

"A little trouble down in Mexico," Joseph said and continued, "Don't need to tell the stories twice. Where's Rod? I can kill two birds with one stone." Joseph swallowed the last bit of the sentence and pushed a cigarette into his mouth.

Skid stared at the cigarette pack a bit too long, and Joseph noticed. "Yeah, they're pretty sweet, aren't they?"

Gold filigree was on both the top and bottom of the pack. A ring of flowers encircled the cigarette near the filter. "Aren't those women's cigarettes?" Skid asked.

A brilliant springtime sun shined across the porch planks painted gray. Joseph was taller than Skid, so the young man looked into the soldier's eyes. A flicker of pain registered and quickly disappeared.

"What difference does it make? They're French, and I like the taste."

"Okay, well, Rod's in the shop. He's been talkin' about your visit for days."

"Yeah, I gotta get him to look at this piece of shit," he said as he pointed to the Jaguar's front hood. "Drivin' a bit rough. Might have run over somethin'."

"Oh, yeah. You said there was a noise or somethin' in the front. What kind of mile..."

"Let's go see what Rod's up to," Joseph said, turned, and stepped off the porch.

***

Rod was halfway into the engine compartment of a '57 Chevy when Joseph bounded through the shop's large, sliding door. He tossed his cigarette over his shoulder as he crossed the threshold.

Skid stepped on the smoldering ash and followed Joseph into the shop. He noticed how the siding needed a new coat of paint and how musty the place smelled following last night's rain. *I hope there's not a leak in the roof,* Skid thought. The top had tin panels with tar paper underneath. That made it hard to find a leak.

"Hey, you son of a bitch," Joseph yelled. He raised his arms and laughed as he approached Rod.

The mechanic pulled himself away from his work and turned. He had thick grease on his hands, trying to wipe them on a shop cloth as Joseph neared.

"Hold on," Rod said.

"I don't care," Joseph said, lowering his arms and wrapping them around his cousin.

Skid hadn't seen Rod hug too many men, and truthfully Joseph didn't give him much of a choice this time. So, they stood there momentarily, and the boy thought he caught Rod's shoulder sinking a bit.

"You're a sight, I gotta tell ya'."

"Rod, my boy, you shoulda seen the other guy," Joseph said as he stepped away from the hug. "What you got goin' on here?" He nodded toward the Chevy.

"Threw a rod at ninety. It churned up the engine somethin' awful."

"I bet it did." Joseph pulled another cigarette from the pack in his shirt. He let the butt dangle and said, "I'm only gonna be here a couple of days. Looks like you're too busy to look at my old rust bucket."

Again, Rod chuckled, something Skid had rarely seen, especially since his mother's death. *So, what is this all about?* Skid thought.

"I can always make a space for you. Let's go get some coffee," Rod said. "Is there anything left from this morning?"

"I'll make some fresh," Skid said, moving away from the car. He bumped into the edge of a workbench and winced in pain.

"You all right there?" Joseph asked.

"Yep," Rod said, "he's clumsy, but he's handy."

Both the men laughed as Skid limped a few steps and walked through the big barn door. He checked his pants and saw a small oil stain. "Damn it," Skid muttered. "That'll never come out."

"What," Rod said, standing right behind him now, "what did you say?"

"I just said these pants are stained now."

"I thought I heard somethin' else. You can still wear 'em, cain't you?"

"Yeah, sure, no problem," Skid said, but he didn't like wearing clothes with stains and rips. Damage often happened in the shop, and Rod saw nothing wrong.

"Look at these cigarettes," Joseph said, pulling his pack from his shirt pocket.

"Ain't never seen nothin' like 'em," Rod said.

The men walked close with only a sliver of daylight between them. "They're from France."

"He says they taste great," Skid said over his shoulder. He glanced back and saw the backs of the men's hands touch and then fall away.

"I tried smokin' once," Rod said, "almost threw up."

"Yeah, you gotta get used to it," Joseph said with a tone of authority.

"Why would..."Skid began but stopped talking as he stepped up on the porch. A swing painted the same color as the planks squeaked in the wind.

"Not too cold to stay out here, is it?" Rod asked.

"Not for me," Joseph said, sitting beside the rock-hewn steps on the porch. He lit the cigarette hanging from the corner of his lips.

Skid went into the kitchen, and by the time he returned with two cups of black coffee, the men were already laughing and joking about things they'd done as kids.

"And you held my head underwater," Rod said.

"You swam like a rock. I was just tryin' to teach you," Joseph countered.

"I come off Tiger Hill on a bicycle with no brakes once," Skid said.

The men stopped and looked at Skid. They seemed to be both astonished and admiring.

"Why would you do that?" Rod asked.

"I don't know," Skid said as he placed a cup on a small table near Rod's chair. "I didn't do it on purpose."

"Good answer," Joseph said, laughing.

"Don't do stupid shit like that again," Rod said.

"Don't worry, I learned my lesson."

The men drank coffee and leaned back in matching hand-woven, willow-strip rocking chairs. Joseph balanced on the curved runners of the chair, hovering in the air for what seemed minutes. He leaned until the spindles at the top of the chair scrubbed the wall.

The sun cast giant shadows from the two large maple trees on each end of the yard. The men reminisced about climbing trees where they grew up, embellishing some accounts, and downplaying others, until Rod said, "So, for real, how're you doin'?"

Joseph nodded ever so slightly and gazed into the distance. A cardinal flitted from one of the maples to the other. "I'm good. Free as a bird."

"What did you do over there?" Skid asked. "I mean, whatever you can tell us."

Joseph took a deep breath and sighed. "Too much and not enough, that's for sure."

"He was in military intelligence," Rod said, allowing a slender tone of pride to creep into his voice.

"Wow," Skid said. Of course, he knew this, but somehow Rod had forgotten that.

Skid had a glass of iced tea and sat on the edge of the porch, looking up at the men as they rocked.

"I picked up some of the language and got roped in. I was called an augmentee to a battalion." He pulled another cigarette from his pack. He laid the box on the flat arm of the rocker and lit a match with his fingernail.

"Did you have to kill anyone?" Skid asked. It was a natural question, which the boy was sure had been asked by others, but he could see Rod wince. He knew he'd get "a-talkin' to" later about that.

"It's not a good-," Joseph began and then stopped, "I mean."

"He means it's not somethin' he can talk about. That's all," Rod said. But, of course, the "that's all" could have covered Skid's follow-up questions or an attempt to change the subject.

"I seen men die if that helps. I was in a paddy one day, clear blue sky, just like today, but hotter. I was standing, and my closest friend was less than ten feet away when a mortar came whistlin' in. When I came to, there were parts of him all around. I had to jump into the irrigation ditch and get his right foot." Joseph said. He forced a slender jet of smoke from the corner of his mouth. "Pretty much all that was left of him."

"Damn," Skid said. His foot slipped off the limestone step leading up to the porch. The sound of his sneaker on the gravel sidewalk made a popping noise.

Joseph winced as a flicker of pain flitted across his cut cheek. "Ain't nothin' but a thing."

"Yeah, and a thing ain't nothin'," Rod responded. "What the hell is wrong with that piece-of-shit car of yours?"

"You drive it and tell me," Joseph said as he tossed Rod the keys. "Hey," looking at Skid, "climb in the back."

The Jaguar convertible sat two people comfortably, but a third had to find a way to serpentine their path between the collapsed top and into the tiny back seat. Skid had stopped growing, but he was still the "kid," meaning his place was behind the grownups.

As Rod drove over the cattle gate and onto the paved two-lane in front of the farm, he said over the engine's whine. "I don't hear it."

"You will," Joseph shouted.

Skid struggled following the conversation in the front bucket seats with the wind noise, the non-existent mufflers, and the accelerating engine. Finally, the talk grew animated, with Skid catching a word or phrase over the growing din.

"Better dead than red," Joseph said, laughing.

"Turn it up," Rod shouted.

At that moment, Skid saw Joseph reach for the radio volume knob as Rod touched it. Joseph's hand lingered momentarily and dropped back to his cockpit side. He pulled his pack of cigarettes from his coat pocket and slipped the filtered end out with his lips.

The speakers behind Skid made it even more challenging to hear what was happening in the front seats, but he finally recognized the music. It was the hit single *Fight the Power* by the Isley Brothers. Skid liked the song, a throbbing beat, and the message harkening back to the protest songs of the 1960s. A few rock stations in Nashville blanketed the mid-state, but Skid's favorite was 103 KDF-FM. On the weekends, they had a DJ named Rockin' Rudy, who played a weird mix of rock, soul, and protest music. He was Skid's favorite. He liked the tone and rhythm of the announcer's voice. He wished he could write that way.

Skid was no hippie, but he now felt a pang of pride in the students who'd protested at his school, even if he were wrongly accused of skipping school during the commotion. Maybe he'd tell Joseph the story and get his opinion.

Skid watched the talk between the two men become more animated. Then the engine stumbled like a racehorse nearing the finish line. Joseph nodded and yelled, "That's it."

"Maybe it's just a tire, like on mom's car?" Skid asked.

"That ain't it." Rod nodded and backed off the accelerator. "I think I know what's wrong." He turned the wheel and made a U-turn.

The mechanic cut the engine as the car crossed over the cattle gate. The vehicle coasted on the gravel driveway in front of the house. Skid had seen him do this before, with other cars needing attention. He called it a "suspension and brake check," which helped him diagnose hard-to-find problems.

"Sure, you can stay a couple of days while I get this tuned up," Rod said. He glanced over at Joseph as he guided the car toward the shop.

The retired Army augmentee dipped his head under the windshield and lit his cigarette. When he sat back in the seat, he smiled and said, "My duffle's in the back."

***

"I took the mule train down the side of the Grand Canyon last week," Joseph said. He put down his fork and pulled a cigarette from the pack on his right.

"How can you smoke and eat at the same time?" Skid asked, at once regretting the question.

"Talent, ability, and a death wish from way back," Joseph said and chuckled.

Skid nodded and raised the tuna sandwich to his mouth. The lunch should have been more elaborate for a war hero. But Skid didn't want to waste time in the kitchen cooking. He wanted to hear some of Joseph's war stories.

"What about..." Skid started to ask, but Joseph interrupted him.

"So, tell me about this time you came off Tiger Hill on a bicycle," he said.

Rod said, "Yeah, I'd like to hear that one, too."

Skid told him about the trek up the hill and how the girls caught him off guard, causing him to let off his brake. Then, he added a new wrinkle by talking about how he felt when he let go.

"It was freeing and terrifying both," Skid said. He took a sip of milk and leaned forward. He was tempted to ask Joseph for a cigarette, but changed his mind at the last second.

"I've felt that too," Joseph said. He leaned over and pulled his shoulder-length hair from the back of his head. He ran his finger over a three-inch scar along the nape of his neck. "I got this when I was leaning out of a helicopter, and we caught some fire from the ground."

"That musta hurt."

Joseph gave him a "Are you joking" expression before he said. "So, that took me out of the game for a month. Not bad enough to send me home, but you know."

"And?" Rod asked.

"Yes, my hair was shorter then," Joseph said with a chuckle.

"Rod won't let me grow my hair out," Skid said, immediately regretting the childish whine in his voice.

"You're a man. Take some shaving cream and wash that Stephan's hair oil from your head. That cut makes you look like Rod," Joseph said, glancing at the mechanic. "You sure as hell don't want that. Be free."

"I used to have some dandruff." Skid nodded and said, "But maybe it's time."

Joseph took a bite. "Man, that's good. What did you put in it?"

"It was my mother's recipe. Red onion and lemon juice makes the tuna taste sharper," Skid said. He took a bite of his sandwich but couldn't hide his smile.

"Your mama was a good woman," Joseph said. "Only met her that once at the wedding. Yep, it's a real shame what happened to her."

Skid nodded and took another bite. "I think about her all the time."

Rod took a bite of his sandwich and stared ahead. He chewed and swallowed, paused a second before taking another bite.

Joseph rubbed the side of his cheek. Skid couldn't tell if he was wiping tuna oil from his chin or trying to keep a tear from sliding down his face.

***

That night, Skid lay awake with memories of his mother playing in his head. Near the end, he knew she was dying, and he'd seen her in pain. She didn't want that, so she tried to avoid him when her symptoms worsened.

He listened to the sounds of the house. It was built in the 1920s. While much foundation settling had already happened, there were still wood-on-wood creaks.

The voices started low, making it impossible for Skid to decipher the words. But he knew the emotional tone, just like every child, and it wasn't good. So first, he heard unintelligible phrases with Rod ending one with "Forever." Then, more garbled words with Joseph ending one tirade with "Again."

What could it mean? Skid remembered a similar talk between Rod and his mother, with long passages wrapped in whispers. He believed some of the argument might have been about him, but his mother wouldn't say a word when he asked about it the following day. Later that day, Rod would look at Skid and raise his newspaper, blocking eye contact.

Skid recognized the tone of the conversation between Rod and Joseph. It sounded significant and urgent. Were they reminiscing about their days overseas? Why would there be an angry tone to their talk?

As the men's voices faded, Skid heard a distant door shut. It wasn't a slam or an exclamation point grown-ups sometimes used for emphasis. It was just an emphatic closing of a door.

***

Skid woke to the sound of birds and a gentle breeze wafting through an open window. He liked to sleep with his window cracked. While the morning temperature hovered around the freezing mark, he felt warm and safe under his bed covers.

The boy rolled out of bed, shuffled to the bathroom, and then into the den. A strange creaking noise didn't match the other sounds he'd grown accustomed to while growing up in the family farmhouse.

Skid wore pajamas and was barefoot as he moved through the house, searching for the mysterious noise. He glanced out the window and saw the small end table that usually sat near the two rocking chairs on the porch sitting upside down in the front yard. He didn't think there was enough wind last night to pick it up and carry it that far.

Skid opened the front door. He noticed the bare feet first. They were ash white and moving in the gentle breeze. Then, the body twisted, and Skid saw the face.

Its tongue was out and seemed too thick to fit in the mouth. The eyes were closed, and the shoulders slumped. The neck stretched against a thin, yellow rope.

"Joseph," Skid whispered. Maybe he thought he could bring the young man back to life if only he could speak with the correct tone. Maybe there were magic words he might say that would make the horrible sight go away.

"Oh, shit," Rod said. He rushed by Skid and grabbed Joseph's legs. He pushed up against Joseph's body and held him there. "Holy Christ, boy, get something to cut him down."

The boy turned and ran back into the house. He found scissors on the kitchen counter and retrieved the end table from the yard.

"You son of a bitch," Rod said as Skid climbed the small table. "What the hell were you thinkin'?"

Skid sawed at the nylon rope until Joseph's body fell back onto Rod. They both crumpled to the floor.

"No, no, no," Rod said. "Call an ambulance! Call an ambulance!" He screamed at Skid.

The boy ran into the house again and called. Soon, two sirens whined in the distance.

Joseph lay on the porch. His eyes fixed on the rafters holding up the porch as if searching for a leak in the roof.

"Why?" Rod asked. "Why'd you do it?"

The ambulance driver and attendant put Joseph's body on a stretcher. Then, they carried the body across the lawn and slid him into the back of the vehicle.

A sheriff's deputy held a notepad and asked Rod questions. "Do you have any idea if something was bothering him?"

Rod shook his head no.

"What about those bruises on his face and that cut?" the officer asked.

"He came here like that. He said he'd gotten into some trouble in Mexico."

"Are you sure you didn't have anything to do with that?"

"No, we always got along great," Rod said, shaking his head in disbelief.

The deputy said there would be a follow-up interview, probably no autopsy, and a full report filed with the V.A. "He coulda gotten some help over at the Alvin York if he'd had a mind to."

Rod said, "I shoulda seen it comin'."

"There ain't no way you coulda known. I've seen a bunch of veterans come back from the war and do this."

Rod nodded and picked up the yellow rope. He twisted it in his hands and looked as the ambulance inched down the driveway.

The officer lowered his hand and said, "I'm gonna need that for evidence."

"He was a good guy," Rod said. He handed the officer the rope. He sat on the edge of the porch and covered his face with his hands.

***

May 1, 1975

Dear Editor,

Something must be done.

Veterans are the best of us. They put their lives on the line daily, and when they return home, they're sometimes shunned and degraded. No wonder many take their own lives instead of facing the derision of serving.

It's outrageous and-

Skid stopped typing and looked at the paper on the typewriter platen. What was he doing? Did he really believe writing a letter to the editor of a small newspaper in a little town would do anything?

He yanked the paper from the roller and crumpled it into a ball. He tossed the ball at a waste can less than ten feet to his left. He missed. Again, confirming what he'd known, basketball wasn't his sport.

Joseph was a good guy, Skid thought. *So why did he do it?* Would Rod know, and should he ask him?

Skid pushed back from the desk that took up a corner of his room. He spun in his secretary's chair and closed his eyes. Sometimes, this helped him think. Finally, he stopped and wondered aloud, "What was Joseph thinking?"

Chapter 26

And then Skid read *Siddhartha* by German novelist Hermann Hesse.

It was so short he finished it in two sittings. He read the first half the night after the coroner's office shipped Joseph's body to Missouri, where his mother waited. Skid read the novel's second half the next day. He was lucky it was a Saturday. He'd been laid off at the department store and was waiting to hear the results of filling out a form and an interview at McDonald's.

Skid knew Siddhartha was the first name for the Buddha from the lecture in Mrs. Wilson's class before she handed out the assignment. She said the book influenced her understanding of life and hoped the same would happen for her students.

The book lay face down on his nightstand. He picked it up and read the last few pages. He looked at the setting sun in his bedroom window and reread the same pages.

Siddhartha was the son of a Brahmin or Minister in Kapilavastu in Nepal, while Prince Gotama sat on the throne. The ruler relinquished his royal riches and responsibilities to become a beggar and preacher. He gathered believers and began wandering the countryside. He taught his wisdom to anyone who would listen.

Skid had read the Bible and attended Sunday School when his mother was alive. He enjoyed the stories, even though some were difficult to believe. He found comfort in knowing there's an afterlife when we die. He realized this was the main selling point of all religions. Skid thought all religions were developed and amplified to ease death anxiety and grow membership.

In Siddhartha's teachings, Skid found this to be the case, but he related more to the text because the minister loved women and had sex. The Buddha's teachings became popular and clashed as his influence resonated far and wide in other parts of the kingdom. Young Siddhartha becomes dissatisfied with the precepts of his father's beliefs. Still, he asks his father's permission to leave his home before he sets out on his journey of enlightenment. He decided to begin his own religion in defiance of the establishment. Siddhartha joins his friend Govinda and Shramanas, a group of traveling Puritans who live in the forests searching for enlightenment.

Did this sound like the beginnings of Christianity? *Of course*, Skid thought. He looked at the darkness outside his window and clicked on a lamp near his bed. All religions start the same way, with a single person, usually a man, with a vision he tells others. Then, they believe his way is the best and join him.

A full moon cast a shadow over Skid's desk and his notebooks. It was his favorite place to write, where he'd put the typewriter he'd rented for a week from Batey's, the local camera shop. He'd hoped to have a new typewriter by now, his mother had hinted he'd get one on his next birthday, but that didn't happen.

Skid looked over the handwritten notes on the plot of the novel. The book report would require him to retell the significant points of the story to prove he'd read the material.

Siddhartha chooses a life of poverty, practicing meditative techniques until he realizes everything he's doing is vanity. He recognizes the Shramanas are nothing but another expression of self-centered fulfillment. He finds their goals are egotistical and not a quest for enlightenment and peace. Soon after, Siddhartha sits under the Bodhi tree and, looking inward for a long time, understands the Buddha. Moved by the compassionate teachings of the Exalted One, Siddhartha resolves to follow the Buddha's path and become his disciple.

As he grows older, Siddhartha becomes the apprentice to a simple ferryman. The old man worships the river he travels on as his most important teacher. There, on the riverbank, Siddhartha finally reaches enlightenment. But, as the story ends, he becomes the Buddha and attains Nirvana. This saddens his disciple Govinda, but he takes over the ministry left behind by the Buddha.

Finally, the two old friends meet, and Govinda and Siddhartha glimpse the essence of the wisdom he'd strived for all his life.

Skid closed the book cover and saw the moon's shadow continue across his desk, creating a pool of white light in the middle of his room. He put his finger to his chin and stared at the pale, shining light. Then, he got off his bed and stepped into the glow. What would it mean? What would happen? Skid wanted something more. He wanted something to happen. He wanted enlightenment and a sense of understanding. Was he expecting to receive some message or sign just from reading a book?

He put one bare foot into the light and then the other. He passed his hand between the light and the floor. He stretched his fingers and clenched them into a fist. He put both hands into the light and opened them.

Nothing happened.

While Siddhartha found wisdom and faith, Skid had not. He'd have to complain to Mrs. Wilson about it in his book report.

Chapter 27

The first day of Skid's job at McDonald's involved following Leon for a few hours. This meant clearing tables, checking the men's and women's restrooms, picking up trash in the parking lot, and emptying the garbage canisters. The management had a system for all these tasks, "Ronald's Rules," and required every employee to comply.

He noticed Tommy had moved from the lobby and lot clean-up to working behind the grill. Skid wondered if that was a step up or a step down. At this point, it was hard to tell.

Leon had met Skid at the time clock. He held the newbie's paper hat and a broom in one hand. "Wait to clock in until as close to your scheduled time as possible," the trainer said.

Skid nodded and stood by the device for twenty seconds before pushing the cardboard with his name at the top into the metal slot.

Then, finally, Leon said, "Hit it," and Skid tapped the button on top. The clock printed the time in blue ink, and Skid pulled it out, looked at it, smiled, and put it back in the rack under his name. "That's money, baby. Make sure you get it right every time," Leon said.

"That's what my boss at Rose's said."

"He was right," Leon said.

The trainer and trainee shared the table in the breakroom at lunchtime. They both had Big Macs, French fries, and chocolate milkshakes. Skid had enjoyed a Big Mac before and wondered if he might learn the "secret sauce" recipe that made the double hamburger both meaty and tangy. "It's Thousand Island sauce," Leon said. "Secret sauce no more."

"Damn," Skid said. "It's obvious now."

"All about the taste," Leon confirmed.

The boss checked in on them and asked Leon how Skid was doing.

"He's good," Leon said around his milkshake straw.

The noise from the grills filled with sizzling beef patties and the bells and buzzers made it challenging to hear. Finally, the young men moved closer across the Formica-topped table.

"It's a lot louder back here than out front in the lobby," Skid said.

"Lots of shouting, too," Leon said, nodding as he finished his fries.

"I know. What's that all about?"

"They have their way of doin' things," Leon explained. "It gets the food out to the counter as quickly as possible."

"I get that," Skid said and then asked. "But why is it so loud?"

"Timing. Makin' sure nobody misunderstands their assignments. It's teamwork," Leon said with a tone of confidence. "Lots of people movin' around the restaurant. You gotta let people know where you are and where you're goin'."

Skid nodded and asked, "When will I get to work back here?"

"They'll slide you in. Then, before you know it, you'll be flippin' those patties and slidin' 'em into those sleeves like a pro."

"I really do like the food," Skid said. "You'd think they would give us a discount or somethin'."

"Yep, not gonna happen. They run a tight ship here, no question." Leon stood and brushed crumbs from his uniform. "We need to get back at it." He sauntered over to the time clock and punched back in.

"That thirty minutes sure goes fast," Skid said as he stood, yanked down the front of his polyester shirt, and stuffed the soiled wrapping papers and drink cups into a garbage can.

"When it's busy, the whole shift goes fast." Leon picked up the broom and handed it to Skid. "When it's time to lean, it's time to clean," he said, smiling.

Skid liked it when Leon smiled. He could see why he was so popular and a walkout and basketball team leader.

When they both clocked out at six, they knew they'd grossed over fourteen dollars for the day's work. But, of course, federal income tax would knock that down a bit.

"Let's go to the Huddle House," Leon said, holding open the back door. Skid had spent most of his pay from working at Rose's over the holiday. So, he didn't have the cash to eat at a restaurant.

"I'm broke," he said. "I'm just gonna go home."

"I'll front ya'. Most of the crew meets there for Brinner," Leon said. "It's a combo of breakfast and dinner."

"No, you don't have..."

"Let me," Leon interrupted.

Skid looked at Leon and his engaging smile. *Again, this is what a leader does,* he thought. "All right, it's Brinner time. Who else usually comes?"

"All the single people at the store. I think we need a chance to unwind after a Saturday rush."

"Agreed," Skid said. He walked to the Nomad and hopped in.

"That sure is a cool, old car," Leon yelled.

He rolled down the window and said, "It was my mom's."

"Even cooler. See ya there," Leon grinned as he closed his car door and cranked the engine.

The trip across town included four stoplights. The boys made sure to drive under the speed limit. They turned on their headlights, even though the sun had just descended below the horizon.

Four cars sat in the parking lot at the Huddle House. It was a small, yellow, white building with twelve seats at the bar and six booths. It was a place where most people came for breakfast. But the McDonald's crew liked that they would have someone else cooking for them, and the breakfast menu there seemed more like regular food than at *their* restaurant.

When Dee Dee walked through the front door, Skid had just chopped his hash browns. He hadn't seen her for two weeks.

She wore the same blue and yellow uniform almost everyone else in the place wore. The orthodontist had removed the last of her braces, and her makeup was flawless. Her eyes popped like irises, and the spray of acne that seemed destined to linger forever on her chin had cleared.

"Hey, goofballs, what's goin' on?" She asked.

Dee Dee smiled at Leon and Skid and slid into their booth. "I didn't know you worked at McDonald's?" Skid asked.

"I work the late shift, seven to one. So, I just wanted to hang for a minute before I go in."

Leon said, "Don't forget to clock in."

"Right, right," Dee Dee said, smirking and glancing around the room. "Hey, is Jeffrey still on the rag?"

"He's okay," Leon said. "His dad gives him a hard time, and then he has to give us a hard time."

"Basic psychology," Skid said. He chopped up his sausage and held a piece up to Dee Dee. She shook her head. He put the meat between his lips and sucked it into his mouth.

"Ohhhhh, gross. I guess you still think that makes you cool?"

"I *am* cool," Skid said. He glanced at Dee Dee, noticing the zipper on her uniform was just a bit low, and he could see the top of her bra. "Hey, you might wanna..." he said, pointing with his fork.

"The girls are growin' up," she said. "Finally."

"Looks like they're expressin' themselves," Leon said. He saw Dee Dee's back stiffen briefly, and then she relaxed.

She yanked at her zipper and scooted out of the booth. "See you losers on Wednesday."

"Are you workin' that night?" Skid asked. It would be his first night on that shift.

"Yep, we're gonna have fun. There's a baseball game that night. Buses expected." She said and walked to the door.

"What's wrong with buses?" Skid asked.

"You'll see," Dee Dee said, chuckling. "Just imagine the gates of Hell opening and every little demon escaping."

She turned to leave and then stopped. It was as if Skid could see the pulleys and gears of her mind working.

She looked down at Skid and said, "I heard about what happened with your cousin there on the porch. I'm sorry."

"He wasn't really my cousin," Skid explained, "I guess by marriage if there is such a thing, but, yeah, it was horrible."

"Suicide is the worst," Leon said. He stopped chewing and looked up at Dee Dee.

"Were there any signals? He just did it?"

"He was troubled," Skid explained. He'd sat down his cup of decaf coffee and looked at his face in the spoon's curve as if it were a mirror. "I liked him and all, but he had a lot of bad stuff going on in his head. He told me some horrible stories."

"I gotta go," she said, "but if you need to talk about anything."

"I know," Skid said.

And she was gone.

"Oh, okay. Say, did you read *Siddhartha* yet? The book we're supposed to have a report on tomorrow?" Skid asked Leon.

"Yeah, well, I read the Cliffs Notes. Sounds like a strange one. I'll come up with something tonight," Leon said as he finished his eggs and moved on to his toast.

"I liked it, but I'm not sure what we're supposed to do with it. I mean, the information," Skid said. He'd finished his eggs, too.

"It's a novel. It's not supposed to be informative, is it?" Leon asked. "It's supposed to keep you entertained and turning pages. Am I right?"

"I don't know," Skid said, "it seems there's more there."

"Ain't no book got more wisdom and knowledge than the Bible. My momma read it to me, and now *I* read it," Leon said. There was a tightness in how he gripped the fork and a scrape as he shoved it back onto the plate.

"Okay, I'm just sayin' it's a weird book," Skid said.

"You got that right. So, what are you gonna say about it?" Leon asked as he stuck his hand into his jeans pocket.

"I'm not sure yet," Skid muttered.

"Let's blow this pop stand," he said as he tossed his keys behind his back and caught them in his left hand as they exited the restaurant.

Skid tried the same but dropped the keys. They made a jangling noise as they hit the pavement.

Chapter 28

Rod had road tested the Nomad after tuning it and rotating the tires, but it still wasn't ready for Skid to take his place behind the wheel. Rod said he had more work to do before he deemed it roadworthy.

So, he picked up Connie for their regular Saturday night date in the convertible Jaguar that Joseph left behind. His mother said she didn't want it, so it sat for days beside the shed. Rod said it needed to be run to keep up the battery. Skid took the keys off a pegboard in the shop and turned over the engine after two tries. "I guess somebody does need to drive it," he said. They planned to go to the drive-in, and it was too cool to drive with the top down. There wasn't much of a back seat. Skid could attest to this, so any make-out session could present problems.

Texas Chainsaw Massacre had been released the previous year, but it was still making the rounds on the circuit. The movie follows the adventures of a band of teenagers looking to get high and have fun until they meet a screwed-up family of murderers. The worst of the lot was Leatherface, a chainsaw-wielding killer who grabbed scantily clad young women and enjoyed roughly spinning them around like tops. Oh, and his mask was made of human skin.

Connie wasn't the biggest fan of this genre, nor was Skid. Still, Battleboro had few entertainment opportunities, and visiting Nashville required more money and time than Skid wanted to commit. And they could always turn off the sound and recline the seats, which they did.

The kissing led to touching, which led to over-the-shirt petting. But, of course, being the over-thinking teenagers they were, they'd already talked about sex and when or if it should ever happen between them. The consensus was that the timing was right. Tonight was the night.

The back windows of the Jag steamed as the kissing, huffing, and puffing grew intense. Connie knew Skid was a perfect gentleman and would never pressure her to do anything she didn't want to.

"Is this really the best place for this?" She asked.

"It's okay with me," Skid said. He looked around at the lines of other cars with similar condensation on their windows. "Looks like it's happenin' everywhere." And returned to kissing her.

"Okay, hold on there, Cowboy. Let's think this through," she whispered between kisses. She wore a white, long-sleeved blouse and a short denim skirt. Her tennis shoes had come off long before they'd gotten to the drive-in. She'd made a point to paint her toenails fire engine red.

"Come on, really," he said.

Skid wore blue jeans, Chuck Taylor Converse sneakers, and a long-sleeved T-shirt. He still wore his shoes, but he'd made himself comfortable by unbuckling his belt. He made sure to wear the belt because Connie had given it to him for his birthday. He didn't care that she'd gotten an employee discount. It was the thought that counted. And he knew she would notice if he wasn't wearing it.

"I'm gettin' kinda, you know," Skid said. It had been a long, grueling day behind the grill, and he could feel the tension in his shoulders and crotch.

"I know. I get it, but..."

"I get the feelin' sometimes that you don't care about me as much as you say you do," Skid said. He'd already pulled away from her on the makeshift bed.

"You know that's not true," she said as she scooted across the leather seat. "I do care for you." She touched his chest as she tried to kiss him. "Just look at where we are. There's a gear shift knob right there. There's no room," she said and then changed her tone. "I just think it can't be done here."

He took her hand and put her fingers on the button below his dangling belt. "Come on, babe," he whined.

"That is not an attractive tone."

"Okay, how about this? I'll do you, and then you can do me."

"What do you mean 'do me'?" Connie asked. "I'm not sure what you have in mind here. I mean, we were goin' pretty good there."

"I'll touch you until you 'feel good,' and you can do the same for me."

"I don't think I'm ready for that," she said as she moved away from him.

"It's just horsing around," he said. He glanced at the movie playing through the windshield. A thin, twenty-something girl was dancing and teasing her boyfriend.

"I get it. But, maybe," Skid said as he reached for her breast and tried to kiss her again.

"No." She was emphatic. "That's enough. Let's just watch the movie. Turn up the sound."

Skid grimaced. The strain on the front of his jeans grew unbearable, and he twisted in his seat. Finally, he flipped the front passenger seat up and scrambled under the wheel.

"Hey," she said. "I was sorry to hear about what happened with that guy visitin' your dad. What was he about?"

"He was troubled. He told me some stuff nobody needed to hear. I found him," Skid said.

"Oh, no," she said and rubbed his shoulder. "That must have been horrible."

"It was," Skid said. "It is." His stomach grumbled, and he felt a tear forming in the corner of his eye. He'd been crying at times in the house and once in the restroom at McDonald's. He didn't think it was a good idea for her to see him upset like that. How manly would that be?

"Maybe it's time we just went home," he muttered.

"Maybe it is," she said. "I'm trying not to lose my temper. I know you're hurting."

"I'm fine," he said between clenched teeth.

She adjusted her seat and buttoned her shirt. She smoothed her skirt and looked for her shoes. "My shoes are up there," she said.

"I don't care," he said as he cranked the engine, yanked the speaker from the window, and tossed it toward the metal pipe with the bracket. He missed.

"I need my shoes," Connie said. A tone of anger and disappointment crept into her voice.

"Come gettum," Skid snarled as he put the car into gear.

He spun the tires as he left their parking space. The torque pushed Connie back into her seat. "Hey, cut it out," she yelled over the sound of the rumbling engine. "What'a you mad at me for?" She asked.

"I can't hear you," Skid yelled, pointing to his ears.

He almost hit a light pole as he gunned the car past the ticket booth and onto the two-lane blacktop. The tires squealed, and he lost control of the vehicle for a second. Then, finally, he wrestled it back between the ditches.

Connie slapped him on the shoulder. "Are you tryin' to kill us?"

Skid's jaw twitched. He couldn't remember the last time he was so upset. Finally, he flipped the headlights to bright and stepped on the gas. He spun right at the intersection of Highway 99 and gripped the steering wheel.

Connie put on her shoes. "You need to slow down, Skid!" She had to yell because the windows were down, and the engine whine and exhaust noise had grown almost intolerable.

He gripped the wheel and pointed the nose of the car to the twin lines on the highway.

"Seventy," he yelled. His voice was stronger than hers, and he knew she could hear him.

"Slow down," she screamed. "I mean it!"

"Eighty," he shouted. Now, the windows captured the roar of the air as they accelerated.

Connie pressed herself into the passenger seat and searched for the seat belt. "Too fast. You're going too fast. You're scaring me!"

"Ninety," his voice almost lost in the moving air this time. He glanced over at her and saw the whites of her eyes as they bulged from the sockets. Her mouth was an oval, and he noticed one of her teeth was crooked compared to the one to the left.

"One hundred," he said. He glanced down at the speedometer to confirm his feat. The dashboard lights shone white against the black metal. The fence posts alongside the road seemed like one long, solid line.

"Stop! Let me out," she screamed. "Right now!"

Skid looked at her again. He could see how frightened she was and that he'd made a mistake.

Highway 99 led from Battleboro to Salem, a small unincorporated community to the west. Like most roads, it began as a rutted trail with the same gauge as a horse-drawn wagon. The road was built to exact specifications to save money, with minor grading over the small hills. Most drivers took those bumps in stride and not at high speed. At times driving on Highway 99 would give the backseat riders a bit of a thrill as you would "lose your stomach" at the top of each rise.

Skid tried to remember if Rod had said he'd fixed the Jaguar. Then, he felt a wobble through the steering wheel. "Oh, shit," he whispered.

Skid was about to ease off the gas when the first mound approached. The suspension absorbed some elevation, but most of the force took Skid and Connie out of their seats, mimicking weightlessness for a second.

Sparks flew from under the car on the downward slope. The second rise in the highway produced the same sensation and more sparks. Then, as Skid slowed the car, the bumps had less effect.

"Wow, that was fun. When's the last time you went over 100 miles an hour?" He smiled at the sharing of the information.

"I'm so mad at you I could wring your neck," She crossed her arms and sat against the passenger side door. Her hair blew around her face as the wind rushed through the window.

"Oh, hell, I'm sorry."

"Pull over here," she said, pointing to a driveway.

"We're in the middle of nowhere. You can't walk from here."

"I think I can."

He slowed the car and pulled into the gravel roadway. "I'm sorry. I don't know what came over me. I just lost my mind." He choked back his tears and stared straight ahead. "I get it. I'm sorry."

Connie opened the door, got out, and closed it with a slam. "I never want to see you again."

"Aw, come on," he whined at her through the open window. "I'm just...."

She squatted down and looked at him through the window. She saw his white knuckles on the steering wheel, red and puffy eyes, and shaking right arm. She realized just how upset he was. She closed her eyes and shook her head. She inhaled and smirked. "Don't make me regret this." She opened the door and got back in.

He wiped his eyes with the palms of his hands and tried to smile. "I really am…"

She covered his mouth with her hand and pulled him into her arms. "You're gonna be all right. Just you wait and see."

He took a shuddering breath and cried. It was the first time he'd felt this level of pain since he'd lost his mother. Through gasps and trembling breaths, he said, "I'm so sorry."

She patted the back of his head. She let him cry on her shoulder for a long time. He finally stopped and wiped his face with the long sleeves of his shirt.

"Let's just go home," she said.

He couldn't think of what to say on the way to her house, so he stayed silent. Skid knew he'd messed up and that it was likely the last time he'd see her.

Skid pulled the car into the driveway and put the transmission in neutral. She patted his hand and opened the door.

"Talk to you later?" He asked through the open window.

"Maybe you should talk to someone about all that, you know," she said. "You've had a lot of bad stuff goin' on."

"Yeah, right, good idea," he agreed.

"Be careful," she said, walking up the drive, down the sidewalk, and opening the front door. She glanced back at him as he backed the car down the drive. The headlights swept across her, and she sighed.

She stood there for a moment longer and then turned off the porch light.

Chapter 29

Skid titled the book report "Hermann Hesse's Siddhartha." And began the essay with, "The novel explores a young man's spiritual journey to search for his place in the world. Siddhartha is the son of a holy man, a preacher's kid as we would call him, but rejects organized religion he sees as corrupt and impure. But, he wants to find out what life is all about, so he and his friend Govinda wander India searching for meaning."

Skid listened as Rod moved plates and pots in the kitchen. It was his night to cook, and most of the time, he'd merely boil some spaghetti and open a can of tomato sauce, but he seemed to be making more effort tonight.

Skid returned to his notebook and wrote. "They meet a group of fellow believers and learn how to fast, pray, meditate, and other physical ways to open their minds to spiritual meaning. Siddhartha leaves this group when the band's actions fail to give him the insights he'd hoped for. He becomes friends with Govinda, another young man searching for enlightenment. Together, they leave their homes to join a group of ascetics who live in the forest.

"Despite living a life of extreme austerity, Siddhartha is still unable to find the answers he is looking for. So he leaves these believers and joins a group of merchants, where he becomes wealthy and indulges in all of life's pleasures. Despite all his material possessions, Siddhartha is still unsatisfied and continues his search for enlightenment.

"Siddhartha eventually meets a wise man named Vasudeva, who teaches him the importance of listening to and learning from the river. So Siddhartha becomes Vasudeva's apprentice and spends many years living by the river, finally achieving enlightenment and becoming the Buddha."

Skid sat up when Rod yelled, "Sheeee-it, dang it. Look at how this pot is dented. How did that happen?" The boy wasn't sure if Rod was directing the question to him or just to the Universe.

Skid knew from the assignment's instructions he needed to end the report with his opinion about the book. But he hadn't really formulated what he thought. It was so strange, and like nothing he'd read before.

Finally, he began, "I believe this story of a seeker who finds inner peace is helpful and challenging to modern readers. Hesse seems to be chronicling his own spiritual journey, and maybe this book is his answer to those questions. It's an interesting story, and I really liked it."

Skid closed his notebook and got up from the dining room table. This was where he did most of his writing, even though he had a desk and chair in his bedroom. He heard breaking glass from the kitchen, and Rod shouted, "Damn it. I'm all thumbs tonight."

The boy stood in the kitchen doorway and watched his stepfather kneel on the floor next to the stove. He was picking up the larger portions of the broken drinking glass and holding them in the palm of his hand.

"Let me help," Skid said as he crossed the room and grabbed the trash can. He placed it next to Rod and walked to the carport. He held the broom and dustpan, waiting for Rod to put the shards in the trash can.

"Let me," Skid said.

"I made the mess," Rod said with a disgusted tone.

Skid handed the broom to Rod and noticed how the older man's hand trembled. He knelt and put the edge of the dustpan next to Rod's foot.

"Did you...," Rod's voice trailed off and then. "Did Joseph tell you anything?"

"He didn't say anythin' to me," Skid said as he gathered the broken glass into the pan. "I heard you guys talkin' that night, but I couldn't make out what you were sayin'."

"You didn't...uh, just as well. He didn't say anythin' to me either. I wish he had," Rod said. His shoulders slumped, and he put the broom next to the door.

"He seemed really upset when he told me about seein' those people being evacuated from the roof of the American embassy," Skid said. He was still waiting to lend a hand with the clean-up.

"I got it," Rod said as he placed the last of the broken glass in the waste can.

"Okay," Skid said. "Did you get cut?"

"No, oh, yeah, I'm okay. He told me he'd worked there, and he recognized some of the soldiers at the gate," Rod said as he stood and twisted the knob that turned on one of the electric stove's eyes. Soon, it was glowing red.

"That musta been hard to watch," Skid said.

"Yeah," Rod swiped at the end of his nose. "Get me that can of tomato sauce," Rod ordered.

"It's spaghetti sauce."

Rod looked at Skid, and his cheeks grew red. "All right, spaghetti sauce."

"It's just that," Skid said as he attached the opener to the lip of the can.

"All right, mister know-it-all. I can do it," Rod said as he grabbed the opener and snatched it away from Skid. The ridge of the half-opened can slid across Rod's hand and left a red line through his palm. "Damn it," he yelped in pain as blood filled the cut. "Picked up all that broken glass, and I get cut from a lid."

"I'm writin' a report on this book for class. It was about letting go and just experiencing life." Skid said. "Kind of like, this too shall pass."

"Horseshit," Rod said, still grimacing in pain.

"I know but think about it. What if Joseph saw all that shit on the TV, and that's why he hung himself?" Skid asked. He took a dish towel and handed it to Rod. The stepfather wrapped it around his left hand.

"He didn't leave no note. So, we'll never know why he did it," Rod said, lifting the edge of the dishcloth. "It's almost stopped bleeding."

"I'll get some MERCUROCHROME."

Skid returned from the bathroom with the tiny bottle. He twisted the top and extracted the medicine-covered swab. Rod opened his hand and watched Skid daub the cut.

"You're a regular Florence Nightingale."

"They showed us a video at the restaurant," Skid said. Then, for some reason, he stuck his tongue out as he administered the antiseptic. And then he said, "Workers get hurt there all the time."

Skid pulled a roll of gauze from his shirt pocket and wrapped the wound.

"That'll last about an hour," Rod said, enjoying his attempt at humor.

"Maybe that's all it needs," Skid said.

The simple dinner filled their bellies; as predicted, the gauze loosened before it was time for *The Waltons*.

"Why are you still watchin' that show?" Rod asked as he rocked in his easy chair.

"I don't know," Skid said, still embarrassed by his dream of writing a script for the show. Finally, he settled into his usual television-watching spot on the couch.

He balanced his notepad on his knees. He watched the teaser that always ran before the theme song and the credits. "Enlightenment comes from within," he wrote on the top line of the ruled paper.

Chapter 30

Skid didn't ask to see the guidance counselor/health teacher, and a part of him was angry about the mandatory meeting. He scanned all the diplomas and licenses he had before on Miss Black's wall as she leafed through a file. She looked up at him. His teachers had noticed he'd worn the same knit shirt for three days, and it was easy to see the wrinkles and catch a whiff of the smell. Oily grime covered his jeans and shoes. His right knee bounced, and his hair hadn't seen a comb for days.

"You've been through a lot lately, and now…." She said. She looked up from the papers. "How are you doing?"

"I'm okay." Skid lied.

"I find that hard to believe. Your stepfather's cousin hangs himself on your porch. You've lost your mother in the last year and are nearing graduation. That's stressful for anyone, but you have more than most."

"I'm okay," Skid said. This time his voice took on a sharper tone emphasizing the last word. "Did Connie ask you to talk to me?"

Miss Black ignored the question. Today, she wore a black sweater top and a red, checkered skirt. She accented her outfit with a red headband and a large silver bracelet on her right wrist. The metal clanged against the top of the desk as she made notes. She glanced up but continued to shuffle papers. She adjusted her reading glasses and smiled as she read. "Did you ever…"

He interrupted her. "Did all these diplomas make a difference in your life?" Skid asked. His gaze flicked from the floor to Miss Black's desktop and back to the floor.

"I was always interested in working with young people. But I needed to study psychology and counseling to become the best I could be," Miss Black said. She glanced at her "brag wall" and grinned. "I also needed the diplomas to get the job. They're not goin' to hire someone to do this job without a degree."

"So, if I want to become a writer," Skid let the last word trail out as he exhaled. It was the first time in his life he'd said the words out loud.

"Well, most journalists these days go to school and get a degree in English or go to a college with a journalism school. It's not required, but most editors hiring news reporters or magazine writers want a college graduate. Is that something you've been thinking about?"

"I wanted to write an episode of *The Waltons*," he said. He could feel the heat rise in his cheeks. "And the librarian got me a copy of one of their scripts."

"Yes, Miss Cardwell." She smiled. She had her hair pulled back into a bun, all business. "She did that for you? That's great."

"She's been very helpful," Skid said, now even more embarrassed. "I tried. I mean, I'm still workin' on it."

"You're still writing the first draft of your script?"

"Yes, the first draft," Skid said.

"How many pages do you have so far?"

"About forty," he said, catching her eye. He smiled. He'd never noticed how green her eyes were. Maybe it was just the light. "You gotta type it out in a special format. It's kind of like a play, but there's more about what the characters are doing. And you have to describe the setting, day or night, and what's goin' on in the room. It's all in the script. It's a weird way to write."

"That's impressive," she said. A shaft of sunlight from behind her desk caught the red crystal in her earrings. "You must be close to the end. I know television scripts run around fifty to sixty pages."

Again, words he'd never spoken before. "I know how it's going to end."

"That's important," she said as she jotted words down on a yellow legal pad. "Do you want me to look into some scholarships and loans for film schools?"

"Maybe. Let me think about it." He felt an ache behind his eyes, and he winced in pain. This was becoming too real, and he felt nauseated. "I'm, uh," he started. Skid shifted his weight as he scooted back in the chair. His paperback copy of *Siddhartha* fell to the floor.

"Oh, I read that in college. It was *interesting*," Miss Black said. She closed the folder and pushed back into her office chair. The slant of the morning sun now glowed yellow behind her.

"Why was it interesting? I thought it was stupid," Skid lied again. Could she tell? He picked up the book and put it on top of his stack.

"It wasn't *stupid*. I think it was just an interesting way of looking at the world," Miss Black said with a cajoling tone in her voice. "It made me think."

"You know I don't like to think," Skid said. He knew it was a lame joke, but he hoped to make the pretty counselor laugh or smile.

She chuckled and adjusted her glasses.

Skid learned long ago making people laugh was one way of convincing others to like him, especially girls. That was one of his worst jokes, but it seemed to work.

He straightened his books and stood.

"If you have just a minute more. I've been reviewing your grades, and you're doing better now, despite your troubles at home. Are you going to take the SATs?"

He re-seated himself and said, "I guess I have to if I want to go to college, don't I?"

"Not necessarily, but it's usually a factor on where you can get in. It's next Saturday."

"I think I'm working," Skid said. His gaze drifted as if he had kept his work schedule on the ceiling. "But I can ask off."

"I think you should," she said.

"Would it help me decide what I would study in college?"

She looked up at him. She could see the pain in his eyes and the tension in his shoulders. "It can be a good indicator."

"Okay. Nobody in my family has ever graduated from college," he said as he stood again. He glanced at the diploma wall again and turned toward the door.

"You could be the first," she said. She stood and picked up another file from the vertical holder on her desk. "If you want to talk to me some other time, it can be about anything. That's my job."

He tried to remember if she'd ever said anything negative to him. Nope, nothing.

"I know," he said with a smile, "it says so on your door, Counselor." He pointed to her shiny, new nameplate.

Chapter 31

Rod's system involved several torn-down cars in different garage bays. He would move from one to the next depending on the parts that arrived or the job's complexity.

He had pulled an engine from a Ferrari, but he'd carefully organized the parts on a bench next to the toolbox. The engine hung from a block-and-tackle with rope encircling a rafter by a large hook and gleamed in the intense light Rod had set up around the garage. He needed the light to see the small parts. His eyesight was still good, but he had difficulty reading the fine print on instruction manuals and daily newspapers. He was too vain to wear reading glasses now, but he knew they'd soon be necessary.

Skid brought the box marked "Fragile" and "Italy" from the porch and set it next to the toolbox. "Looks like belts."

Rod focused on the pulleys before him and said, "Just in time."

The manufacturer recommended pulling the engine from its compartment every thirty thousand miles. A man from New York, the owner, was a stickler for regular maintenance. The job with parts and labor would cost well over one thousand dollars. Rod had promised the job would be finished at the end of the week, and it was already Wednesday.

"So, the guy's coming on Friday," Skid said. The stepfather shrugged at his attempt at making conversation. "Are you gonna make it?"

"Sure," Rod said as he ratcheted a bolt that seemed welded to the motor. "Sleep is for suckers."

Skid looked skeptical. Rod looked up and caught it. He returned to his wrenching.

"I've never missed a deadline yet."

"Right," Skid said. Again, thinking he could take a stab at a conversation with Rod. "Did you know a deadline originally meant a boundary or fence around a military prison? The guards could shoot if prisoners crossed the line or over the fence."

Rod stopped and glanced over his shoulder at Skid. "When did you get so tall?"

"Mostly at night," Skid said, "probably when you're asleep."

Rod ignored the attempt at humor and focused on the intricate engine. "Goddamned Italian engineers."

"Oh," Skid said. Not sure how to respond to the remark. He glanced down at his tennis shoes. The blue-with-yellow piping of his polyester McDonald's uniform stretched across his chest, and his biceps tested the elasticity of the short sleeves.

"And you're filling out a bit. Not just skin and bones now."

"I eat at the restaurant," Skid said. "Lots of meat and empty calories."

"Right, how do you like workin' there?" Rod asked as he continued wrenching. It was like he was in a trance, and his hands moved without him having to think. This was the most extended conversation between the two of them since Joseph's suicide.

"It's okay. They said I might have management potential. They have a training program in Chicago. Hamburger U."

"Well, all right, then," Rod said with a smile.

"I'm not sure it's right for me," Skid said, looking at his nametag. He was glad they'd let him use his nickname. He was proud he'd been named after his grandfather, but "Clarence" seemed too formal. "But it's nice to be asked."

"It's always nice to be asked," Rod parroted Skid. He didn't say it mockingly or with any enthusiasm, but the boy frowned.

And then Rod grunted as he applied pressure to a bolt. Under the bandage he'd changed that morning, the cut in his palm was almost healed, but for some reason, his left hand seemed to not have the strength it once had.

"I'd have to turn eighteen and finish school and such to go to Chicago."

"Of course," Rod said without looking up from the levers and pulleys. He plucked the old belt from the engine and threw it toward the work table. It landed short and fell to the concrete floor.

"Did you want me to throw this…"

"No, just leave it. I'll decide later if there's anything else I can use it for. There's hardly any wear, and it might fit somethin' else."

Skid nodded. "So, I guess you're happy to get rid of me soon."

"You're my boy," Rod said. He slipped a screwdriver under a clasp and pulled up. The spring snapped and leaped into the air. Mechanics sometimes called them 'Jesus' clips because that's what was usually yelled when they were released.

Rod snatched the clip out of mid-air and laughed. "I promised your mother I'd take care of you. I really need your help here in the shop."

"I'm not really good at…"

"No problem. Just thinkin' out loud. I'll be happy to train you."

"Great," Skid said. The tension in his shoulders relaxed. But, deep down, he knew that would never happen.

"And eventually, you'll have to pay some rent. That's fair, isn't it?"

For some reason, this surprised Skid. This was his ancestral home, and Rod was a man married to his mother for three years. He felt now wasn't the time to remind the old man of this. "Sure, I get it."

Rod transferred the spring into his still-bandaged left hand and offered his right hand to Skid. The young man shook it.

"It's a deal," Skid said.

"All we got left is each other."

Skid nodded and turned. "Gotta get to work."

"Hamburger University," Rod said, turning back to his engine. "The shit they come up with these days."

Chapter 32

Connie explained to Skid he was on probation because of his reckless driving away from the drive-in. He would have to earn her trust and promise never to do something like that again. She asked him if he'd had a chance to talk with Miss Black, and he assured her he had. However, he didn't say what they'd discussed and lied that he'd scheduled another session.

She mostly accepted his apology because she wanted to go to the concert. He crossed his heart and swore never to do anything stupid like that again. "You scared the shit out of me."

"I wish I could go back in time and fix it."

"I know," she said. "Just don't go crazy like that again."

Skid looked at her and gave her a quick grin.

"It's not fair that you're so cute." She said, "All right then. Let's go to the show."

She wore high-rise, bell-bottom jeans and a T-shirt reading "Joe Walsh Barnstorm Tour," which she bought following the last time she saw the band. Her father had taken her to that show, but this time she'd roped Skid into buying tickets and, possibly, another T-shirt. This time the art would have a picture of Joe wearing aviator goggles, a scarf, and a puzzled look followed by the album's name, "So What."

"This is the second time I've seen him in concert," she said. She wore her hair long, touching the top of her shoulders.

"Right," Skid said, "your dad took you."

"He didn't care for the music but sat there and pretended he was having a good time."

"He's a good dad."

She nodded. "Yeah, the old man really is."

But Dad wouldn't have approved of her outfit tonight. She'd forgotten to wear a bra under the 'Barnstorm' shirt. Connie filled out the shirt, but not to the point of distracting men approaching the couple. Skid wondered if her going braless was a protest of some kind. Had she burned it? That seemed out of character. Was it a fashion statement? He didn't know how to bring up the subject.

"Should we get some earplugs?" Skid asked. He handed the parking lot attendant a dollar and drove through the gate. Another attendant waved him into a slot not too far from the sidewalk.

"I borrowed some cigarettes." She said, smiling. She opened her shoulder bag and showed him the pack.

"You don't smoke now," Skid asked, "do you?" Connie seemed to be changing right before his eyes.

Skid wore bell-bottom jeans and a T-shirt, too, but his was plain white and didn't have a logo or the cover of an LP. Maybe he'd buy a shirt from the vendors on the way out. As he walked, his belt had a large, silver buckle peeking from under his shirt. It was one of his mother's last presents, and he only wore it on special occasions.

The setting sun cast a yellow light over the crowd as they moved through the late afternoon heat and humidity.

"Smoke, no, of course not. You can snip off the filters and stick them in your ears if it's too loud."

"You are *so* smart." Skid gripped her hand tightly.

"I just listen to people."

"You'd be surprised how rare that is."

Skid pulled the tickets from the back pocket of his jeans and handed them to the ticket ripper. The bored teenager said, "On the right and down six rows." He pointed to the section.

They both nodded and walked down the concrete steps. The gymnasium was home to the college basketball team and doubled as a concert hall when the team's schedule allowed. This was Skid's first time attending a show here, but Connie was a veteran. The gym's maximum capacity was three thousand for basketball; attendance could reach four thousand for concerts.

"This is so great," she said as she shuffled through the crowd. She bent her head back and gave Skid a kiss on the cheek. No seats were on the floor, but the pull-out bleachers were filling. Skid wanted to sit in their assigned seats, but Connie had convinced him earlier they'd have a better view if they stood before the stage.

"You're welcome. I got them from Miss Black. She knows Rockin' Rudy from the radio station."

"I bet there's a story there," Connie said.

"Yep, and the price was right, too."

"Free is good."

"Free is always good," Skid said.

"So, if you saved all that money, does that mean you'll buy me a T-shirt?" She asked. She tugged at the edge of her shirt and smiled as lasciviously as possible.

"Sure," he said, trying not to be distracted by the slope of her breasts and symmetrical nipples. "I can guarantee you'll look great in it."

"And nothin' else?" Again, with the tone.

"Especially in nothin' else," Skid teased.

A long-haired young man stumbled onto the stage. He'd forgotten his shirt, and his low-ride jeans showed his chest, belly hair, and just the start of his "happy trail." The kids were calling that the beginning of a person's pubic hair. Undoubtedly, he'd seen a picture of Robert Plant of Led Zeppelin and was trying to affect the look.

He moved into the spotlight at the center of the stage. The now-darkened arena quieted as he grabbed the microphone.

"Hello, there. I'm Charlie Fallon with the Student Events Committee, welcoming you to the best rock and roll show ever. And we've got a surprise for you."

"Uh oh," Skid said.

"Yeah," Connie said, "that can't be good."

The people grew restless. Skid and Connie were straight, but they knew some in the crowd had planned their drugs to kick in for the main artists, not a "surprise" opening act. Now, everyone's timing would be off. The crowd erupted, thinking they were just moments away from Joe Walsh taking the stage.

"We've got a special surprise for you. Opening the show tonight is a singer/songwriter of the new hit song *Doctor, My Eyes*. So, Ladies and Gentlemen, here's Jackson Browne."

"Boo," yelled the crowd.

Jackson sauntered to the piano and sat down. His guitar sat on a tripod stand stage left. He began playing the first cut from the new album. The two microphones were plugged into the house's public address system. The speaker stage right sounded like the screws holding it in the cabinet were loose, and the cardboard cones rattled.

"Get off the stage!" one well-pickled audience member shouted.

"We want Joe!" screamed another.

Jackson finished the song to a smattering of applause. Skid looked around the gym and noticed most concertgoers talked amongst themselves and ignored the artist on stage.

"This will not end well," Connie said.

Skid nodded and waited for the downbeat. He liked this song. It had a great rhyme scheme and tempo. Lots of heart, and clearly, it was written by a talented poet. He'd bought the cassette tape and was playing it in his car. He also bought *So What* and played it even more.

The booing grew louder, and Skid could see Jackson's hands shaking from the fourth row. Was it nerves, or was he pissed?

"Shut up, motherfucker," someone behind Skid and Connie yelled.

Jackson stopped singing and turned to the crowd. He shielded his eyes from the spotlight and said into the microphone, "*You* shut up shit head."

Crowd members who ignored Browne's act looked like they had rehearsed the next move. A wave of "Boos" and "Get off the Stage" comments echoed off the concrete walls and large windows.

Jackson stood, flipped off the audience, and stormed from the stage.

The crowd cheered, and the house lights came back up. Skid looked at Connie and said, "I've never seen anything like that."

"Me neither," she said.

"So, now, what do we do?" Skid asked.

"I'm not leavin' until Joe plays."

"So, I guess we're stayin' here."

Skid shifted his weight from his left foot to his right. While working the grill at McDonald's, he'd found that doing this was the only way to keep his feet from hurting. Unfortunately, he had to wear horrible black shoes with non-skid rubber soles at work. They were cheap but didn't have much arch support. The "Chuck Taylors" he wore tonight felt better. Still, it had already been a long day, and a temperamental musician wasn't in the plan.

The house lights dimmed, and the single spot returned to the piano and guitar sitting center stage. The announcer returned and picked up the microphone in front of the keyboard.

"Let's do better this time," Charlie said, scanning the crowd. He returned the mic to the holder as Jackson came out and sat at the piano.

The artist banged on the keys and crashed into an upbeat song, *Rock Me on the Water*. The crowd listened, and this time when the song ended, they responded with cheers. The singer looked out at his new fans and smiled.

Jackson nodded, waved, and exited the stage. The roadies took only six minutes to push the piano off and pull the equipment for Joe Walsh to center stage.

Joe stumbled to the microphone and said, "Thank you. Thanks to Jackson Browne, a fine singer and songwriter. You're gonna hear a lot more from him in the future." He nodded to the drummer, and they launched into *Rocky Mountain Way*.

"Now that's what I'm talkin' about," Skid screamed at Connie. The music was so loud she couldn't hear what he said and smiled, offering two of the pinched-off cigarette filters. He took them and placed them in his ears.

He mouthed "thanks" and felt the thumping bass, crashing drumbeats, and Joe's screaming guitar.

"You gotta feel it," he yelled at Connie, but he was sure she didn't hear him. So instead, she stared at the stage, raised her hands over her head, and screamed.

Chapter 33

Two weeks had passed since the concert, but they still talked about how unprofessional Jackson Brown was and how great Joe Walsh performed. At dinner, again at McDonald's, they enjoyed the relaxed atmosphere past the rush hour.

"So, what'a ya wanna do after this?" Connie asked.

"I don't know. What do you wanna do?"

"Well," she said, eyes averted and smiling, "we've been talkin' about it for a long time."

"Oh," Skid said. "You mean…."

"Maybe," she said, inching closer to him. They were sitting at a booth on the same side to be closer. "Maybe, if you're ready."

"Oh," Skid said, "that, ready, ah, with the thing."

"We can talk about it," Connie said, squeezing his arm.

"So, I guess I'm off probation."

She pinched his cheek and said, "You've been a very good boy."

***

As the familiar landmarks heading toward their favorite make-out place passed, Connie stared out the window and twirled the ends of her recently dyed midnight-black hair. She liked to experiment with her hair and makeup. The song *Dreams* came up on the cassette tape.

"I've listened to this song so many times, but for some reason…." Her voice trailed off. Maybe it was the beer or the joint they'd smoked fifteen minutes ago.

Skid tapped the steering wheel as he swapped out the completed Fleetwood Mac tape for *The Smoker You Go; The Player You Get*. The jet engine level of the concert continued to affect their hearing, so he had to crank up the knob on the stereo. Unfortunately, the cigarette filters didn't stop *all* the deafening sounds in the sweltering room where the guitar god slashed his silver strings. Joe staggered a bit as he stalked the stage. *Was he drunk?* Skid asked himself. How could he perform that well if he was intoxicated?

They'd been discussing sex for a few weeks, but the subject took a back burner as the concert grew closer. All that was put on hold after his acting out at the drive-in and their fight. The issue floated to the top of his mind as he drove through the mist.

"I don't think I want to grow up," Connie said.

"Me neither," Skid agreed.

He turned down the volume as he turned the steering wheel. He felt the front wheels sink into the muddy ground and the back wheels spin and catch hold.

"I don't think we need to go into the cave tonight," he said without looking at her. The exploration of the mouth of the cave had become a ritual for them. They enjoyed finding something new before their make-out session in the back of the Nomad. "With all the rain and such."

Skid turned off the headlights and turned to look at her. Moonlight diffused by the fog provided a soft glow to her face and T-shirt. He'd always found her attractive, but he could see her changing before his eyes. She wasn't just a girl anymore.

"Maybe it's not the right time," she nodded slowly.

"Well, we've talked about this. It's not that big a thing."

She giggled. "It's not that big, but it's okay."

"That's not funny," he said. He turned his head toward the cave entrance. A cloud passed over the moon, and he remembered how the light looked in his room.

"It doesn't have to be tonight, does it?" She asked.

"It's time," he said. He turned back to her. He lowered his gaze and tipped his head forward. He snaked his hand behind her and pulled her close.

"Wait," she said.

He started kissing her, covering her mouth before she could say anything more. He felt her body stiffen and her hand push on his shoulder. He kissed her harder and let his hand wander under her shirt. Her left breast felt warm and soft.

"Wait?" He whispered as he kissed her ear.

She took a deep breath, circled his shoulder with her left hand, and pulled him to her. "All right, I guess. How about we…"

He already knew what that meant. The pattern was kissing, heavy petting in the front seat, and even more, making out in the back. Finally, she slipped a condom on him the last few times, bringing him to climax with her hand.

Skid pulled away from her and tumbled over the back of the front seat. He couldn't get a stupid grin off his face. He hadn't felt as free and relaxed with the beer since Joseph killed himself.

Connie clambered over the seat and slid into his arms. The kissing continued as the music stopped. The machine whirred, and a thin ribbon of brown tape spit out around the sides of the cassette.

"Oh no," Connie said, looking up and seeing the player eat the tape.

"It's okay," he said, pulling his shirt over his head. He knew he could replace the tape with next week's paycheck and maybe buy something else.

She pulled her shirt over her head and unbuckled her jeans. They were tight. "I had to lay on the bed to get the last button." She sucked in a deep breath and yanked at the fastener.

They kissed, and he felt the cool vinyl of the seat against his back. He'd noticed how a spring had poked through the bottom cushion yesterday. He'd meant to fix it but had gotten busy and lost track of time.

"Here," he said as he handed her the condom. Again, this had become part of their routine. He'd lean back as she kissed his face and chest. She unrolled it onto him and let her hand linger there momentarily.

She started moving her hand, but he caught her wrist and shook his head. "I don't think I need that tonight."

He pulled away from her and reached under the driver's side of the front seat. He yanked a white towel from the opening.

"Just in case," he whispered. His cheeks turned red.

"You've thought of everything," she said with zero enthusiasm.

"I try."

They began kissing again, and her resistance to his hands on her breasts eased. Her jeans were now half off.

"What do you need?" She asked.

"I need you. All of you."

"Gosh, Skid," she said as he tried to cover her mouth with kisses. "Wait. I'm not..."

"C'mon. It's time." He said as he pulled off her jeans and underwear.

He'd seen her naked three times and loved how her breasts were like hills leading into her stomach and pelvis valleys.

"Wait," she said.

But he kissed her. He slipped his tongue into her mouth, and she tried to pull away. Then, finally, he said as she put her hand on his chest. "I love you. I want to make love with you. It's the perfect time."

Connie looked at him. She paused a moment. The windows had fogged.

It was like they were the last two people on Earth. Then, finally, she took a deep breath and said, "Okay, but take it easy. It's probably gonna hurt."

"I know," Skid said. But he couldn't wipe the smirk from his face.

He spread the towel under her butt, pulled her lower body down, and positioned himself above her. This time, it was *him* pausing for a moment. But with the blood rushing from his head, it was impossible to rationalize what would happen.

He moved against her. She let her hand fall from his chest and rubbed him against her. "Slow and easy," she whispered.

He nodded, but with all the excitement, he pushed too fast.

"Ouch. Come on. Slow, Skid," she said. This time she was a bit louder, with a tone of apprehension. Even with the towel, her naked bottom scraped the tiny wire from the broken spring. "Ouch."

"Are you okay?" He asked. He really didn't want to hurt her.

"There's a, what is it?" she asked. She pushed up against him and searched under her bottom. "There's a..."

"Okay," he said. But he couldn't slow down and was too far along to stop.

He was inside her. Skid felt the warmth and the gentle pulse. He couldn't help smiling, and when she pushed his chest, he didn't stop.

"Okay," she said, "that hurts. What is that pokin' my ass? That's enough."

"No," he said. This time louder than a whisper and insistent.

"Okay," she said, "pull out. Get off me. That's enough."

He could feel himself near the end. It was less than a minute, but for Skid, time slowed.

"I'm almost there," he said.

She shoved him, and he climaxed.

"Dammit," she screeched. "I said get off. There was somethin' pokin' me."

"Yeah, I know."

"There was somethin' sharp pokin' me in the ass. It's not funny. There's a needle or somethin'." She pulled up the corner of the towel. There was a spot of blood the size of a tennis ball. She ran her hand over the surface of the bench seat and flicked the top of the broken spring.

"Oh, man, I'm sorry." He pushed himself into the driver's side corner and slipped on his shirt.

He slipped off the used condom, tied a knot in the top, and slid it under the floor mat. Again, this was a habit of his from earlier sessions of petting.

"So," she said, pulling on her jeans and T-shirt.

"So."

"You can take me home now," she said as she dressed and climbed back into the front seat. She'd left the top two buttons of her jeans unfastened.

"Oh, okay," he said as he joined her. He turned the engine over and pulled on the knob for the headlights.

Without music from the tape player, Rockin' Rudy on the radio supplied the music. His usually eclectic song choices seemed off tonight. A slow song followed a fast one. He was known for ending one tune and crossfading into another seamlessly. It was as if he had perfect pitch and could anticipate where one song ended and the next picked up the key.

"He seems off tonight," Skid said. He intuited Connie would know he was talking about the DJ.

"You should have stopped when I told you." She said as she looked out the window.

"You're right. I'm sorry. It could have been a perfect night."

"*Should* have been," she said, putting her naked feet on the dashboard. She knew he didn't like her doing that, but she did it anyway.

"Should have been," he repeated. He knew how he felt about putting her feet on the dashboard, but he held his tongue.

"No Brinner tonight," she said.

Going to the breakfast-only, late-night restaurant was also part of their routine. But not tonight.

"Okay," he said as he twisted the wheel and pressed the accelerator.

"Go. I kinda like it when you drive fast," she said. "But not too fast."

He pushed the gas pedal harder, and the car whizzed down the wet streets. Her house was just a few blocks ahead, and there was no traffic. He parked in her family's driveway.

Connie jumped out of the car and slammed the door. She didn't give him a chance to say goodnight or give her a kiss.

"Goodnight," he said to the empty seat. He pulled the cassette tape from the player. "Great. Just great."

Chapter 34

Rod noticed it without Skid saying a word. He looked up from under the hood of a '57 Chevy he was rebuilding for a collector in Kansas City and said, "There's the man."

Skid wore his McDonald's uniform top and black pants. He'd polished his horrible and uncomfortable black shoes and had already attached his name tag.

How did Rod know? Skid thought.

"It's okay. I've seen it with guys in the Army. Their dicks hang a little lower like they've conquered Everest or somethin'. Congrats."

The air in the garage felt heavy, and Skid considered challenging Rod's observation. Should he fight his stepfather for his girl's honor? A real man would ask him to step outside, wouldn't he?

"Surrendered was more like it," Skid said with a defeated tone.

"That works too. I bet she's angry with you now," Rod said. He grunted as he twisted a rusted nut. He picked up a can of penetrating oil and sprayed it on the joint.

"Mad as a hornet," Skid said. But then realized he was in trouble with Connie and not the kind a simple apology or a Big Mac might fix.

"Give her some time. She's a virgin, right? Was?" Again, Rod asked without looking up from his work.

Skid noticed he always had a hard time making eye contact with him. Maybe he was that way with everyone.

"Yes, of course. I'll call her tomorrow."

"Good idea," Rod said, again with a grunt as he gripped the wrench and pushed. "Hand me that rubber mallet."

Skid searched the workbench for the tool. He found it under a hand saw and picked it up, letting the heft of the hammer rest in his hands.

"Give it," Rod said as he turned. He held out his hand and nodded at Skid.

"Here you go," Skid said. He tossed the hammer across the bay, and Rod caught it.

"Nice toss. I don't know the girl well, but you'll work it out if you like her and she likes you."

Rod turned back to the engine compartment and whacked the end of the wrench with the hammer. The nut still didn't budge. He sprayed more penetrating oil on the bolt. "Let that soak in a bit," he said more to himself than Skid. "Don't want to break that thing off in there," he said, thinking for a minute, "kinda like what you were thinkin' last night. Har. Har. Har."

Skid wouldn't have reacted to the joke, it wasn't funny, but the lascivious laugh at the end was all he could take. He picked up the rubber mallet and swung. He wasn't aiming for anything and was surprised when the black rubber hit the fender.

"Boy," Rod said, "what the actual fuck?"

The hammer missed Rod's shoulder by two inches and left a dent in the fender of the vintage vehicle. It wasn't a big deal, but the stepfather wasn't having it. He backhanded Skid across the face.

The blow stung Skid, and he reacted by swinging at Rod. The Army vet had been in several bar fights and even had a tussle with his father growing up, so he was more prepared to take on the adolescent. But instead, he stepped back as he peppered Skid with three punches to the stomach before the boy could move.

Skid sucked air and stepped back, leaning against the table with Rod's carefully arranged tools. He scanned the assortment and picked up a screwdriver.

"Now, boy, you don't want to go there," Rod said with a menacing tone. He'd been cut while losing a fight in a German Bier Haus and didn't want to hurt Skid.

"I d-d-d-don't know what to do," Skid said, tears filling his eyes as he stammered.

"Of course, you don't," Rod said, taking a less threatening tone this time. He raised his palms and moved toward the teen. "It's been a tough couple of months."

"Years," Skid wheezed between gulps of air and snot bubbles.

"Okay, yes, years, I get it. But we can't have you swingin' a screwdriver with bad intentions." Rod moved toward Skid and put out his right hand. "Let's just forget about the whole mess, and we both get to work."

Skid dropped the screwdriver, and when he did, he balled up a fist and let Rod have it in the jaw. The older man, a veteran, stopped, grinned, and touched the side of his mouth. He felt warm liquid and saw blood when he looked at his fingers. "Good one. Let's see what else you got."

Rod punched Skid in the gut again, but the boy moved to the side, slipping much of the punch's force and jabbing Rod on the chin this time. "Come on," the old man said as he spat blood. "You think you're a man, now!"

Skid lunged at Rod with his arms wide. Rod moved to his right and stepped under the attack. He grabbed Skid and put him in a headlock. "I could put you to sleep now. You wanna take a nap?"

Skid struggled, pushed back against the older man, but couldn't get his hand under the vice-like grip around his neck. He struggled to breathe as his cheeks grew red.

"Give up, boy," Rod whispered.

Skid's ears and cheeks reddened, and his shoulders slumped. He pushed back against the bigger man and tried to step on Rod's toes. It didn't work.

Rod eased his grip. "Okay, I'm gonna let you go now, but behave."

Skid stepped away and bent over, trying to catch his breath. "Y-y-y-you," he stuttered.

"I know. I'm sorry to have to get rough," Rod said. He turned his back on the boy and returned to his project. "I'll have to charge you for takin' out that dent."

Skid turned and moved through the shed. Sunlight from the dormer windows on both sides of the roof shone on him. He felt the heat, cool, heat, cool as if gaining energy with each step. "Son of a bitch," he whispered as he stepped through the double door at the end of the building. "Son of a bitch."

Chapter 35

Connie wouldn't take Skid's calls for two days. He'd talked with her mother and once even spoke with her father. Finally, Mr. Palmer said Connie was as mad as he'd ever seen her and should leave her alone.

Skid knew she worked that Saturday at Goldstein's, so when his shift ended at McDonald's, he changed clothes in a gas station bathroom and pulled into a parking slot in front of the store.

There was a two-hour limit to parking on the square around the courthouse, with a meter maid placing chalk marks on the car's tires to prove there was a violation. Skid didn't think he'd need that much time to apologize to Connie.

He opened the glass door and stepped in from the bright sunlight. His eyes adjusted to the dimmer light, and he swept the store looking for his girl. At least, he hoped she was still his girl.

Skid didn't see her, but he saw Mr. Goldstein working with a customer in front of the tri-pane mirror that showed every angle of a man's body. Skid didn't know the customer. So many people were moving into the town that keeping up with all the new faces was hard. Finally, Mr. Goldstein saw Skid and tipped his chin toward the storeroom.

Skid found Connie standing on a ladder and putting away shoes into a huge wall rack. She stood on a step stool and didn't hear him approach.

"Need any help?" He asked.

She didn't turn her head and said, "Not from you."

"I just came by to apologize. I lost my mind for a minute."

"It was longer than a minute," Connie said, still not looking at him. "And when I asked you to slow down, you put your foot on the gas."

"I was just," Skid stammered, "I-I-I don't know."

Connie slammed a box into a slot. A single light bulb illuminated the storeroom, and she realized it was in the wrong spot. The force of her jerking the shoes from the storage place caused the ladder to wobble. She regained her balance.

"That was close," Skid said.

She jerked the box out of the wrong place and jammed it into another.

"You'll need to listen to me more next time." But, again, she wouldn't look at him.

"You mean, there'll-."

"Don't push it. I'm still angry with you."

"Please don't be mad anymore," Skid said with a pleading tone. "What are you doin' after work? We could just hang out."

She glared down at him. "Goin' home and washin' my hair."

"What if we went to the big town and had a late dinner?" He asked. Skid knew their favorite restaurant and her usual order. He gambled that she'd be hungry after working all day.

"You have that kind of money?"

Skid pulled a roll of ones from his pocket. He'd gotten paid the day before, and while he needed new underwear, he thought spending on Connie would be the better investment.

Connie glanced at his open hand at the cash. "That should be just enough."

She turned, and her foot caught the edge of the ladder. Skid rushed toward her and put out his arms. He grabbed her arm as she fell, and she landed hard on her right foot. Her ankle didn't break, but it did make a crunching noise.

"Owwww, damn it," she said, a bit too loud for the store. Connie knew Mr. Goldstein didn't like his pitches to his customers to be interrupted.

She sat on the wooden floor and rubbed her ankle. Mr. Goldstein opened a curtain and looked down at his employee.

"I heard from the other room. Are you all right?"

"I've sprained it before, so don't worry about it. I'll be fine."

He looked at Skid. "Why don't you let this big, strong boy take you home?"

"I can do that," Skid said.

Connie shook her head in disgust. "I can't believe I did that." She offered her hand to Skid, and he helped her to her feet.

"Take her home and put some ice on it," Mr. Goldstein said. He knew she was a good worker, and those were hard to find.

"Will do," Skid said.

"You're not comin' in the door."

"Oh, how about I dump you on the porch, and you can crawl into the house?"

Again, an icy glare from Connie. "That'll do."

She leaned on him as they moved through the curtain. He pushed the cloth aside and felt her lean against him.

"I love you," Skid said.

"You're all right, too," Connie said. "Idiot."

Chapter 36

Skid hated working the drive-through. Some customers would mumble or change their minds during their orders. Some would even challenge the orders they made when they got to the window. Some would even get mad because they made a mistake. However, the customers needed to be served quickly and efficiently. They were right, no matter what.

He adjusted the headset and picked up the drinks. Skid knew Leon's memory was better than his, and he could count on him to get the orders right.

"Hey," Leon asked during a break in the line. "Your neck is red."

"Are you callin' me a redneck?"

This had become some of the witty banter that got them through slow periods of their shifts. There was a rumor that a team bus would be arriving soon, and when that happened, it would be chaos in the store. So, it was joking now, but all business later.

"Yeah," Leon said. He leaned against the fountain drink counter. He crossed his legs and arms. "Whatcha gonna do about it?"

"Ha, ha, I'm not gonna get my ass kicked twice in one day," Skid said. He mirrored Leon's stance and looked at the slightly taller man.

"Who kicked your ass?"

"My stepfather and, I guess you could say, my girlfriend. We did it last night."

"Did it? You mean, oh, right. And..."

"It did not turn out great."

"That's not unusual. Too much goin' on, and your dick takes almost all the blood from your brain." Leon said with a professorial tone. "So, you can't think."

Skid chuckled and said, "I guess you're the expert here."

"I was eleven. A girl in the neighborhood liked to take a boy's virginity. Kind of a collecting scalps situation. I had just gotten my first pimples, and she saw that. I guess she thought I was ready."

"That's weird," Skid said.

"And kind of sick," the young athlete said. "If you think about it," Leon said. His gaze dipped to the floor before the cash register and back to Skid.

"Well, I think..." Skid began.

He glimpsed movement to his right. The video monitor showed a pickup truck rolling to the menu board next to the window. Skid turned on his microphone. He would return to the conversation later, hoping to get more of Leon's wisdom.

"Hi. Welcome to McDonald's. What can I get you?"

The camera couldn't pick up the face in the truck's window. Sunlight slanted across the cab and plunged the opening into darkness. A deep voice crackled over the intercom.

"Big Mac, fries, and a Coke."

"That's a number one," Skid said. After that, he modulated his tone because he knew some people didn't like being corrected.

"Okay, whatever."

"That'll be three, fifty-three. Pull around to the window."

Leon lifted the Coke from under the dispenser and sat it on the counter near the sliding window. Skid turned to the crewmate at the fry station. "Large Fries." He nodded at the front window chief and said, "Big Mac."

"Please and thank you," the assistant manager said.

"Please and thank you," Skid parroted him. He knew being courteous to the customers and crew was important, but he forgot sometimes.

The pickup pulled up to the window. The driver, an overweight man with a scruffy beard, held four dollars out his window. Skid took the money and gave him change.

Skid wasn't watching when the frontline chief put the Big Mac in the white paper bag and how she picked up the French fries from the back of the rack. The hot lights would keep the fries warm for only so long before they got cold. There was a protocol for wasting fries that had been too late out of the fryer, but the assistant manager liked less waste and more profits.

Skid took the bag and handed it through the window. The driver opened the bag and pulled out three fries. "I thought so. You fooled me one last time."

He took the Coke and threw it at Skid. The driver hit the gas and sped away.

Skid tried to move, but the drink caught him on the chin and drenched his uniform. "God damnit!"

Leon turned, and so did the Crew Manager. It was against the rules for crew members to use foul language no matter what happened.

"Hey," the Crew Manager said. He moved toward Skid with his eyes squinted almost shut, and his fingers balled into fists. "You can't..."

Leon stepped in front of the Crew Manager and put his hand on the young man's chest. The Crew Manager glanced down at Leon's hand and then looked up. "Really."

"Skid's havin' a hard time right now," Leon's tone was soft and deferential, "I'll get him a towel and a mop to clean up in front of the window."

The Crew Manager glared at Leon until the larger man dropped his hand. "I'll have to write him up."

"You do that. Be sure to say that the fries were cold, too," Leon said. His tone was sharper than before, and he grinned as he looked down at the manager.

"Good grief. Okay, get on it."

"Will do, yes, Sir," Leon said. But, of course, if he'd been a soldier, this would be when he'd snap off a salute to a superior officer.

Leon picked up a towel from the break room and brought it to Skid. He was still wiping the liquid from his eyes and shaking his uniform top. "That's new."

"We're all about customer service here," Leon joked. He wasn't sure it was time to poke fun at Skid and the incident, but he felt it was the right move when he saw Skid smiling.

"Just when you think it can't get worse," Skid said as he took the towel from Leon.

"Don't say that. It can always get worse." Again, an attempt at humor.

"True," Skid said, agreeing. "That is true. But let's hope it doesn't."

"You got that right." The young peacemaker said.

Chapter 37

"Mrs. Anderson is dead," Dee Dee said.

After homeroom, she'd rushed through the stream of students to catch up with Skid and Leon. The young men walked with confidence and verve. It was payday, and they were already considering ways to spend their money. Dee Dee matched their stride and looked at them for reactions to the news.

"The principal didn't mention it in morning announcements," Skid said.

"They're telling her next of kin first. She has a sister in Alaska, and the police are having a hard time getting ahold of her."

Leon bumped into a fellow basketball player, and they smiled and high-fived. "Damn, that's cold. I'm in her Monday and Wednesday speech class." He asked, "What happened?"

"She was driving on New Nashville highway, and another car went down in the ditch between the four lanes, flipped over, and landed on top of Mrs. Anderson's car. She died instantly."

"Wow," Skid said.

"She was mindin' her own business, and poof, gone," Dee Dee said. They turned the corner and approached the biology lab on the right.

"Good Lord," Leon said. He pulled a pencil from behind his ear and put it in his shirt pocket.

"Shit happens," Dee Dee said, "but that's just weird and..."

"Awful," Skid finished her sentence. "What, I mean, how are we supposed to make sense of this?"

"So much of what goes on in the world doesn't make sense," Dee Dee said.

"Trust in the Lord," Leon said as he peeled off and walked into the Physics lab.

"I'm havin' a hard time trustin' the Lord when somethin' like this happens," Skid said. He approached the lab door and let Dee Dee enter ahead of him.

Skid remembered all his long walks and conversations with God after his mother died. She was a good person, and it didn't seem fair that she had to suffer as she did. The only conclusion Skid could reach was that life was hard and unfair.

Mrs. Jenkins stood at the chalkboard and stared at the piece of chalk in her hand. Dee Dee and Skid walked past her and then looked back at the board. It was blank.

"Settle down," Mrs. Jenkins said, even though the students could hear each other's breathing. "I wanted to talk about human biology today." He noticed how several of the pupils had picked up their pencils. "You won't have to take notes today. None of this will be on your test."

Skid remembered how he was in Mrs. Anderson's speech class last year. He'd even been cast in a play she was producing, but he'd caught the flu and missed performing. Nevertheless, she had done one thing for him that had changed his life in many ways. He said something in class in response to her question about an attainable life goal. Skid wanted to speak about how he felt walking through the woods near his home. She gave him the podium, and he began recanting how he'd walk along the stream and enjoy how the water sounded. He didn't mention the conversations with God about his mother. He knew it would have been too much for the audience.

The room grew still, and his descriptions and words enthralled the students. Until he mentioned how he liked listening to the leaves rustle as he walked. A student named Russel was in class, and Skid got an unintentional laugh, most likely to relieve the tension of the scene he'd set. He finished the oral essay and sat down. His gaze dropped to the floor in shame even though he'd fulfilled one of his aspirations.

After class, Mrs. Anderson told him his impromptu speech had a good beginning. It was building to a nice ending before the unfortunate joke that wasn't really a joke.

"Teenagers can be so cruel," she said.

She told Skid that speech competitions were coming up and he should consider applying. "You might win a scholarship."

Skid didn't believe her, but he appreciated the support. He'd had several teachers pointing out his strengths and encouraging him. Finally, Mrs. Wilson suggested he try a writing competition sponsored by the local power company. Again, his teachers saw something in him he couldn't see himself.

"Do humans have a soul?" Mrs. Jenkins asked. "There's no biological evidence of this. Were we created six thousand years ago, or did humans evolve over tens of thousands of years? As someone who teaches science, the fossil record shows that we and millions of other species evolved over billions of years. That said, there's something in humans that makes us want to believe in a higher power. You can call it God, Allah, Mother Nature, or whatever, but most of us need something to explain why things happen."

She stepped from behind the podium and sat on the corner of the desk. Mrs. Jenkins folded her hands in her lap and scanned the room, looking each student in the eye. "What happened to Mrs. Anderson was an accident. She wasn't being punished or paying the price for an ancestor's sins. She was in the wrong place at the wrong time and had no control over the situation. It's sad, and we all will deal with her death in our own ways. It would be nearly impossible to recreate what happened in an experiment as far as science goes. Her accident was a random, one-in-a-billion chance of happening. There's nothing we could do about it."

Mrs. Jenkins brushed a tear from the corner of her eye. "We have no one to blame. We may get angry, deny reality, cry, and laugh when we remember something funny someone said or did and move on with our lives. That's the way life is, but people's memories in our lives will live on."

Several girls in the class had tears in their eyes. So did some of the boys. Skid glanced at Dee Dee and saw her pull a handkerchief from her purse. She dabbed at the corners of her eyes as the teacher finished her speech.

Skid looked down and saw his hand shaking so hard that the pencil he held fell to the floor. He bent over to pick it up, and when he straightened himself, he felt hot tears drip down his cheeks. Who was he crying for? Mrs. Anderson, maybe his mother, and perhaps Rod's cousin, Joseph?

Mrs. Jenkins took a deep breath and circled her desk. She sat down and opened the attendance roster. She started calling off the names but was too choked up to get past Jules Anderson.

"Let's just call it for today. Everyone should take this time to stay here and talk with friends or go to the library. This is hard, and as you get older, you'll find more and more of your friends and family will die. Science can explain a lot these days, but some things are out of our control in this world and may never be explained."

Dee Dee gathered her books, still sniffing and touching her handkerchief to her eyes. "Are you going to the library?"

"I think I'll stay right here," Skid said. He couldn't bring himself to look up at her.

She put his hand on his shoulder and squeezed. "I've lost people in my family and friends, and it never gets any easier."

He looked up at her. "Thanks,"

She turned and walked out of the classroom.

Soon, Skid and Mrs. Jenkins were the only ones in the room. Dust motes floated through the air, and a soft breeze moved through the open windows. It was going to be a day full of sunshine.

"It looks like Spring has sprung." Skid's attempt at humor fell flat, but Mrs. Jenkins looked up and smiled at the boy.

"It looks like it'll be a nice day," the teacher said.

Chapter 38

Connie stepped back from the front door and waited for Skid to answer. She'd thought about breaking up with him but with the death of Rod's cousin Joseph and now Mrs. Anderson. She was worried about him.

She pulled down the hem of her untucked shirt and looked up, surprised when Rod answered the door.

"Hi," the stepfather said. "Skid 's out in the shed doin' some inventory."

"He wasn't expecting me. I mean, I didn't call."

"Oh."

"We had a little fight. So, I thought we might talk about it."

"Talkin' is always good," Rod said. He swung open the screen door and stepped back so she could come in.

Rod looked like he'd just woken up. She noticed he had oil stains on his white T-shirt. Had he slept in it? "I usually get a nap after lunch. Keeps me goin'."

"I'm sorry. I didn't mean to wake you."

"I was about to get up. Only need about ten minutes. One of those things they taught us in the Army. Gotta be sharp when you're waitin' for the enemy to shoot at you." His attempt at a joke didn't land with her. "Should I go get Skid?" He asked.

"No," she began, "well, I can go out to the shed."

"Okay," he said. "How's your car doin'?"

"Great," she said with a smile. "I wish you'd let me pay you for your time," she said. She sat in a rocking chair, snapped open her pocketbook, and searched for her wallet.

"Like I said before. You get the family discount."

She closed her purse. "Thanks."

"Besides, that was an easy one. I've got a Ferrari in the shop that refuses to turn over. I can't figure it out."

"Fuel, spark, and air," she said. Connie had heard Skid quote Rod. It was what it took to get a gas engine running. It was as simple as that.

"Huh, I guess he *was* listenin'. Maybe I can turn him into a mechanic after all."

She tapped her sneaker on the floor, setting the chair in motion. She added more momentum. *Why am I sitting down,* she thought.

"Skid looks up to you," she said. She smiled again. *What's with all the smiling, Connie?*

She remembered how impressed she was when Rod diagnosed her car's problem. She put her index finger to her bottom lip and looked up as he stood across from her. *What's with his mouth, Connie? You've kissed lips like those before.*

Connie had looked so helpless there in her parent's driveway. The temperature was cool that morning, and frost still covered the grass. She pulled her sweater closer to her body. Her always white Keds, no scuffs allowed, were thin. She wasn't wearing socks, and her feet were cold.

Rod told her to get back in the car and try the ignition. When it failed to turn over, he pulled jumper cables from his trunk and attached them to the two car's batteries. Then, he told her to turn over the engine again. But, again, it made a clicking noise.

Rod hooked a tow chain from the back of his car to Connie's and towed it the five miles to his shop. She'd protested at first. "I don't know how to do this," she said.

"We'll go slow, and it'll be fine. Just tap the brakes and turn the wheel. And don't forget to put on your lights. We don't want to get run over."

A few cars passed them, but it was an uneventful tow. Finally, they crossed the cattle gate and pushed her car into the shed. He told her to hop in, and he'd drive her home. She saw Skid cutting the grass at the church back to her house but didn't get a chance to wave at him. Instead, she told him the story of her broken car that night.

"Rod's a good mechanic," Skid had said.

"He knows his business," Connie agreed.

Now, the mechanic stood looking down at her.

"I love these old rockers," she said, pushing against the floor.

"Can I get you somethin' to drink? You want some water or somethin'?"

"No, I've got to get goin'."

She stood and walked toward the door. She turned quickly and bumped into him as he followed. "Oops, sorry," Rod said.

"It's okay," she said without turning. "I really wish you'd take some money for fixin' my car."

"You paid for the parts and the battery," Rod said. He stepped back. A wedge of light fell across the floor from the open front door. Connie stepped toward him and put her arms around him. "At least I can give you a hug."

Rod stood still and kept his arms at his side. "That's not necessary. Happy to do it."

Connie looked over his shoulder at the sofa. A tangle of a colorful quilt lay at one end, and a red pillow sat at the other. He did say he'd been asleep.

Her right foot was between his legs, and she felt something hard in his loose-fitting coveralls. *What was it?* She asked herself. It suddenly dawned on her he was semi-erect. She backed away and turned her head. She felt her cheeks reddening, and her left hand shook.

Connie didn't have much experience with men. Still, she knew from her time fooling around with Skid that penises were complicated. Did Rod know she felt him? Did he find her attractive, and was that just something that happened?

"Let's go see if we can find Skid," Rod said. He opened the front door and held it for her. She stepped through and into the sunlight crossing the porch. She was just a few feet from where Joseph had hung himself. She turned and jumped off the end of the porch. Rod took the steps and followed.

Was it because he was sleeping, he had an erection, or was it her? She asked herself. She'd heard older girls call them "dumb sticks," and there were times when men had no control over how they might react. Curious.

Skid stood at the shed's door and rubbed his hands with a towel. He smiled at her and walked across the grass. The frost from just minutes earlier had made it now wet with dew. "Hey," he said.

"Hey, back at ya'," she said. "I'm still mad at you."

"I saw you skippin' across the porch and then jumpin' off. I guess your ankle's all better."

"All better," she said, grinning.

"I'm sorry. It won't happen again," Skid promised.

She hugged Skid. *No erection,* she thought.

She looked over Skid's shoulder and watched Rod walk past them and into his workshop. First, she saw Rod glance back at them. Then, she noticed a sly smile as the stepfather turned his head.

Chapter 39

"So," Dee Dee began, "how did the big night go?"

"Funny you should ask," Connie said.

They sat opposite each other in the cafeteria, eating the same lunch, a hot dog and fries. Connie had water, and Dee Dee had a Coke. Unfortunately, the room's maximum capacity was four hundred, making it impossible to serve the classes simultaneously with the current enrollment. As a result, some students began lunch at eleven while others had to wait until one. Dee Dee and Connie were lucky they were in the group that ate at noon.

Connie parted her hair on the left side this morning, and her makeup featured thin mascara and pink lipstick. Dee Dee liked going without makeup unless it was a special occasion. So instead, she sported a short, pixie cut she'd seen on a model in an old magazine. So, she'd asked the beautician for a "Twiggy," which she got.

"What's funny?" Dee Dee asked. She took a bite of her hot dog. Mustard leaked around the edge of the bun and smeared her mouth with yellow.

Connie motioned with her napkin, and Dee Dee swiped at the errant condiment. She nodded, and Dee Dee smiled.

"We did it," Connie said, barely in a whisper.

"No, really. I wasn't sure he had it in him," Dee Dee said with just the right tone of irony. "I knew you were talkin' about it, but-." She tried to hide a twitch of shock flashing across her face.

"So, Skid talks to you about stuff like this?" Connie asked.

"Who else is he gonna talk to, Monte?"

"Good point," Connie said, "he's an idiot."

"Right, I need details."

"Well, we'd been kind'a foolin' around for a little while, but we decided it would happen Friday night."

"How did you bring it up? I mean, how did you talk about it?" Dee Dee asked. The noise in the room made it impossible to have a quiet conversation, so the girls heads got closer.

"We, you know, just talked," Connie said and sipped her drink. "We went to our place and did it in the car."

"Just like that?" Dee Dee asked. She took another bite of her hot dog.

"Pretty much. There was kissing and such, and I had him put on the condom. He was very excited. Even in the dark, I could see his cheeks gettin' red." She smiled and said, "So cute."

"What was it like?" Connie was so close she could smell the Jean Naté on Dee Dee's neck.

"Did it hurt?" Connie said. "Oh, yeah. Bad. I asked him to go slow at first, and he did."

Dee Dee said, "He's a sweet boy."

"Yeah, he's got every reason in the world not to be, but he is." Connie nodded and took another sip of her drink. "The weirdest thing was there was a broken spring in the seat, and it was pokin' me as he was doin' it. But, of course, I moaned and stuff because the spring hurt, so I guess he thought he was doin' it right."

"Was he?" Dee Dee asked. She stuffed some fries into her mouth. Her head almost touched the table now.

"He was gentle, but, man, he was determined. Little head takin' over for the big head, I guess."

Dee Dee nodded. "Right. Well, now what?"

Connie smiled and said, "Now we don't have anything to do on graduation night."

Both girls laughed and took a bite of their lunch.

"It's strange. Have you ever, I mean..."

"I've seen one, no, make that two. The first," Dee Dee said, "was in the second grade, and Jimmy Dodge asked to see mine, so I asked to see his first. We got caught, and the teachers told our parents. I don't really count that one because, you know. The other one was after work one night. We were in the parking lot at the Huddle House, and this boy from out of town and I started kissing. He was in training, so I knew I probably wouldn't see him again. I was curious. We were sitting in the front seat messing around and stuff, and bloop, there it was."

"Weird, isn't it? It's like they have a mind of their own."

Dee Dee nodded and smiled. "What about you?"

"Pretty much the same as you, but Skid was my third. The first was a 'show me yours' kind of thing at a church camp, so it was tiny. The second one was at a sleepover where this boy and me ended up in the closet. So he put it in my hand."

Dee Dee said, "That's pretty much all you need to do most of the time. All you gotta do is hold on."

Both girls laughed. "They do the rest, don't they?"

Connie said. "What about the different shapes and sizes? What's that all about?"

"Weird, ain't it?"

"I mean, somethin' happened the other day. This one was huge."

"Not Skid?" Dee Dee asked.

Connie shook her head. "I mean, it was a weird situation. Just one of those things."

"Like at the doctor?"

Connie chuckled. "No, not like the doctors. It was just, I don't know. It was Skid's stepdad. I gave him a hug, and I felt it."

"It's gotta be pretty big to feel it like that."

"Yeah," Connie said. "Weird."

"But interesting," Dee Dee said with a giggle.

Both girls nodded. They both took French fries from their plates and chewed as they thought about what all this meant.

"I've heard they wake up like that sometimes," Dee Dee proffered.

"Just wake up, and boom, there it is?"

"Pretty much. I mean, I've had cousins sleep over, and you can't help but see it when they get up."

"Oh, really, cousins," Connie teased.

"No, silly, through their PJs. You know. Good grief." Dee Dee raised both hands and said, "Okay, I give up."

"So, what happens after that?"

"I think they pee, and it goes away."

"Until needed," Connie said. She took a bite of her hot dog and smiled as a group of cheerleaders passed the table. "And then boom, there it is. Dumbstick. Have you heard it called that?"

"Yeah, the name really fits, doesn't it?"

Connie smiled and glanced around the room. There were boys everywhere, and she began mentally undressing several of them. How different would each 'dumb stick' be? "Oh, yes, profoundly dumb."

"You done?" Dee Dee asked.

"You're gonna keep this between us, aren't you?"

"Of course. Tick-a-lock," Dee Dee said, using her index finger and thumb before her mouth, indicating she'd keep the information to herself.

"Good. It's nobody's business and all. I don't care, but I just don't wanna have to deal with the hassle," Connie said. "You know."

"Lots of meddlin' dumbos here."

"Ain't that the truth," Connie said.

They both grabbed their trays and stood. The swirl of adolescent boys and girls encircled them as they moved toward the waste cans. Then, finally, they tossed their trays on top of the stack and moved towards the open double doors. The next group of diners stood in line, waiting to get in. Skid stood next to Jacob. They both wore bell-bottomed jeans, 'Chucks,' and T-shirts.

"Lookin' good, boys," Dee Dee said. She held Jacob's gaze a bit longer than she did with Skid.

Connie touched Skid's arm as she passed him. He nodded at her and smiled.

"Life is good," Jacob said.

Skid agreed, "So good."

Chapter 40

Miss Black stood in front of the door to the Vice-Principal office. Her hair was blown out to resemble the *Charlie's Angels* actress Farrah Fawcett. She didn't have the same toothy grin or the big, expressive eyes, but the cut looked good. Skid wondered if she had a date since it was Friday.

She pulled him out of the stream of students passing and turned him toward a corner. The clamor from all the students made it hard to talk, so they stood closer than might have been socially acceptable.

"I was talking with Mr. Salman. "He said he announced the Middle Tennessee Electric essay contest to your class."

"So?" Skid asked. He brushed his hair from his forehead. He was trying a new look, like the Beatles, the "mop tops." He wore a knit shirt, bell-bottom jeans, and Converse All-Stars, just like the other boys.

"I think you should give it a try." She said, talking a bit too loud. It was impossible to speak at the normal volume with all the chattering.

"Why?" Skid asked.

"I think you'd be good at it."

"No, I don't think so," he said and turned to go.

"There's a one-hundred-dollar prize for first place," Miss Black said. Several students' heads turned at the mention of the prize amount.

Skid turned back and looked at Miss Black. "You think I can do this."

"I think you can."

"I'll consider it," he said, turning to ford the stream of students packing the hallway again.

She tapped her temple three times and said with as much volume as possible. "Serious thought, Skid."

Skid remembered Mr. Salman's announcement from earlier about the contest and how the teacher had pinned the notice to the bulletin board near the door. He had to move along. His next class was History in Mr. Lewis's classroom.

No, he thought, *I've got no shot. I don't have the time or energy to write.*

He entered the room, and there on Mr. Lewis's bulletin board was the same announcement that also hung on Mr. Salman's. Skid couldn't avoid it.

And then, he read the subject of the essay and the requirements. The topic was "How Has Rural Electrification Changed the South?" The piece had to be no more than fifteen-hundred words.

The notice got him thinking. It had elements of history and economics that intrigued him. In addition, the subject included societal and environmental issues.

Skid took his seat and opened his notebook. He wrote down the subject of the essay contest and the phrase "one thousand words" at the top of a ruled sheet of paper.

How did rural electrification change the South?

And what would he do with one hundred dollars?

He knew tuition at the local college would be around one hundred and ten dollars this summer semester, not counting any books he'd have to buy. So that check would put him well on his way to higher education. *Besides,* he thought, *what've I got to lose?*

Mr. Lewis liked the Socratic teaching method, so he'd usually follow his lectures with a question-and-answer period until the bell to change classes rang. Skid waited until everyone else had gone.

"Don't be late for your next class." Mr. Lewis said. He pushed his glasses up his nose. They always seemed to be slipping down. Skid knew that would drive him crazy. So why doesn't he just get them adjusted to fit his face?

"I won't be. It's P.E. We always, wait, no, never mind. Okay, I'm thinking about writing an essay for the Middle Tennessee Electric contest."

"Thinking? So, you haven't fully committed yet?"

"All right, never mind," Skid said. His chin dipped, and he shuffled toward the door.

"Wait, Skid, I'm sorry." The teacher looked genuinely remorseful that he'd been so short with Skid. "So, what can I do to help?"

Skid turned, smiled, and walked back to the teacher's desk. Mr. Lewis's books and papers covered the desktop. He'd already opened his well-worn briefcase.

The teacher leaned back in his office chair and put his sandals on the edge. He wore a blue work shirt and jeans. Skid couldn't remember Mr. Lewis wearing anything different in class, even in the winter. He wondered if different versions of this outfit were his entire wardrobe.

"The subject is how rural electrification changed the South. I'll need to research the history and develop a solid argument for both sides."

"Who told you that?" Mr. Lewis asked. He picked up a well-chewed pencil and put it between his teeth.

"Mr. Salman. He said every great work of art tells both sides of the story. Electricity made life easier for most people and harder for others. That's my premise."

The instructor looked up at the fluorescent light overhead and the air conditioning vent at the end of the classroom. "I can see how it helped, but what did it hurt?"

"I'm goin' to make a list and write about what I think are the top three. That should limit the essay to the right length." Skid said. His books shifted against his chest, and he had to move his hand up to steady them.

"That's great. Good start," Mr. Lewis said. He sat up and shuffled the papers on his desk. He shoved them into the briefcase. "I've got a book at home I can lend you. And I'm sure Miss Cardwell in the library can help."

"Right," Skid said. "She's always been very supportive."

Mr. Lewis stood and patted Skid on the shoulder. He remembered all the tragedies the boy had experienced lately. He took a chance that a bit of encouragement might be helpful now.

Skid hadn't felt an act of kindness and empathy from an authority figure in a long time. It caught him by surprise, and he started crying. The tears trickled down his cheeks, and he felt his bottom lip quivering.

"I'm sorry," Skid blubbered. He tried to continue, "I don't know…"

Mr. Lewis didn't remove his hand from Skid's shoulder. In fact, he started rubbing the boy's back and whispered, "It's okay. It's okay."

Skid tried to stop crying and wiped his nose on his sleeve. "I can't stop."

"It's okay. Just let it out. Let me get you some tissue," he said, turning back and opening a desk drawer. He pulled out a tissue box and pulled three from the pack.

"It's just..."

"I get it. Lots of stuff's goin' on," the teacher said. He rubbed Skid's shoulder as the boy finally pulled himself back together.

"I'm gonna be late," Skid said, forcing the words between diminishing sobs.

"You're lucky you're here and not in P.E. Imagine Coach Billings if you started crying."

Skid chuckled a shook his head. "That would be epic."

"Although, the way the basketball team played last year, I'm sure he's seen a lot of students crying."

Skid had to chuckle at the teacher's attempt at humor. He knew it was a distraction but a welcome interruption with everything he'd been through.

"That would be funny if it weren't so sad," Skid said between fading sobs.

"I'll write you a note." Mr. Lewis said and pulled a sheet of paper from his notebook. "Dear Coach Billings," he said as he wrote, "Skid was late because he was blubbering too hard to walk."

They both laughed as Skid took the paper from Mr. Lewis. "Thanks," he said, "but that's not what you wrote, is it?"

He opened the folded sheet of paper and tried to read the words, but he couldn't focus his eyes on the excuse.

"Of course not," Mr. Lewis said as he pushed Skid toward the door. "I was just trying to lighten the moment. I wrote that you'd peed your pants and needed to change clothes."

Again, both young men laughed and entered the hallway. One went left, and the other went right.

Chapter 41

Skid felt he'd need his full attention to write the contest essay, so first, he wrote the last two scenes in his *The Waltons* screenplay. He hadn't looked at it for a couple of weeks and needed to create an ending that worked for him and the show. When satisfied he had a draft that worked, he put it away. Then, he picked up the library book about the creation of the Tennessee Valley Authority Miss Cardwell had selected and started reading.

He sat in the oversized recliner and tilted the lampshade toward the book. The information was a bit dry, but he knew he'd need a solid, historical foundation for his essay. He'd add his own thoughts and opinions later in the piece.

The screen door slammed, and Skid glanced up at the clock. It was only four o'clock, and Rod usually didn't come in for dinner until six. So, either something had gone very well today, or something had gone wrong.

"Hey," Skid said, not looking up from his book.

"Hey, yourself," Rod said. He walked past the recliner and toward the kitchen sink. He turned on the water and grabbed the soap and a brush.

Skid didn't like when Rod washed up in the kitchen sink, but there wasn't anything he could do about it. When his mother was alive, she put her foot down, and Rod washed his greasy hands in the garage. Now she was gone, and the stepfather did whatever he wanted.

"Too early for dinner," Rod said as he sat on the sofa. He clicked on the television and turned up the sound.

"I'm not hungry. I've got too much to do," Skid said, still not looking up from his reading.

"Oh," Rod said. Cartoons flashed across the television screen as he changed the channels. A closeup of the face of the Lone Ranger in black and white filled the screen. "Ain't nothin' on."

"It's mostly kid's shows until the news."

"I can't handle this," Rod said as he turned off the set. He picked up the weekly shopper and unfolded the paper. He bent the paper toward a shaft of setting sunlight. He "tromboned" the article in the light. "Can't see this," he muttered.

"Maybe you need glasses," Skid said without looking up from his book.

"What did you say?"

"Nothin'."

"I asked you, 'What did you say'?"

"And I said maybe you need glasses."

Rod snapped the paper and turned it to another angle. "I don't need fuckin' glasses."

"Just because you say it doesn't make it so," Skid whispered.

"What?" Rod asked, a growing irritation on the edge of his voice.

"I said you're gettin' old."

"Bullshit. I'm not old."

"I didn't say you were *old*. I said you were getting old."

"Get up," Rod commanded. He shot to his feet and walked toward the recliner.

"That's okay. I'm fine."

"I said, get up, boy. I need to sit there to read the paper."

"I'm busy. Go outside. There's plenty of light out there."

"Look, *Clarence*," Rod said, looking down at Skid. "I pay the bills around here, and you need to do what I say."

"I'm almost eighteen."

"So?"

"That means I'm a man."

Rod chuckled and said, "You have no idea what it means to be a man. Until you have that birthday, I'm still the head of the family, and that's that. Now, get up."

Skid looked up, closed his book, and stood. "I'm not happy."

"I don't care," Rod said as he sat in his easy chair.

"Let me know when dinner's ready."

"You'll know 'cause you're cookin' it," Skid said as he stomped out of the room. "Old man," he muttered as he walked out the door onto the porch.

Skid sat in the rocking chair and tried to focus on his book. But the words skittered across the pages instead of explaining the history of rural electrification. They did not make an impression on his mind. He was too mad.

He tried to analyze why he was feeling this way. So many things in his life seemed out of control and beyond his influence. How was he supposed to handle all this?

And Skid remembered the fight in the garage and how Rod had handled him like a child. He considered how to better prepare for their next fight. It seemed inevitable. Skid vowed to find a book in the library to help him learn to protect himself. He needed to learn how to fight.

Chapter 42

Rod's customers rarely came into his shop to check on the progress of their cars. Instead, they usually waited until they received a phone call or a postcard telling them the project was finished.

But Larry Cox was different. He would take the two-lane highways from Chicago to Tampa twice a year. He was a snowbird. After his wife's death, he made the trip alone. He would point out different sights and changes in the landscape to the empty seat next to him.

His Airstream had everything he needed and more for a trip that would only take a few days for most travelers. However, he never felt comfortable in either of his homes, so he would stretch the journey to weeks.

Larry had his 1940 Mercedes-Benz 320 Cabriolet A placed on a flatbed truck and shipped to Rod before his last trip south. Unfortunately, one of the hinges on the passenger side, "suicide door," had rusted to the point it needed to be replaced and the metal around the frame repaired. It was a tedious and delicate job, and Rod was one of the few mechanics in the world who could do it right. In addition, the dashboard's wood grain finish had dulled and even rotted in a few places. But, again, Rod was one of the best in the restoration business.

"Welcome," Rod said. "Good to see ya' again."

"Proud to be here," Larry said as he entered the shop.

"It's been a long time. How ya doin'?"

"If I had your head, I'd throw mine away," Larry said with a chuckle.

Rod had never heard that phrase, but it seemed like a compliment. He let it slide.

"The engine checks out," Rod said. He stood next to the car and patted the fender. The shop was his element, and he felt he could speak with confidence when talking about cars. "I put new points and plugs in and replaced all the belts. Where'd you say you found this?"

Larry hitched his pants over his protruding belly. He smacked his lips as he recalled the car's provenance. "It was in a barn in Pennsylvania for over thirty years. This German farmer had inherited it from his father and had it shipped over from Berlin. He didn't need it. He drove a truck, so he just parked it. Finally, his widow let me have it for a song."

"Thirty-five hundred miles on the odometer. You're one lucky s-o-b. It looks pretty good," Rod said. "I put in a new battery, and it cranked right up."

"Them goddamn Germans know their business."

"That they do," Rod agreed. "For the most part, German cars were well-built and would last long if cared for properly."

"That's great. You're the expert. When can I have it?" Larry always wore a cowboy hat on his "snowbird" trips. He'd told the story to Rod about how his wife had picked it out for him in this little town in Georgia. Rod listened, but truthfully, he couldn't care less. He'd found it a good idea to feign interest in whatever customers wanted to talk about over the years.

"I'll have it ready in two weeks. I'm waiting for parts for the dashboard from Germany."

Larry nodded. Before retiring, he had been in the import/export business and was sympathetic to shipping delays. He raised his bushy, gray eyebrows and said, "I could make a call if you think it'd help?"

"I don't have a problem with that, but I don't think it would make much difference. I'm sure they're workin' just as fast as they can." Rod said. He leaned against the Mercedes fender, wiping his oily hands on a gray towel. He parroted the customer, but without the curse word, "Them Germans know their business."

"Well, you deal with these folks all the time. People I used to work with are probably all retired or dead by now."

Rod nodded and stuffed the towel in his overalls' front pocket. "Patience is a virtue. At least, that's what my old man said."

"It's funny what sticks with you, ain't it? I mean, what your parents say," Larry said. He hiked up his pants again and shuffled his cowboy boots on the concrete floor. "Say, what about the undercarriage? I never even looked at it."

"I had it up in the air. It looks pretty good. There is a small bit of rust on the frame near the back, but not enough to cause any trouble. I'll buff it off and repaint it with some rust retardant."

"I might wanna sell it someday," Larry said, giving Rod a wink. "Can't give a customer a reason to say no, can ya'?"

"That's business in a nutshell, ain't it?" Rod answered Larry's question with a question.

"So, I guess I'll see you on the way back from Tampa," Larry said. He polished the toes of his boots with the back of his jeans.

"I'll see you then."

As he was about to leave, Larry turned and said, "You ain't gonna believe this. As I was turnin' onto your road, I almost got run over."

Larry passed his hand over his face from his forehead to his chin. Rod knew this was a way of showing a racial slur for some people in the North.

"No," Rod said. "I'm sorry to hear that."

"It's not like when we were overseas, is it?" Mr. Cox asked, passing his right hand over his face again as if it were a window shade being lowered. "Know what I mean?"

Rod had seen an old M.P. do that on one of the Army bases. He quizzed the man on what it meant and was told it was a sign cops would sometimes use to indicate a Black person was involved. The "shade" is the optimum image in the motion.

"This jigaboo in a white Camaro. He was flyin' low, I tell ya'. Ain't you got no cops in this town?"

"Most of them seem to be relatives of the Chief."

Larry nodded and said, "We've been *there*, haven't we?"

"What did you do?" Rod asked.

"I flipped him off. If I had a gun, I'd have taken him out right then and there." Larry frowned and said, "Them Black bastards are gettin' too uppity. They don't know their place, I tell you."

"Yeah," Rod agreed, "too uppity, no question. Some of 'em need to be put back in their place."

"Might be time to send the whole lot of 'em back to Africa." Larry nodded and said, "No doubt." He scanned the interior of Rod's shop. "You gotta nice little operation goin' on here. But, say, ain't you got a son? Is he as good at wrenchin' as you?"

"Stepson. He's got a good head on his shoulders, so I think he'll most likely end up workin' here in the garage. He's still tryin' to figure out what he wants to do."

"Every child has their own path, no question about that, I tell ya'."

"Right, well," Rod said. He hooked his thumb over toward the stall with the Mercedes. "Gotta get back at it. These cars ain't gonna fix themselves."

Larry turned and walked away. Then, over his shoulder, he said, "Keep me posted when I can come to get that thing."

"And you be careful out there," Rod said. He considered not falling to Larry's level of racism. Then he remembered the bill from fixing the Mercedes-Benz would buy groceries for the next four months. "Don't let none of those jigaboos run you off the road."

Chapter 43

Skid began work on his essay for the contest. His premise involved how electrification changed agriculture. He started his argument with the line, "Food production, crop management, and quality of life all improved when the Rural Electrification Act of 1936 provided funding to bring electricity to poor and underdeveloped parts of the country."

In his first, second, and third paragraphs, he used the ideas proposed in the first line, food production increases, overall farm efficiency, and improved quality of life for farmers. Wells that served animals and plants would grow bigger and faster when electric pumps fed irrigation and feed troughs.

Skid sat at the kitchen table and looked out the window. The setting sun cast shadows over Rod's shed, which family history had told him was a livestock barn when the property was a working farm. Rod had cleared most of the stalls and moved in several workbenches where he could keep tools and parts organized. Skid tapped his pencil on his front teeth and focused on the land behind and around the barn. He imagined what it would look like with kerosine lamps lighting the structure instead of bright, electric bulbs. He knew kerosine light was mainly yellow and electric bulbs cast white light. How would faces look in yellow light? What electric tools and equipment would ease the farmer's burden? How would an electric pump pulling water from a well improve the farmer's family's quality of life? What would indoor plumbing mean to men, women, and children?

He explored the three ideas in his premise. He concluded electricity changed life on the farm for the better in so many ways. The essay was now over three thousand words. Skid knew it was three times too long, so he put it aside and went to his room to prepare for work at the restaurant. His experience writing told him he would need several drafts before he would feel the essay was finished. The letter to the editor about the injustice of his punishment following the student walk-out and the television script had informed him well. He wasn't a perfectionist, but something inside him knew when the last draft was his best effort.

There was a mustard stain on the bottom of his uniform, so he ran soap and water into the bathroom basin and dunked it in. It wasn't noticeable, and his shift manager likely wouldn't have seen it. Still, Skid had, and he took pride in his appearance and work at the McDonald's.

Rod was still in his shop when Skid left. The tense air in the house kept them apart, and now they even found ways to miss having meals together. Rod had become adept at warming up Swanson's TV dinners. Skid usually ate cold cereal or something he'd brought home from the restaurant.

He passed several cars he recognized as he drove down the two-lane blacktop leaving the farm. It wasn't a busy road, and he knew almost all the neighbors. The common practice was to throw up your hand and wave at drivers as you drove by them on the opposite side of the road.

Skid saw a farmer he didn't recognize coming toward him. The tractor's top speed was twenty miles an hour, so several cars were behind him. Skid waved at the farmer, and the man dutifully replied. He wore a wide-brimmed hat covering his face and overalls. Skid smiled, trying to think of new ways the farmer's work is aided by electricity. Grain silos and their feeders all ran on electricity. Milking machines and fans to keep livestock cool in their stalls would run on electric power. He'd have to make even more additions to his essay if he added all these new ideas.

Skid considered the changes he'd make to his next draft, throwing up his hand at the line of cars behind the tractor and checking his watch to see if he would be on time. He knew it would be close but believed he'd clock in as scheduled.

He neared the end of the line of traffic when he noticed Connie's car. Where was she going? She must have known he'd be at work, so why was she on this road? He slowed as he neared her car and threw up his hand as he approached.

She looked forward, focusing on the car and the line of slow traffic ahead of her. He noticed her lips were tight, and she wore sunglasses even though the sun was almost set. She didn't respond to his greeting. Instead, she turned her head toward the ditch on the right as he passed her.

That's strange, he thought. Where could she be going, and why didn't she notice him?

Skid pressed the gas pedal down a bit more. His mother's car lurched forward, and he twisted the wheel as he approached a sweeping curve shaded by a big oak tree. When it rained, water puddled under the massive branches. During ice and snowstorms, dozens of drivers would find themselves in the ditch before the tree.

Locals continually begged the county road supervisor to regrade the curve and make it safer. Unfortunately, that would take a massive effort by the already overworked road crews and cost thousands of dollars. County officials didn't feel the political pressure required to fix the problem. Instead, they put up a sign warning of the "Dangerous Curve," but that was the extent of their efforts.

Skid twisted the steering wheel as he drifted around the corner. Finally, gravity grabbed him, sliding him sideways on the smooth, vinyl bench seat. Pulling out of the corner, he released the gas and glided down the hill.

He felt a knot in his stomach, but he couldn't figure out why. He glanced down at the stain on his uniform top, and the wet, discolored place was now dry. No one would notice. He'd fool the shift manager into thinking his uniform was clean and fresh.

He pulled into the parking slots reserved for workers and turned off the engine. Skid paused a second. He thought about the essay, the farmer on his tractor, and his smiling face. He wondered about Connie and how she had ignored him. He wanted to give her the benefit of the doubt. Of course, she didn't see him, but that twist in his guts continued until he turned off the car engine, walked across the parking lot, and opened the employee's entrance.

Chapter 44

Skid thought of the three of them and sometimes Dee Dee as Monte's posse, something he'd picked up from watching "Gunsmoke." In Skid's mind, the death-defying plunge on his bicycle should have anointed him with the mantle of leadership. Even after that, though, Monte still held the post.

Monte was usually the first to do "grown-up" things like smoking cigarettes, drinking beer, or having sex. He would recount the event to anyone who couldn't witness it. He'd say he enjoyed smoking but threw up after four puffs. He burped and almost threw up after his first beer. The only thing that had gone well for him was his first sexual experience.

The posse met most school days at a shrub to the left of the main entrance. They had no uniforms or distinguishing pens or badges. Only their friendship, which had developed since grade school, contrasted them.

This was near the beginning of their sophomore year, long before Skid had his job at the department store or the restaurant. In that 'fallow' period, he had lots of free time for reading, watching TV, and hanging out with the guys. Scattered rain throughout the two days of the previous weekend kept them from riding bicycles or bumming rides with older siblings. So, there wasn't much news of activities until Monte showed up.

Most boys in school wore short hair slicked back with Stephans anti-dandruff hair tonic just like their fathers did. But Monte's naturally wavy blond hair wouldn't work with the oily liquid, so he just left it natural. By the way, the girls loved his gold-tipped, curly waves.

He rushed up to the group, barely awake and wishing they were elsewhere. "I did it," he announced. The phrase was delivered flatly to not arouse suspicion in the students passing them.

"What?" Skid asked. He stood next to the bush and scratched a pimple near his ear. "Did what?" This time a little too loud.

Monte shushed him. "Come on, man."

Eddie, a buzz cut his mother kept high and tight with mail-order clippers, stood across from Monte. He used Stephan's to help support his hair standing up straight.

He was also the most observant of the group and already knew what Monte had "done."

"You did it?" Eddie asked. "Holy shit."

Dee Dee approached, looking sad and needing something from her 'boys' to make her feel better, but Skid stared her down. So she kept moving along with the hundreds of other students.

Monte nodded. "Yep, my uncle brought his stepdaughter for a visit. You know how it was rainin' and all."

Nods all around.

"When it stopped, we rode bikes down to the creek behind our house," Monte began. His family worked hard but never got the chance to own a home. They rented the house just down the road from Skid. He was very familiar with the site of the "incident."

"What are you talkin' about? There's nowhere to do it down there. It's all rocks, thorn bushes, and trees," Skid said. He glanced down at his foot, where he'd felt something strange on the ground. *What is that?*

"The trees," Monte nodded.

Eddie said, "So, let me get this straight. You did it in a tree?"

"No, from the tree."

"Wait a minute, hold the phone, 'from the tree'? How does that... *What?*" Eddie asked. It was starting to sound like a made-up story to his virgin ears.

"We rode down to the creek and was throwin' in rocks and talkin' and such," Monte began. Then, "'afore you know it, we was talkin' about," in a whisper, "s-e-x."

Skid said, "Just talkin'..."

Monte smiled and shifted the book stack from his left arm to his right. "More than just talkin'. 'Afore you know it, we was kissin' and..."

"Come on, that's gross," Eddie said. His face looked like he'd just bitten a lemon. "You're related to her."

"She ain't a real cousin. She's a stepcousin? Is that a thing?" Monte asked.

"Just go on," Skid said. He checked his watch and realized the morning bell would ring in just a few minutes.

"Well, we was talkin' and sex..."

"Yes," Eddie said, agitated by the story's pace. "Get on with it."

"Awright, awright, we start kissin', you know, just to see what it's like. And it was good. She really got turned on."

Skid wasn't familiar with the term 'turned on' about sex. But he didn't want to interrupt now that Monte's story had gained momentum.

"She started runnin' her hands through my hair. She said she didn't like it when boys had all that greasy stuff in their hair."

At that moment, the other boys stopped using hair oil.

"And then she put my hand on her boob," Monte said. He tried but couldn't control his lips, which had curled into a lecherous grin. "We keep on kissin', and I feel it gettin' stiff."

"Her nipple," Eddie said as if his addition might help the story along. But unfortunately, they were all aware of the impending school bell, and this story took too long.

"Right, right, and then I started to get...you know...and that's when she put her hand on my...you know. First on the outside of my jeans, and then she unbuckled my belt and grabbed it."

Skid asked and regretted it immediately, "Grabbed it?"

"Yeah, man," Monte said. "Like she was yankin' a pump handle."

Giggles all around, but if he didn't hurry, the story would still be unfinished when the bell rang.

"And then what?" Eddie asked.

"She dropped it, yanked down my pants, and grabbed it again. We was still kissin' when all this was happenin'. Anyway, she's wearin' this little dress, and she pulls that up and tugs down her panties. She pulls me under a tree limb and jumps up, grabbin' a limb. She puts her legs around me, and 'afore you know it, I'm in there."

An audible "whoa" from the boys. "Just like that?" Eddie asked.

"Yep, just like that," Monte said. His eyes darted from one posse member to the other. "She's got her legs around me, and she's movin' up and down. Anyway, it don't take long 'afore I'm done. Wow, it was so good."

"Wow," the posse said in unison.

Skid looked down at the ground and closed his eyes. *Would his first time be as exciting and weird as Monte's?* He asked himself. It wouldn't be possible.

"Did you, you know?" Eddie asked. While the interest level in the group was even, Eddie was the one asking the most questions.

"Hell yeah," Monte said. This time a bit too loud, drawing the attention of several other students as they entered the main entrance.

"What about, you know, gettin' her pregnant?" Eddie asked.

"I don't know. Whatever. You know, it ain't like cows. Girls cain't get pregnant from just doin' it one time. You gotta do it three days in a row. At least, that's what I heard." Monte added a tone of authority to his last sentence. His knowledge of the subject would not be challenged until years later during "health" classes conducted by the pretty, new school counselor, Miss Black.

The bell rang, and it was time for everyone to go to class. Skid looked down at the object next to his foot. He picked it up and studied it for a moment.

The rain-soaked condom had a milky, translucent appearance. This was long before his relationship with Connie had begun, and Skid had never seen a used one before, so he didn't know what to make of it. A strange balloon?

"Put that down," Eddie screeched.

"Throw that away," Monte said, slapping the condom from Skid's hand.

Skid picked it up again, tossed it behind the bush, and rubbed his hand against his jeans. "All right. All right. Weird," he said, "why was that there?"

"Looks like somebody was fuckin' there in front of the school," Monte said as he shifted his books to his left hand and grabbed the big door handle leading into the common area. "I guess it's happenin' everywhere."

The boys lined up and entered the school. A day that would live in infamy. A day filled with education, and not just the 'book learnin'' kind.

Chapter 45

This was the fourth time Skid had a dream about his mother in less than two weeks. It always began the same. She was cooking in the kitchen when he came home from school. She liked to have warm cookies waiting for him at least once a week. This was one of those days.

Baking from scratch seemed so "yesteryear" because there were grocery aisles filled with milk and egg mixes for cakes, pies, and cookies. Still, Donna was a purist, and there was nothing she wouldn't do for her son. So, she kept up the routine until she became too sick to stand.

The aroma of the baking cookies met Skid at the door, and he couldn't help but smile. "Is there milk?" Skid asked as he placed his stack of textbooks on the table's edge.

He'd dressed himself that morning without any fashion direction from his mother. When she made a comment after glancing at him over her shoulder, he said, "It's what all the kids are wearing." The creased, clean blue jeans and white T-shirt had become a de facto school uniform for sixth-grade boys. White Converse All-Stars also dominated the fashion trends.

"Just make sure your clothes are clean before you leave the house," she said, fulfilling her motherly duty.

"Oh, I'm clean," Skid said as he snatched an oatmeal chocolate chip cookie from the cooling rack.

Donna closed the refrigerator door and picked a glass from the dish rack beside the sink. She poured half a glass and set it next to Skid.

"What does that mean?"

He considered the fallout if he didn't tell her about the "incident" with Eddie on the playground. Would his teacher send home a note or call his mom? He knew the punishment would likely worsen if the news went that way.

"I said a curse word on the playground," Skid said, trying to mask the admission with the cookies and milk as much as possible.

"Oh," Donna said. She leaned against the counter and wiped her hands. "You don't have to tell me what you said, but you know better, right?"

"It just slipped out. Ass. I said Eddie fell off the monkey bars and busted his ass. I guess the teacher heard it."

"So, what happened?" Donna asked. "And you know you're going to be punished."

"I've already been," Skid said and gulped some milk. "Punished."

"Okay," Donna said. She sat across from him.

"I had to wash my mouth out with soap."

Donna nodded. She was still pretty, and time was being kind to her. There were pictures of Donna as a baby with her mother in her thirties, and Donna now looked like her twin. Her sharp cheekbones, thin arms, and legs were precursors to the cancer that quietly ravaged her body. Detected too late, she'd be dead in less than five years.

"So, no TV tonight."

"But they're playin' a rerun of *Andy Griffith* I really like," he whined. "Isn't soap in my mouth enough? I can still taste it," he said as he picked up the glass of milk and took a sip. His face twisted into a grimace, clearly an attempt at melodrama.

Donna turned her head and allowed a fall of black hair to hide her smile from him, but he could still detect it from where he sat. She was so pretty. How did he get so lucky?

"I'm not happy about this," she said and stood. She put her arms around him and smiled. The boy stood and felt the heat of her shoulder as they embraced.

"Everything's going to be okay," she whispered, tightening her arms around him.

***

When Skid woke up, he looked at the alarm clock. He was early again. His dream of six years before was both comforting and disturbing. So much had happened. So many changes. He hoped everything would be settled soon, and he could fall into a dull rhythm of work, play, and sleep.

He checked the calendar that hung next to his chest of drawers. He'd circled Graduation Day in red. The rented cap and gown hung on a hook on the back of the door.

Another day, not circled, finally jogged his memory. It was a year since Donna's death. Maybe that was why he kept having the same dream. Was she speaking to him from beyond? He didn't believe in such, but it was nice to think that maybe his mother was still somewhere.

It was a silly thought. But why could he still feel Donna's hand on his face?

He prepped for the day and came into the kitchen to the coffee and burnt toast aroma. Unfortunately, Rod's talent for fixing machines failed to translate into cooking. He would joke he couldn't even boil water, though that seemed unlikely given his knowledge of physics and experience. And he made coffee every day, so the joke wasn't true.

Skid stood at the kitchen sink and drank a glass of water. He watched Rod walk across the backyard and toward the shed. The morning dew soaked the mechanic's brown shoes and the cuffs of his coveralls. Spring had sprung, and Skid was glad to see winter fade.

He closed his eyes and swore he could smell Donna's cookies as they were cooling on the counter. How could that be? Do we all leave behind bits and pieces of ourselves after we die, or was it just her?

Skid recalled details of the dream and relished each morsel of the cookies from so long ago. He'd have to remember that recipe and try to recreate that sometime in the future.

"I bet Connie would like those cookies," he said as if speaking to a ghost.

He nodded, opened the bread bag, took two slices, and slipped them into the toaster. He refilled his water glass and waited.

Where am I going? He asked himself. Somehow, he believed his mother would have had an answer.

The toaster popped, and he picked up the slice on the left. "Hot, hot, hot," he said, placing it on a plate. So, again, with the other one.

He slathered butter on the toast and picked up the plate. The toast tasted good, and when he was finished, he put the plate in the sink. He drained the water glass. He hadn't acquired a taste for coffee yet.

Skid dressed, the cap and gown again capturing his attention momentarily. Finally, he picked up his keys and made his way out of the house.

He glanced up at Rod's streetlamp at the end of the driveway. What would life be like without that light? His mind flicked back to his essay on electricity. What did it all mean, and what would life be like without the light and energy provided by the electric company?

He'd work on a final draft of the essay tonight and turn it in tomorrow, just in time to meet the deadline. What he had was good, but he wanted to make it better. He wanted it to be as close to perfect as possible. He would try to make his mother proud.

Chapter 46

Few problems in Skid's life couldn't be answered by a trip to the library. But unfortunately, the book with the answers wasn't always in the school's collection. Still, public and university libraries usually had whatever he needed.

He remembered during their fight how Rod's arm felt around his neck and how helpless he felt. He could have died, and the reality was too much to let go unacknowledged.

Skid started with Miss Cardwell. She'd been so helpful in his curiosity about writing a script that he believed she would help solve this problem.

"I need a book on self-defense," he said. Skid had placed his books and notebook on the table behind them. Miss Cardwell sat behind her desk, checking in books and replacing the stamped cards.

"Self-defense. Why would you want a book on that?"

"Well, I need to work out. I'm tryin' to stay in shape." He said as he flexed his long, thin arms. Six feet tall and one hundred and seventy pounds looked like it needed a few more milkshakes and not additional exercise.

"I see." She looked at him over her reading glasses. "You're not being bullied, are you?" She asked.

"No, no," he lied. He didn't want to bring up the fight with Rod. It was too embarrassing.

"Well, the most popular books are on jiu-jitsu," she said as she stood and circled her desk. "Follow me."

He left his books at the desk and trailed behind her like a lost puppy. "It's just for exercise."

"I know," she said without looking back at him. "You already told me."

She walked down the space between two tall bookcases and stopped near the end. "These two shelves are what we have. Look through the titles and check out the most promising one."

Skid scanned the book spines and pulled out "Beginning Jiu-Jitsu." He opened the book and found black and white pictures of men in poses representing the accompanying text.

"This looks pretty good," he said.

"Let me know if you have any more questions," she said. She was about to leave when she asked, "How did your script turn out?"

"It's finished. At least a draft is done."

"Good for you," she said.

"Would you be interested in," Skid began to hem and haw, "ah, I guess you don't have the time to read it?"

"We're getting ready to close out the school year, so I'm pretty busy. Sorry."

"It's okay," again with the hemming and hawing, "it was just a thought. It's fine. What are the odds of me getting it to the show? Pretty high."

"Astronomical is more like it. But did you enjoy writing it?" The librarian asked.

"It was fun to try and think like the characters. I can't tell you enough how much I appreciate your help."

"My pleasure," she said, picking up a book from her desktop. She opened the cover and slipped the small white card into the manila envelope.

Skid turned and let his books drop to his hip. His shoulders slumped, and his tennis shoes scuffed against the leg of a table.

"Wait, Skid," Miss Cardwell said. She could read his disappointment like the cover of the book she held. "I've changed my mind. I'd be happy to look at your script."

The boy straightened his spine and reached for the paperclip-bound script. He'd copied the title page from the sample script. It read "John-Boy's First Kiss."

"Oh, would you? That would be great," Skid said. He slipped the script from the top of his books and held it out to her. The pages fanned out over her desk. She shuffled them like a deck of cards and replaced the clip.

"I like that show. Watch it almost every week," the librarian said.

"Don't expect too much from my script."

"I think I can expect just the right amount," Miss Cardwell said, pleased with her little joke.

"I'm finishing my entry to the rural electrification essay contest."

"How long is it?" She asked. She'd returned to the chair behind her desk.

"Not too long," he said with a tone of a puppy whine in his voice.

"Okay, let's shoot the moon," she said, smiling.

"I've never heard that phrase before."

"It's from the card game Hearts," she explained. "Go for all the points."

"I see. Okay, then," he said as he handed over another four pages.

"Come by tomorrow."

"Okay," he said again," and thanks."

"My pleasure," she said, smiling up at him. "Oh, by the way, how did your genealogy research turn out? Family trees are a hobby of mine. I've traced my people all the way back to Ireland."

"Kind of a dead-end right now," he said. "I talked with a woman at the state archives, and she promised she'd look. No guarantees."

"Records can be hard to track down, but she should be able to find census, marriage, and death records. Sometimes there's even heritage information in a family Bible."

Skid thought for a moment. There was a beat-up old Bible in his mother's things. He'd have to dig it out and look.

"Whatever you find could add to the researcher's final outcome."

"I'll do that," Skid said, his head wagging like a puppy.

He honestly believed helping him was a pleasure for her. How come there aren't more nice people like her in the world?

Chapter 47

How come there are so many mean people in the world?

Skid never got a chance to read the book on Jiu-Jitsu. However, he did look at the black-and-white pictures at lunch.

Later, he waited for Rod to pick him up after school because his mother's car needed a battery, which was on backorder. Then, he saw Leon and a group of his friends approach.

They all wore bell-bottomed jeans, as was the fashion. The young men wore polo or tennis shirts, and the lone young woman wore a black top and pink slacks. Leon led the troop and had a swagger from his finely tuned athletic body and confidence gained from a recent victory on the basketball court.

The famous parents' pick-up spot was under a giant oak tree at the south corner of the campus. Unfortunately, the rain from the night before left the ground around the tree soggy. The bare branches would soon be covered with leaves, but for now, the tree's bark was black, slippery, and dotted with mold. Skid thought about how the tree had witnessed the comings and goings of all the students who attended this school. It must have been thousands over the decades.

It was late. Skid believed Rod had gotten busy with a car and had probably forgotten about picking him up. He was just about to walk down to the drug store and make a call from the pay phone on the sidewalk.

"Hey," Skid said to Leon, "you got a dime?"

"Okay, moneybags, what'a you need a dime for?" Leon asked. He glanced over his shoulder and found the girl smiling at him.

"I gotta call Rod. He probably forgot about me."

"That's not very nice," Leon said. The one girl in the group giggled. She was taller than three of the four boys and parted her hair on the left. She could almost see eye-to-eye with Leon.

"He's just busy. I'll pay you back."

Leon reached into his pocket and fished around for the change. "Hey. What's that book?"

Embarrassed, Skid shifted the library book in his hand. "It's nothin'."

"Naw," Leon said, "that says Jiu-Jitsu. So that's some kind of Japanese fightin'?"

"It's nothing. Don't worry about it."

"Naw, it's somethin'," he said and grabbed the book on self-defense from Skid's stack. The rest of the books fell to the soggy ground around the tree. Leon thumbed through the book as Skid gathered the rest of his things.

"I was just curious," Skid said without looking up.

"Interesting pictures. Men wearin' white robes and throwing each other to the ground. That can't be good," Leon said.

"Humm, they got hoods on?" the girl asked.

"Naw," he turned and looked at the girl. But then, he told Skid, "You don't need this."

"I *do* need it." Skid stood up and glared at Leon.

"Naw, you don't," Leon said, tossing it into the tree limbs.

The girl giggled and covered her overbite with her hand. Her big eyes flashed at Leon.

"Aw, come on, man," Skid said. He stared at the book now wedged between two branches.

"Let's go. I got a Big Mac waiting with my name on it," Leon said as he walked past Skid.

"It's not funny. I know it's ironic, but it's not funny."

The athlete stopped, turned, and glared at Skid. "I say it *is* funny."

Leon and his posse strolled toward downtown. Their laughter could be heard over fifty feet away.

"Okay, jeez. It's kinda funny," Skid said.

He moved to the base of the tree and found the footing slippery. He looked up at the limb. Skid theorized that getting his feet set before grabbing the lowest hanging branch could be problematic. Besides, he didn't want to embarrass himself by falling in the mud.

Finally, Rod drove up in the Jaguar. It had become a humid, sticky day, and he had the top down. The English roadster slid to a stop at the corner of the sidewalk.

"Hop in," he said, smiling.

Skid looked at the car and then up at the book dangling from the limb. Finally, he shuffled his notebook and texts and opened the passenger side door.

"Why are you drivin' Joseph's car?" Skid asked. He regretted bringing up the name. They hadn't talked about Joseph since he died.

"Why not?" Rod asked but winced for a split second. Then, "Hey, how was your day?"

Skid glanced one last time at the book in the tree. "Just great. Big day." And closed the car door.

Chapter 48

Skid found the self-defense book lying in a puddle under the lowest tree limb the following day. He winced as he picked it up and shook the soaked pages. Finally, he put it in his locker, standing upright with the pages fanned open, and hoped it would dry before its due date.

Saturday was the SAT, Scholastic Aptitude Test, a college entrance exam you could study for but didn't seem necessary. So, Skid would just do his best and let the chips fall.

Skid had his number two pencil stuck behind his right ear. He'd gotten a good night's sleep and a complete breakfast, as Miss Black had advised all the Seniors.

He breezed through the Social Studies, English, and History sections with time to spare, but when he got to the Math section, he lost his way. He'd never been good at Math, struggling with Arithmetic and Algebra One, getting "D's" in both. Good enough to graduate but not good enough for prizes or recognition.

He could feel the sweat on his brow and under his arms as he tried to remember how to answer the multiple-choice questions. You could use note paper to work the problems, but as Skid glanced up at the clock in the auditorium, he knew he'd never have time to finish. So, he started picking "A's," "B's, and" C's" in rotation. He felt he'd at least get half of the problems right using this method.

He found out several weeks later that wasn't the case. Out of a possible 800, Skid scored 735 in English, 700 in Critical Reading, 700 in History, and 256 in Math. The scores would be averaged together. Luckily for Skid, the testing company had provided the answer to that math problem. Because of that average score, he could enter any state-sponsored school and several private ones, assuming he could get the money together.

Skid found Connie in the cafeteria the next day and pulled out his scorecard. "What did you get?"

She had brought her lunch that day. She almost always did and sat with the windows to her right. He sat across from her and plopped down his tray.

"I did okay," she said.

"I did pretty good on everything but Math, as expected. Miss Black says I can still get into college with my average. I'll have to take the minimum Math class there and hope for the best."

"That sounds like a plan," she said as she unwrapped her cheese sandwich and took a tiny bite.

Lunch for him today was a hot dog, tater tots, and an apple. He picked up his hot dog with no mustard and took a bite.

"So, *tell* me," Skid said. He elongated the "e" in tell, hoping to soften the blow to her if her score was lower than his.

"780," she whispered.

"What, what was that?" Skid asked. He couldn't hear her over all the other conversations around them and *his* chewing.

"I said," raising her voice a bit over the surrounding din, "780."

"You're kiddin', right?" The difference between their scores was a deep academic chasm. He blinked and said, "I mean, that's great. So that's your average?"

"Yeah," Connie sighed.

"So, you can go-I mean, wow, that's great."

She glanced around the room. "My parents are goin' to start in on me about goin' to U-T or Vanderbilt, God forbid. They always wanted to go there but didn't have the money."

"What about you?" Skid asked. "You sound like you don't want to go to either of those schools."

"I wanna be closer to you. I mean, U-T's in Knoxville. That's three hours and a different time zone. And Vandy, that's just a bunch of rich kids and legacy losers."

Skid thought carefully about what he would say next but blew it anyway. "I want you to go wherever you like. We can still date."

"Long-distance," she said, wincing at the thought. "It hadn't occurred before the test that I might do that well."

"You're smart. Smarter than me, for sure." The thought that she might be out of his life reverberated through his teenage mind. Skid knew what a good boyfriend would say. "You should go to the place that's best for you. We'll figure out somethin'."

"Sure, right," she muttered and finished her sandwich. She picked up an apple and took a big bite. Skid chuckled at the sound of the crack as she bit and the gnashing as she chewed.

"It's good news. Finally, you've got proof of just how smart you are," he said, again, trying to be a good boyfriend.

She swallowed. "I didn't need that. I know I'm smart," she said as she put the sandwich wrapper in her paper bag.

"I know. Listen, it'll work out," he said, reaching for her hand. She put her hand palm up in his.

"I had a plan. My parents had a plan. I just don't..."

He shook her hand, trying to be encouraging. "It'll work out. You've got a bright future."

Connie stood and turned. He watched her leave the room and knew big changes were likely coming for them.

He finished eating, glared at Leon as he left the room, and walked to his locker. He opened the door, and the book looked like a crinkly fan, though dry now.

Skid weaved through the meandering students filling the hallway. Finally, he opened the door to the library and searched for Miss Cardwell. He wanted to put the damaged book into a stack of others on her desk. Maybe she wouldn't remember how she'd advised him on which book to check out. But he still had to get his essay and script from her. He somehow knew he could trust her to be honest about the quality of both pieces.

He looked around the room. Three other students occupied tables and the stacks. Miss Cardwell was in the back of the room and saw Skid. She arrived at her desk just as Skid slipped the Jiu-Jitsu book under a Steinbeck novel and a history book.

"I have your script and your essay," she said as he sat down. "I made some notes in the margins and on the back pages. I hope that's okay."

She wore a black skirt and white blouse again today. It was almost as if she chose the outfit as a uniform, though there were no rules on what staff wore.

She pulled a manila envelope from a drawer and held it to Skid. He took it from her.

Miss Cardwell began her critique with, "It was like watching an episode of the show. I think you've got a real talent."

"I hope so. Maybe I'll get lucky."

"You don't really need luck," she said. She saw the self-defense book in the stack and the wavy lines in the spine. She pulled the book from the pile and fanned open the pages.

"That was an accident."

"I see. It does look like an *accident*." She looked at him over her reading glasses and said, "You weren't going to tell me?"

"Well, I don't want to get anyone in trouble." He brightened as he said, "I can pay to replace it."

"It looks like you were trying to hide what happened, and I might not notice. That's bad," she said. Skid was amazed at how much she sounded like his mother when he was a kid and was about to discipline him. "I'm not sure how I feel about that. I'll let you know if I choose to replace it. You can pay for it then. Okay?"

"Deal," he said.

"Smells like hot dogs are featured in the cafeteria today," she said.

Skid stepped back, embarrassed his breath smelled of the mystery meat tube steak. "I'll drink some water."

"Drink a lot," she said, twitching the corner of her mouth twice.

"I'm sorry," he stammered.

She didn't acknowledge his apology and began checking in books from the stack on her desk.

Later, he stepped back into the hallway and waited for the stream of humanity to part. *It was just a book,* he thought, *no big deal.* Unfortunately, he missed the part where he'd failed to thank her for reading over his work.

Chapter 49

The banquet was held at McKnight's Restaurant on Mercury Drive. Friends and families from all over the county filled the banquet room. Skid sat at the dais next to the other finalist in the essay contest. He looked over his work as he ate. He glanced at the other writers and noticed they were reading their work, too.

The salad came first, with rolls on the side. Skid glanced up at Connie as she sat with Rod on her right. Rod wore his only suit, black tie, and white shirt. Connie wore a white sweater top with a "V" neckline, gray slacks, and flat shoes. Skid couldn't swear she was wearing a bra. He'd become accustomed to seeing it but wondered if this was the most appropriate place for that choice. He could see Rod and Connie talking, and, at times, they seemed interested in the subjects. Could they be talking about him?

Skid picked at the edges of his salad. When the entrée and side items arrived, he ate his Salisbury steak and mashed potatoes. The smell of the meat and gravy made his stomach flip. Was he nervous? Why would he be worried?

And green beans. He was never a fan of green beans, but his mother had almost always had them on the weekly menu. She would encourage him to eat them. She stated, "They're good and good for you." Skid was never convinced.

He looked up as Connie got up from the table. Rod stood, reseated himself, and glanced at her as she left the room. *It would be nice if those two could get along,* Skid thought.

The emcee for the evening was the local radio reporter that had covered the walk-out so many months ago. He was tall with a scraggly beard and large hands. His fingers encircled the microphone as he made announcements. *How could he be nervous,* Skid thought? *He talks on the microphone all the time.* He made sure to include a thank you to the staff and owner of the restaurant.

Connie came back in, and again, Rod stood while she sat down just as the first entrant began reading her essay. Skid wasn't listening. He continued focusing on *his* essay, hoping he wouldn't stumble as he read. He had a problem with stuttering as a child, and at times under stress, he could feel that tug when he had to speak to a crowd.

The first reader finished to a smattering of applause. Then, after a short introduction, the reporter stepped away from the microphone and waved Skid to the podium.

He began reading slowly initially with a history of the Tennessee Valley Authority and how the Roosevelt administration believed cheap, electric energy would lower poverty in the region.

"Congress created the Tennessee Valley Authority or TVA in 1933 as part of President Franklin D. Roosevelt's New Deal programs to stimulate economic growth during the Great Depression. TVA provided construction and economic development jobs aiding in the exploitation of the region's natural resources, including the construction of hydroelectric dams and the irrigation of farmland."

Skid continued reading, looking up at the audience, occasionally maintaining eye contact for a second when possible. Rod and Connie looked at Skid from below the dais. It was as if he could feel them pulling for him.

"Access to affordable energy would provide rural communities in the Tennessee River Valley with a markedly improved quality of life and economic well-being."

He kept reading. It mainly was facts and figures he'd discovered in the library; when he looked up, he could see the statistics boring his audience. Unfortunately, it was too late to make any changes. Still, he wished he'd had a chance to rewrite the essay into a more personal and easy-to-understand argument.

Skid continued. "The Tennessee Valley Authority pioneered regional planning and land management principles, including coordinating economic, social, and environmental development across multiple states and communities. The influence of TVA can still be seen today in modern approaches to regional planning."

He ended with, "The creation of the TVA was substantial because it helped to transform a region that had been economically and socially neglected after the Civil War. In addition, TVA laid the foundation for sustainable development practices that would impact future projects in the United States for decades."

Skid returned to his seat before the last of the applause died. He put his cards on the table and looked at Rod and Connie. They both smiled, but he believed their reactions were more supportive than their actual belief in what Skid's essay delivered.

The third and last contestant began reading slowly, keeping her delivery in a deliberate and authoritative tone. Finally, she sat down to an ovation, a bit louder than the first competitor.

The radio reporter returned to the podium, smiled, and congratulated all the essayists. He praised their work and used " talent " to describe the three writers. It was the second time Skid had heard that word describing his work. He smiled. He liked that word.

The reporter pulled an envelope from his jacket pocket and opened it. He explained how the panel of readers had decided which essay was the winner and who would get second and third place. Then, he read a description of the third-place entrant and her theme. She accepted the twenty-five-dollar check and smiled at the audience as they applauded.

The second-place essay obviously had a similar theme but a different timeline describing how rural electrification came to the county. But, again, its focus was on the people involved and how hard they'd worked to make the miracle of rural electrification happen. Skid stood and walked toward the podium. He accepted the fifty-dollar second-place prize, waved at the crowd, and sat down. The first-place entrant, coincidentally the restaurant owner's son, took home the check for one hundred dollars. He stood next to the podium, shook hands with the reporter, and posed for a picture as he accepted his prize. A second picture with all the finalists would appear in the middle of the page of the local section of the newspaper the next day.

The crowd applauded, took their napkins from their laps, and soon there were pockets of people around the room congratulating the winners with hugs and enthusiastic encouragement.

Rod stood next to Connie as she hugged Skid. She said, "I'm so proud of you," as she kissed him on the cheek.

The stepfather offered his hand, but not a hug and Skid took it, shaking the clammy fingers. *How is it he's nervous?* Skid asked himself.

Connie put her arm around Skid's shoulder and grinned. "Let me see it?"

He pulled the envelope from his coat pocket and showed her the check. "Better living through electricity," Skid said.

"You need to hang on to that," Rod said, "do somethin' nice for yourself."

Skid nodded but had already concluded he'd likely cash the check and spend the money on Connie. He wasn't getting rich working at the restaurant and believed she deserved something nice.

In the parking lot, Connie clung to Skid's side. She even took his arm as they strolled past their fellow classmates. They were all *so* dressed up and looked like adults. How could that be? Wasn't it only yesterday they were children on a playground?

Rod walked behind the happy couple and pulled the keys out of his pocket. The Jaguar sat at the end of a line of cars in the parking lot. Light rain from earlier left the asphalt wet, reflecting the yellow streetlamps at the edge of the lot. He patted the canvas top as if congratulating himself on saving the car interior from the rain, opened the door, and slid under the wheel.

Skid opened the driver's side door to his mother's car and slid under the wheel. He scooted across the seat and pulled the lock on Connie's side. "Sorry," he said. He was still nervous and could still feel the adrenalin from delivering the speech.

"It's okay," she said.

Rod pulled alongside them. He'd put the convertible top down and revved the engine. "Race ya home," he said over the roar of the sports car motor.

"That's okay," Skid shouted.

"You sure?"

"I'm just goin' to take Connie home. I'll see ya later."

The tension at Skid's home had been tight as a violin string for so long. Finally, this might have been a moment where all three could come together and relax.

"It's good that you and Rod are getting along now," Connie said as she watched the Jaguar's taillights turn right and disappear.

"Do you think he wanted to hang out with us or somethin'?" Skid said as he turned the steering wheel left.

"No, he's old. He's got better things to do," Connie said.

"I can't imagine what," Skid said and rolled down his window.

"I was really proud of you up there."

"I was nervous."

"You didn't look it. And that coat and tie." She smiled and said, "I could get used to seein' you in that."

"Or out of it," Skid joked.

"Ha, ha. Okay. It's a school night, so we better go straight home," Connie insisted.

He glanced at her with the wind blowing her hair. She'd rolled her window down, too. The night air hung with moisture, and her face took on a glow in the flashing lights.

"Okay. Well, rural electrification. Big, huh?"

"Yours was the best one," Connie said, sticking her hand out the window. She let her arm wave as if her hand was a bird flying through the black sky.

"That's not true. I needed at least one more draft, but I didn't have the time." He glanced at her and saw his remark draw her frown. "I mean, thanks, but the winner picked a single farmer and told the story from his perspective. That's what made it better." He paused momentarily, " That's what makes *all* stories better."

He considered complaining about how the restaurant owner's son took first place and that the contest might have been rigged, but it was a "blind" read, and the judges didn't know who wrote which essay. Now, he knew better.

"How about that Salisbury steak? It reminded me of the school cafeteria."

"I had the chicken," Connie said, not looking at him. "The chicken was good."

"What did Rod have?" Skid asked.

A half-second passed before she said, "I don't know. I mean, I wasn't paying attention."

"Oh, okay, just wonderin'."

She continued to wave her hand through the damp air. Then, finally, she pulled it back in and rubbed her palm on Skid's face.

"What's *that* for?" He asked, drying his cheek with the shoulder of his jacket.

"Felt like it." She giggled and stuck her hand back out the window.

"It was kinda gross," he said, but the air rushing through the car windows drowned out his comment.

He reached across the bench seat and, because he knew exactly where it was, pinched her nipple. Yep, no bra.

"Ouch," she shrieked over the rushing air in the cabin.

"Before you ask," he said, grinning, "felt like it,"

She shook her head and stuck her hand out the window again.

Chapter 50

Skid had a night shift the next day. It was his first time working with Leon since he'd taken his library book and tossed it in a tree. They'd seen each other in the hallway since then but not spoken.

Working the grill on Saturday meant the restaurant could be busy or dead, with nothing in between. It would all depend on events that might draw kids to the area. This Saturday night, a concert at the university featured Elvis Presley. It was the last of a series of shows scheduled for the new basketball gym. Tickets sold out quickly, and while Skid liked Elvis's music, he wouldn't pay to see him.

The assistant manager, the owner's son, ran the restaurant that night. So, when two school buses pulled into the parking lot, Skid knew the small weekend crew was in trouble.

"Drop twelve Big Macs," he yelled at Skid, now on the grill, "no, make that 24. And give me fries. I need fries."

Skid peeled the paper from the singles and covered the large, flat, metal grill with meat. The whirr of the vent over the grill made it hard to hear, but the crew chief increased the volume of his orders to overcome the roar.

"Let's have everyone off break right now and get Leon off the lot. We need him in here."

Leon entered the grill area just as Skid began pulling the burgers from the grill and sliding them into the paper silos holding the three-layer bun in place. The owner and the assistant manager's father came in from the break room and surveyed the action behind the counter. Finally, he nodded to his son and walked toward the office near the break room.

Leon wielded the caulk gun-like Bid Mac sauce dispenser. Skid slid the meat into the paper tube and turned to get the next patty as Leon slid the middle section of the bun into place. Skid held the meat patty with one finger and waited for Leon to clear the area. Then, he slid the second burger into the tube, where Leon would squirt more secret sauce and place cheese and lettuce into the tube. This constantly happened for several minutes as the two dozen sandwiches made their way over the countertop holding the vents and to the warming shelves on the other side.

Leon nodded and smiled at Skid, but the smile wasn't returned. Skid still didn't know why Leon would throw his book on self-defense into a tree. Finally, Skid swallowed and said, "Let's get another twenty-four buns ready to go, just in case."

Leon connected the two sides of the Big Mac paper tubes and placed them on a tray. He flipped over the plastic bag holding the buns, removed the bottom layer one by one, and put them in the bottom of the tubes.

"Give me twenty-four more Big Macs," was the order from the assistant manager. Skid and Leon nodded, presaging how busier they would become.

This was a gamble on the part of the assistant manager. If people didn't order Big Macs or the crowd went next door to the KFC, he'd be stuck wasting a lot of meat and buns.

The routine of Skid cooking while Leon prepped began again. The hot burgers were sizzling, and the shouts and alarms from the rest of the crew made it difficult to hear, much less think. The good news was that thinking wasn't required to do the job. On the contrary, the more machine-like the cook and prep team were, the more effective.

Skid nodded at Leon but didn't speak. Instead, he began removing the hot burgers from the flat surface of the grill. He could smell the rehydrated onions to his left as they sat in an aluminum bowl. Scattering the onions by hand onto the burgers was the finishing touch and his least favorite part of the job. The smell would cling to his fingers until the following day, no matter how often he washed his hands. It reminded him of Rod trying to clean the grime from his fingers.

Skid held the burger with his index finger while Leon squirted Big Mac sauce onto the bottom bun. Leon pulled back as Skid swept the hot spatula over the back of his hand. The young man winced in pain but wouldn't let Skid see it hurt. When it happened the second time, Leon said, "Come on, Man!"

"Yeah," Skid said sarcastically, "come on, *Man*."

Leon shook his head and continued prepping the buns for the meat delivery. Skid continued pulling burgers from the grill and waiting for Leon to prep the buns. Again, he avoided Skid's spatula, and the rest of the rush ended with no further injuries.

Chapter 51

Skid stood in front of the full-length mirror in his mother's bedroom and checked the length of his graduation gown. He'd grown a few inches since ordering it, but it still looked good. Of course, he wouldn't wear shorts and sneakers on graduation day, but he felt the gown fit.

"Why do they tell us we're all educated individuals now and make us all wear the same stupid dress and flat-head hat?" He asked the image in the mirror.

"Isssa mortar boat," Rod said. "I mean, a mortarboard."

Skid jumped, surprised by the sudden appearance of his stepfather at the door.

The day's work had ended. Because Rod had been welding all day and it was already hot, he'd stripped off his yellow coveralls. He was wearing "tighty whities" and nothing else. Rod's penis stretched against the cotton crotch, and Skid could see the outline of the head. Seeing him in this outfit often, Skid knew Rod's penis was bigger than his.

"Holy crap," Skid said. "You really scared me. And how would you know what they call the graduation cap?"

"I know about more stuff than just cars," Rod said. He took a sip of brown liquid from a clear tumbler." Ask me somthin'."

"No," Skid said as he adjusted his mortarboard. "You're drunk."

"I know. I'm a gown up," Rod said, laughing. "Get it, a gown up."

"Ha, ha. You can leave me alone now."

"I don't gotta," Rod said as he sat on the bed. "You're in my room."

"This is where the mirror is."

His hands and arms up to his elbows were dirty. He was supposed to wash his hands in the sink in the shed. He had liquid Lava soap, and while it wouldn't get his hands "Sunday morning" clean, it worked well. Rod's dirty fingernails had been a running argument with Skid's mother, and now he'd taken up that mantle.

"And you're gettin' the bedspread dirty," Skid said. He glared at his stepfather, believing the threat in his eyes was enough to make him get up and leave him alone.

"I don't care," Rod said and took another sip of the liquor. "Ah, Tennessee's finest."

It was something Rod always said at least once when he drank. "Sippin' whiskey."

"Okay, that's it," Skid said. He took the mortar board off and unzipped the graduation gown. "I gotta go to work."

"Stay here," Rod said. "We can talk."

"What do we have to say to each other?"

"How 'bout," he said, setting the glass on the bed. "The future." He waved his hands across his face as if he were a magician.

"I'm gonna try to go to college," Skid said. "Somewhere."

"No, no, no. You'll work whiff me until you know everythin' there is to know 'bout engines. Simple as that." He picked up the glass and drained the contents. "You're smart. Won't take you long at all."

"I'm not interested."

Rod's face fell. "But I promizzed your mo-mo-mother I'd take care of youse."

Skid turned and looked down at Rod. He'd crossed his legs and draped his left hand over his knee. A beam of light from the setting sun caught the grime under his fingernails.

"No, I may not know what I want, but I do know what I don't," Skid said as he took off the gown and hung it on a hook on the closet door.

"I shee. Unglateful little twat," Rod said.

Skid's hands balled into fists. "It's my life."

"That it ish. That it ish, loser."

Skid wasn't sure if Rod was referring to the essay contest and the banquet they'd all attended or a general view of his stepson's overall choices in life.

"Me," Skid said, still glaring at his stepfather, "look at you."

"I make a goosch livin'."

"I'm not you," Skid said with a tone of pride and disgust in his voice.

"You're not even mysh son."

"Thank God for that," Skid said. He stepped toward the door, but Rod caught the back pocket of his black work pants.

"Yoush need to apologise."

"For what? Tellin' the truth doesn't deserve an apology. Let go of me."

Rod's line of work made his hands and arms extremely strong. He'd wrench all day, picking up heavy car parts, and pulling metal, sometimes more than his weight.

"Not until you say youse sorry."

"I'm not," Skid said, his voice rising an octave as he pulled. The pants strained at the seams but didn't rip. Instead, his sneakers squeaked on the hardwood floor as he pulled away.

Rod held on but lost his balance. He slipped from the bed and fell to the floor. "Help me up."

Skid looked down at him. The whiskey glass tumbled to the floor and bounced on a throw rug that was a family hand-me-down. It was empty and didn't break.

"I've got to go to work," Skid said as he pulled away. "You're pathetic."

Rod curled into a ball and chuckled. "Now, thash's my boy."

***

Skid worked the grill that night. Leon was off, but Dee Dee took orders just the other side of the massive vents dividing the prep and sales areas.

Skid lost himself in the routine. Three buses parked in the back of the lot; the rush meant non-stop cooking for over an hour. At break time, the crew sat at the table in the breakroom, almost too tired to eat.

"He was so drunk," Dee Dee said. She sat opposite him. The room was decorated with posters encouraging the workers to think the "McDonald's way" and be a team member. One poster promoted "Hamburger University." Dee Dee continued, "He tried to keep you from coming to work? Maybe he was lonely."

"I don't think that was it," Skid said. He picked up a double cheeseburger and took a small bite. He looked at the fries on the tray and picked up two. His hand shook as he put them in his mouth.

"He's an odd duck," Dee Dee said. Most of the crew had developed spots of acne because of the greasy atmosphere of the restaurant. But she had somehow figured out how to keep her skin clear.

"To say the least. He was always 'different,' but he's gotten a lot worse since Mom died," Skid said.

"And don't forget about Joseph," she said, taking a bite of her sandwich. "That might have stirred the pot."

Skid hadn't forgotten about Joseph. Rod had seemed even more on edge and dark since the suicide. He leaned back in his chair and took a deep breath. "I've gotta get out of there. Somehow, some way," Skid said between bites, "He's drivin' me nuts."

"You could stay with us. I mean, I'd have to ask my folks, but there's a day bed in the basement," Dee Dee said. She glanced at him, then her gaze returned to her Big Mac.

She'd dyed her hair a lighter shade of blonde, and her new eye makeup made her brown eyes large and expressive. She felt the boys looking at her now, and she liked it.

"No, but thanks. I'll figure it out."

"Offer stands," she said and sipped her diet soda.

"It may come to that," Skid said in agreement.

"So, have you heard from any colleges?"

"Waiting," Skid said, "U-T would be good. Connie says it's on her list."

"Go, Big Orange," Dee Dee said.

The noise from the grill area grew. Skid tried to ignore it and said, "How about that cap and gown?"

She smiled and said, "It looks weird, right?"

"Yep," Skid said as he took another bite of his sandwich, "so weird."

The assistant manager came to the door. "You two need to clock in early. We've got a big rush."

Dee Dee and Skid looked at each other and frowned. "It never ends," Skid said.

"Until it does," Dee Dee said and balled her wastepaper into a ball. Then, she took a sip of her drink.

"Until it does," Skid parroted her and stood.

Chapter 52

Skid found the envelope on the kitchen table. The return address caught his attention. The first line read Tennessee Department of Vital Records. Rod had put the letter there after he picked up the mail on his way in from the shop to eat lunch. It wasn't addressed to him, and the data inside would not have interested him.

But Skid did find the information interesting. He read the heading first and the explanation of the research. He'd lied about writing a report on his family tree. Unbeknownst to Skid, the university librarian had sent the request to the state agency with access to birth, death, marriage records, and, most importantly, census records.

The paragraph began with listing his mother's name and her husband, Skid's father. The couple's grandparents were listed and verified by birth and death records. Documents from the turn of the century revealed four more grandparents and their mates. Remarkably, the papers went back even further to a time before the Civil War. Skid sat down and tilted the letter into the light to read the captivating information. In the census for 1870, names he'd never heard ran down the page. Sure, his father's surname continued to track, and his mother's given name also appeared on the list. But in the 1870 Federal count, Skid saw something that stopped him from reading. It was a single letter that changed his perception of his family and himself. Next to the boy's name, who would be Skid's four-times great-grandfather, was the letter "M." All the people up to a point, going backward, and when designated by the census taker, had a "W" by their names, ages, and their professions. Eugene Walker was the boy's name, and he was six years old at the time of the count.

The letter stated that information on family members before the war was spotty and unreliable. Finally, the researcher ended the report with a salutation. She hoped the student would receive a good grade for the report.

The wooden chair squeaked as he leaned back and looked out the window. In his research, he already knew what the letter meant. A story explaining how his ancestor came to be began to swirl in his mind. Was the pregnancy planned, or was force involved? Was the offspring merely the chance to provide a restocking of the labor on the plantation?

Skid stood but wobbled a bit as if the blood in his brain had left him. He steadied himself by putting his hand on the tabletop. "Whoa," he whispered. After a few moments, the wooziness cleared.

He put the letter in his notebook, picked up the novel *The Scarlet Letter*, and walked out to the Nomad. He cranked the engine, still dazed by the letter and the implications. When he reached school, he parked and entered the main doors with the other students, but today he felt different. He needed confirmation, and the only person he could think of that might give it to him was Miss Cardwell.

He walked by the auditorium and saw students in conference with volunteer tutors. He recognized Leon from his broad shoulders and growing Afro.

Skid walked to the library and found the librarian pushing the book cart near the non-fiction section.

"Miss Cardwell," Skid said. He'd affixed a smile to his face, but his mind was churning so much that he had difficulty concentrating.

"Yes, Skid," she said. She stopped the cart and walked to her desk. "Do you have another damaged book to check in?"

If he hadn't been so distracted, Skid would have laughed at her joke about his mishandling of the Jiujitsu book. He handed her the novel he'd been carrying, and she put it on her desk.

"Oh, well, no, I'm sorry about that. But, like I said before, I'll pay for a replacement if that's what you need."

"It's fine. We buy new books all the time," she said. Unfortunately, her reading glasses had slipped down her nose. "Although, of course, that one had a bit more life in it, but, oh well."

"You were really mad at me, weren't you?" Skid asked. He wanted to stay on her good side because he had to ask her another favor.

"No, just disappointed. I'll get over it. What can I do for you today?"

"I got this," he said, pulling the envelope from his notebook. "I didn't know the university librarian would do this."

"I'm sure she was just trying to be helpful. What is it?" She asked. She sat behind her desk and held out her hand.

Skid gave her the envelope and watched her open it, adjust her glasses, and read the first few lines. Then, he waited for her to experience the same shock he had as she read.

"Very interesting," she said. She folded the letter and handed it back.

"But the Census. Did you see it? Do you know what it means?"

"It looks like sometime before the Civil War, one of your ancestors was Black. Is that what you mean?" The librarian asked.

"How I mean, what, ah, I don't know what I mean."

"At the time, slave owners believed they controlled every aspect of their workers' lives. The pairing of slaves was sometimes decided on how strong or smart the children might be. It wasn't unusual for the slave owner to impregnate their women to improve their stock. Very much like breeding pigs and cattle to bring out positive traits."

Skid felt lightheaded. He looked for a chair to sit in before he fainted.

"Or, they felt the women were merely pieces of property, and they could do with them as they pleased."

Miss Cardwell saw him go pale and rushed around the edge of her desk. She took his arm and guided him to a pale, wooden chair. It scraped against the pine flooring as he sat.

"Tha 'M' m-m-means," Skid stammered.

"That means Mulatto. Your ancestor was half-Black."

"I kinda thought that was," he began, and his voice trailed off.

"It was over a hundred years ago," she said, putting her hand on his shoulder just as Mr. Lewis had. "It doesn't mean anythin' today."

"I know. It's still a shock," he said. He couldn't look at her. "My people, my ancestors, were owned by other people."

Miss Cardwell stood and looked down at him. "Look around. There are lots of us around here. So, you're in good company."

"You?"

"If you go far back enough on my family tree. It's not unusual at all, but for some reason, it's heartbreaking."

Skid considered what the news would mean to Rod. How would he feel about marrying a woman whose ancestors were Black? Skid had difficulty believing it wouldn't be a significant issue for him. He said he had Black friends in the Army and wasn't prejudiced. But he wasn't supportive of the school protest and always seemed to give Black folks he met a disdainful look. On any level, Skid believed that Rod would not have accepted his mother or him if he knew they were of mixed race, no matter how many generations had passed in between.

Skid glanced around his favorite room in the school. He was just weeks away from graduation, and this was the place he would miss most. He also knew how supportive Miss Cardwell was and the impression she'd made on him.

"Thank you," he said, "for everything. I always felt like this was home."

He stood, but his knees were still watery. She took his elbow and said, "Just take deep breaths."

They both inhaled, looked at each other, and eventually smiled. "There," she said, "that's better."

He nodded, gathered his books, and walked to the door. Skid could see Leon through the large pane of glass as he ambled up to the door. He opened it and held it for Skid.

He glanced up at Leon, nodded, and walked through the door. While he knew only a tiny amount of his blood was from his ancestor so many generations before, he had a new perspective. Maybe he'd write a story about it one day.

"See ya' at work," the athlete said, but Skid was still lost in his thoughts and didn't hear him.

Chapter 53

Skid wasn't sure what driving up Tiger Hill might mean to him now. He'd told Connie how he'd accidentally risked his life riding his bicycle down the steep incline years ago. She was duly impressed by his bravery, or was it stupidity? Even he had a hard time discerning what the incident really meant. Was he chosen because he survived? Was he a skilled and talented bike rider? Was he just *lucky*?

They both stopped talking and looked up at the hill through the windshield. Skid's mother's car ran like a sewing machine now that Rod had focused on all the minor problems that plagued many old, high-mileage vehicles. First, he'd cleaned the carburetor and flushed the fuel filter. Next, he changed the coolant, oil, and oil filter, finding no shavings showing metal-on-metal wear. The master mechanic deemed the car was in top condition.

"That's steep," Connie said. Her right hand shielded her eyes from the brilliant setting sun.

"Yep, pretty scary," he said, putting the car into gear.

The engine whined at the struggle but soon topped the grade. He put on the brake and looked down the road to the fire tower.

"Do ya think anybody's up there?"

"It's not fire season, so I'm guessin' no," Skid said.

"Should we climb up the tower?"

"I don't see why not."

He parked the car at the bottom of the structure. It was the same place Monte's posse had parked their bicycles so long ago. Skid opened the door and walked around the back of the car. Connie opened her door and stood by the fender. She looked up. "Man, that's really tall."

"How high is up?" He asked as if the philosophical question might be answered by someone like him.

They crossed the parking lot and began climbing the zig-zag stairs. They stopped on every other landing, taking in the view. The sky was azure, and wispy clouds dotted the horizon. It was late afternoon, but there was still plenty of light.

"Keep goin'," he said, poking her in the side.

"I'm goin'," she said, laughing as if she were being tickled.

Skid walked behind her, watching her butt swish from side to side in her tight, pink shorts. Finally, he glimpsed the start of the cup of her bra through the arm hole of her sleeveless blouse. "Wow," he whispered.

"What?"

"Oh, nothin'. Just thinkin' out loud."

"That thinkin' can get you in trouble. You need to stop that immediately," she teased him. She looked down as he trudged up the flight of steps. Her eyes caught the light from the setting sun. His breath lodged in his throat. Skid fought the urge to say, "Wow."

"Are you okay?"

"Yes, yeah," he said as he stepped on the last landing before the locked hatch leading to the lookout cabin and turned to look at the forest. "It's beautiful up here, isn't it?"

He looked at her. In that light, her eyes shone, and her pale skin seemed almost translucent. Her hair flew around her shoulders, and he could see her heartbeat throbbing in her neck.

Should I chance it, he thought. In his heart, in his mind, in his soul, it seemed like the right time.

"Connie," he said, this time with as serious a tone as he could muster, "I love you."

He'd said the words before, but there was always a feeling of playfulness and humor behind his delivery. She'd always reciprocated with the same attitude.

He felt her flinch at the words and her resistance as he held her hand. Skid leaned in to kiss her, and while she kissed him back, she didn't close her eyes. He jerked back when he noticed.

"What..."

"I'm sorry. It's just not a good time," Connie said as she pulled her hand from his grasp.

"I know, graduation and all that, but I just thought..."

"Let's just enjoy the view. Isn't all this just amazin'?"

He turned and followed her gaze at the setting sun. Skid had so many questions.

"Can we just talk?"

Connie took his hand and placed it on her heart. "Feel that. That's love there. I just can't think about anything else right now. I've got too much goin' on."

He nodded. "I know. I do too. I just wanted..."

"Please," she said as she touched his lips. "Let's not talk about it."

"Okay," he said, but his voice was disappointed.

"I-I, it's just too much right now. There's, aww, shit," Connie said.

He nodded. "I know. Let's just watch the sun go down."

They held hands and watched the sky turn red. The orange light of the horizon filled the space between them and the forest.

Chapter 54

"I told her that I loved her," Skid said. His voice was a whisper, even though the noise in the lunchroom reached near jet plane engine volume.

Dee Dee stopped chewing her pimento cheese on a white bread sandwich and stared at him. "What possessed you to say that?"

"We've said it before, but it was always with a goofy, playin'-around tone."

"So, you wanted to lock her down?" Dee Dee said, this time around, a potato chip.

"No, I don't think so. I mean, I just wanted to let her know how I felt."

She set the sandwich on the paper bag and folded her hands before her face. "And what did she say?"

Skid flinched as he called up the memory. He glanced at Dee Dee and smirked. "What'a you think?"

"Oh, man, that's rough. Where did the deed go down?"

"Fire tower on Tiger Hill. I thought it was the perfect spot. The sun was going down, and the horizon was red and orange. It was beautiful."

"Then what happened?" Dee Dee asked.

"I stood there, and she took my hand," Skid said. He picked up one of his potato chips and then put it back down.

"That sounds good."

"No, it was like she was consoling me. Like people would take my hand at my mother's funeral. I hope you feel better soon, kinda thing."

"Ouch," Dee Dee said. She resumed her sandwich and checked her watch. "Okay, I've got biology and a meeting with Miss Black about my *future*."

"Why did you say 'future' that way?" Skid said. He put his sandwich to his lips and lowered it to his plate without biting.

"Who knows the future, Clarence?" Dee Dee stood and picked up her tray. She balanced her books on her hip and said, "Nobody knows."

Skid smiled. He liked it when Dee Dee called him "Clarence." It was their inside joke.

He looked around the room at all the other smiling and laughing students. Different faces reflected changes in relationships, friendships, and disagreements. The school year was nearly over, and the county would soon open two new schools on opposite sides of town. There was even talk of knocking down the current building.

He saw life continue, and hope and promise filled every mind except Dee Dee's.

"Are you lookin' at colleges?" Skid asked.

"That's what Miss Black wants to talk about. She'll have my file in front of her." She looked down at him. Leon bumped into her with his tray as he searched for a seat.

"I can see it now. Nothin' but heartache."

"Been there. You know, college isn't for everyone," Skid teased her. He knew she was college material, but he couldn't just give her that compliment. "There are trade schools where you could learn how to spot weld or drywall."

"Ha-ha, and maybe you could learn how to fix cars," Dee Dee teased.

The comment could have stung if his mind wasn't already tangled with his thoughts about Connie.

"That's what Rod wants," Skid said. There was a tone of resignation in his voice as the words leaked from his lips.

Dee Dee asked, "Do you really want to work with him?"

"No, I don't know, maybe," Skid said as he pushed his paper plate to the center of the table. "It would be easy. I can see myself doin' that now, for sure. It's just… I don't know anything. It's what he wants. I think he believes he'll get cheap labor forever if I stay. Does any of that make any sense?"

"No," she said as she picked up her tray and swung a cloth bag holding all her cosmetics. The bag also had money, pencils, a small notepad, and a wallet over her shoulder.

"First stage of enlightenment is to enter the stream," he said. He looked up at her standing there and realized how beautiful she'd become.

"Where did that come from?" She asked.

"Buddha," he said and took a sip of his drink. "I've been reading up on it."

"Okay. You know, some Buddhists believe in reincarnation."

"Sorry," Skid said. "I can't go for that. For me, it's one shot, and you're out."

"Just sayin'. Sometimes folks need a second chance."

About twenty people lined up to put their wastepaper and trays in the bins. Dee Dee took a deep breath and sighed. "One thing I do know. I'll be glad to get out of this shit hole."

Chapter 55

Skid found himself in an empty hallway, a rare occurrence on the usually overcrowded floors. It was a Saturday, and he wanted to soak up the atmosphere he knew would soon end with the closing and demolition of the school.

At the end of the black tile corridor, he saw Mr. Salman juggling the keys to his classroom. He wasn't wearing his usual white shirt, black tie, and black slacks. Today, he wore a Grateful Dead T-shirt and jeans. His Converse Chuck Taylors had black and brown scuff marks, and he hadn't bothered to shave.

"I can never get this," he said as Skid approached.

The teacher held a stack of books and papers in his left hand as he fumbled with the keys in his right.

"Let me," Skid said and held out his hand.

Mr. Salman nodded and gave him the keys.

"What are you doin' here on a Saturday?" Skid asked as he opened the door.

"I could ask you the same thing," the teacher said, nodding in thanks to the student and entering the classroom, but there was tension and exasperation in his voice.

"I'm graduating and will never see this place again."

"That's true," Mr. Salman said. "They're bringing in the wrecking ball this summer."

Skid leaned against the bookcase near the line of windows filling the outside wall of each classroom. "What are they going to do with the land?"

"I think part of it's going to be a park. And I believe they're building a new fire station on the north corner."

Skid looked out the window. From this angle, he couldn't see the big oak tree. "What are they gonna do about the tree?"

"Probably cut it down. It's too big anyway."

Skid felt a pang of payback in the back of his mind as the tree that snagged his self-defense book would soon be felled. *But, sometimes, the universe provides*, he thought.

"It's always good to have a firehouse nearby," Mr. Salman said. He was still searching for something on his cluttered desktop. "Ah, *ha*," he said. He opened the middle drawer and pulled out a red pen. "Glory be."

"And you're here because?" Skid asked.

"I'm sorry, Skid," Mr. Salman said. He opened a manila file. His red pen hovered over the title and first line on the paper. "I don't have time to talk with you right now. My father and his new wife are visiting with their three children. So, the house is overrun with sticky, loud, little people. And, most importantly, I have final essays to grade, and there's no quiet place there."

"Oh, I'm sorry," Skid said, putting his hand on the bookcase. He steadied himself and looked out the window. "I'll leave you alone then."

Even the harried and distracted Mr. Salman could tell the young man's mind was troubled. "It's okay. What's goin' on?" Mr. Salman asked.

"I was just walkin' around and thinkin' about this place." Skid's gaze traveled from the floor to the ceiling to the open door. "It's so weird that it's not goin' to be here next year."

"Yes, but time marches on, as they say in the old newsreels." Mr. Salman noticed the quizzical look on Skid's face. "In the olden days, newsreels were shown before the movie started. They were in black and white and usually only told one side of the story."

"I see. So, which of the new schools are you goin' to?"

"I'm not sure." Again, Mr. Salman said, not looking up from his paper. "They both want me, so that's nice."

"Yes," he swallowed hard and said, "it's nice to be wanted."

Looking up and catching Skid's eyes, he said, "Clarence, you've had a rough time lately. I wanted to let you know that the teachers have noticed, and you're handling it well."

"I don't know about that."

"You have," Mr. Salman said. He pushed the papers on his desk into a stack and twirled his red pen. "You've displayed grace and maturity for a man your age."

"I still feel my mother's presence. Is that crazy?"

"No, of course not. We carry our loved ones who have passed with us forever. Now, I've got to get busy. I wouldn't want to be the teacher holding up graduation." He made a flipping motion with his right hand. His red pen clattered to the floor.

Skid bent to pick it up and handed it to the teacher.

"Thanks. Don't worry. Everything will be fine."

Skid glanced out the window. "I'm not so sure."

"Your electric cooperative essay was excellent, by the way."

"Oh, you were one of the readers? Thanks. I think it could have been better."

"Everything can be improved with rewriting," Mr. Salman said. "But you lost focus near the end. It was a very close competition."

The contest wasn't rigged after all, Skid thought. "Okay, good to know," he said as he left. "How did you know you wanted to be a teacher?" He stood in the doorway and looked at his soon-to-be former instructor.

"I was helping my little brother with something. I think it was a math problem that he just wasn't getting. I tried several ways to explain the solution, and finally, he got it. The look on his face." The teacher looked up at the ceiling as if reliving the experience. "I decided then and there to see that look as many times as possible."

Skid nodded. "That's a good look."

"Nostalgia is a two-edged sword. So be careful as you walk these hallways. By the way, I remember your book report on Siddhartha. You liked it, if I recall."

"Yes," Skid said. He looked at the small window in the door. Silver metal wire laced the clear glass. "It was life-changing in many ways."

"It's not one of my favorites, but it's good." Mr. Salman said with a smile," Ah, the river. Yes, we're all on a journey, and the river is the symbolism Hesse uses."

"With many twists and turns."

Both nodded. They looked up at the sound of a child laughing. Then, they saw a girl and her mother skip to the swing set just past the slide through the window.

"There are times I wish I could return to that time," Mr. Salman said.

"Simple," Skid said. "But you just said children were sticky, little creatures?"

"I did, didn't I. Maybe if I ever have any of my own, I'll change my mind," the teacher's bottom lip quivered. "All right, Clarence, I've got to get busy here."

"So, my stepfather says, 'I'm shit, and I ain't worth killin'.'"

The teacher stopped looking at the sheet of paper in his hand and stared at Skid. "And do you believe that?"

"No," Skid said. The word escaped his mouth with more force and emphasis than he'd meant. At that moment, the school's air handler kicked on, and he felt a breeze of cool air strike him in the face. He blinked. *Does Mr. Salman think I'm crying?* Skid thought. *I'm not crying.* It was embarrassing enough with Mr. Lewis.

"Good, you're not. I have a complicated relationship with my father. His father, my grandfather, was a difficult man to live with, and it shaped my father negatively. The way people treat you doesn't require you to accept it."

"But I'm not sure..."

"Sometimes," the instructor interrupted, "you can define yourself by discovering what you're not."

Chapter 56

Where is she?

Skid weaved the '55 Chevy Bel Air Nomad through the downtown traffic. He had the windows down because the sun shone bright, and the forecast did not mention rain. The upholstery glistened from the conditioner he'd spread over the roll and pleat bench seats. He'd fixed the broken spring that had poked poor Connie in the ass as they did it that first time. Now, the machine was perfect.

Rod had installed the cassette player for Donna as a birthday present. He knew she liked to listen to music as she drove, and he even bought her first tape, Frank Sinatra's *Strangers in the Night*. So Donna had handed down driving and listening to music to Skid, just as he'd inherited her car. Today, Skid played Joe Walsh.

Slid parked his mother's car and strode up the steps leading to Mr. Goldstein's store. Two manikins, one in a stylish tuxedo, stood next to a plastic woman in a wedding dress in the front display window. He glanced at the couple and opened the glass door.

He moved from the men's section to the women's, scanning the racks, hoping to see Connie. He believed she was working today, but their communication had become sporadic after the trip to the fire tower.

The store was empty, but he knew boys and girls would soon fill the aisles. There were wedding and graduation outfits on many parents' lists. Now was a time of celebration and euphoria. It was the season of promise.

Mr. Goldstein opened a door marked "Office" to Skid's left. He always looked like he'd just stepped out of a men's fashion magazine, today wearing a plaid suit, red shirt, and white tie.

"Come on in, Skid," he said with his toothy salesman's smile. "Are you looking for Connie? Sorry, she's not scheduled today."

"Oh, sorry to bother you," Skid said, fingering a cashmere sweater on a black wooden table.

"That's two-hundred dollars," Mr. Goldstein said. He smiled, knowing a kid Skid's age likely wouldn't have that kind of money.

"Oh," Skid said, pulling his hand away as if he'd touched a hot stovetop. "I didn't mean…"

"It's okay, Sonny. Is there anything I can help you with? Maybe an outfit for the graduation dance. Something smart and classy?" Mr. Goldstein asked, fingering the lapel of his chic and stylish suit.

"I'm not sure I'm goin'."

"Oh, I see." He left the office with Skid trailing behind. The little man, barely over five feet tall, circled the table full of sweaters and stood next to a rack of sports coats. "Connie is such a good girl. So smart. She accepted that scholarship to Johns Hopkins, but that doesn't mean you'll never see her again. Some couples can make long-distance relationships work. Besides, she'll visit her parents on holidays, Thanksgiving, and Christmas. And breaks. So, I mean, it's not like you'll never see her again."

"Johns Hopkins," Skid said barely above a whisper. "What's that?"

"Once she completes her undergraduate degree there," again with the salesman grin, "she says she'll stay and study to become a doctor. It's probably one of the best medical schools in the world."

"Oh, I guess I could look it up at the library." But, again, Skid couldn't keep the forlorn tone from his voice.

"It's in Baltimore. She's going to be a great doctor."

"A doctor," he whispered.

"I graduated from there on the G.I. bill in '50, not medical school. I wish I was that smart," Mr. Goldstein said, his chest puffing out under the red shirt. "I'm glad I could help her with the paperwork and recommendations."

Skid's lower lip trembled momentarily, and then the boy pulled his mouth tight. "Baltimore," Skid said. "I've never even been north of Kentucky."

"She'll do really well there. And like I said, you'll see her on holidays."

"I want her to do well and be happy. I just didn't know it was goin' to be so far away."

Mr. Goldstein slapped Skid on the shoulder and said, "If it's meant to be, you'll work it out."

"They asked me, the brothers who own the restaurant, they asked me to join the management program." Again, he had a downtrodden tone in his voice. "I'd have to go to Hamburger University."

Mr. Goldstein let his hand slip from Skid's shoulder. "That's not the same as Johns Hopkins, is it?"

"No," Skid said. He pursed his lips and turned toward the front door. "If you see her, please let her know I'm lookin' for her."

"Sure thing," and then the store owner offered his standard response to everyone who visited his store, "Y'all come back real soon."

Skid cranked the engine, and the cassette player sprang to life. A song from the concert filled the cabin. Skid looked out the windshield momentarily and turned off the player without looking for the knob.

"Baltimore," he whispered.

Chapter 57

Rockin' Rudy worked weekends, sometimes as many as sixteen hours in two eight-hour shifts. Skid listened to the rock station because the music spoke to him. Hits like *Fame* and *Shining Star* made his toes tap and freed his fingers to hit the steering wheel.

"Where is that girl?" he asked as he drove by Connie's parent's house. He'd visited a couple of times and could tell they disapproved of their dating from how they looked at him.

He swung by the school and saw the empty parking lot on the east side. And Connie's car wasn't there, so he moved on.

Skid turned up the radio when the song *Late for the Sky* by Jackson Browne came on. It was a song about lovers leaving for a better life together. It was not an upbeat song you could dance to if you wanted. But the words spoke to Skid as he crisscrossed the grid of streets and roads of his hometown. How much longer would he search for her? "As long as it takes," he answered.

The guitar solo in the bridge of the song sounded so plaintive. What would he say to her if he did find her?

On the radio, Rudy said, "That's good for all those dreamers looking for something. But do you know what you need? You need to Rock!"

The rhythmic, chopping guitar licks began "Whole Lotta Love," followed by Robert Plant's voice. Then, the drums and bass kicked in, and Skid tapped his fingers on the steering wheel. What am I going to do without her? He asked himself.

He wasn't the world's biggest Led fan, but the song fit the afternoon's mood. He'd continue his search for his girl, and when he found her, they'd have a long talk about their relationship and future together. He took the small ring from his pinkie finger and looked at the tiny chip of diamond in the setting.

"Thanks, Mom," he whispered.

He put the ring back on his finger. He'd found it when cleaning out his mother's cabinets and chests after she'd died. Rod didn't or couldn't bring himself to go through her stuff. Skid had given away most of her clothes and shoes, but he kept photos and some of her jewelry. He hadn't considered what he might use from her effects until now.

He turned the wheel and rehearsed, "Connie, will you marry me?"

Chapter 58

Skid concluded there were times when people didn't want to be found. First, he'd left messages with Connie's parents that he wanted to speak with her. Then, he'd tracked down all their common friends and told them he was looking for her. He didn't tell anyone, but his demeanor and tone of voice made it clear he had something important in mind. Finally, they all said they'd tell her he wanted to talk with her when they saw her.

He turned the wheel on his mother's car and crossed the cattle grid at the beginning of the property. Skid's grandfather was a cattle rancher, and while it had been years since cows had grazed on the pastures, the barrier to them leaving the lot was still there. He liked how the pipes rattled when the car wheels crossed the indention. It was a signal he was home.

He parked the car in the usual spot and rolled up the windows. There was rain in the forecast, and he didn't want the rehabilitated seat covers to get wet. He noticed Joseph's Jaguar's top was down, so he walked across the gravel lot. He was about to pull the levers allowing him to raise the canvas covering, but he stopped. "Why am I doin' this?" He asked himself. And then he said, "Rod wouldn't piss on me if I was on fire."

The air swept down the small valley behind the shed. The sun sat low on the horizon. Skid saw dark clouds gathering across the azure sky. He took a deep breath, felt the thickening humidity on his face, and smiled. He thought *life was good and it was about to get better.*

Skid knew Rod would expect him to start supper soon but wasn't in the mood. So instead, he was in favor of warming some TV dinners instead of cooking.

The noise caught his attention and diverted him from his walk to the house's back door. The sound came from the workshop. He'd heard lots of weird scraping and sawing noises from there in the past, but this was a different kind of rhythmic noise. Finally, curiosity got the best of him, and he walked toward the shed.

As Skid approached, he noticed how the sun's angle made the sliding door look like the cave opening he and Connie had explored so many times. He noted how it was funny how one thing makes you think of another.

Skid stopped, listened as the sound continued, and walked into the shop. His eyes adjusted, and he walked past a red Ferrari in stall number one. Rod had scattered parts and tools across the table to the machine's right. The old man had a natural talent, no doubt. Skid knew there was no way he could keep the information needed to put the machine back together in his mind. It wasn't his thing. What was? Mr. Salman said sometimes you can define yourself by discovering what you're not? Skid nodded and said, "Bud, you are not a mechanic."

But it was Rod's gift. Skid marveled at his ability to fix and sometimes even improve complicated machines.

"Hey," Skid said. But the noise continued.

He walked by a hot rod in pieces, and a Farmall Cub tractor a local had brought in for a tune-up. Rod did favors like this for friends, and Skid wasn't surprised when he saw the red battery cover sitting on a workbench.

As he approached the source of the sound, his stomach went queasy, and he stumbled over a raised crack in the concrete floor. "Hey," he said again, but with a bit less volume this time.

Skid turned a corner.

The creaking sound came from a red leather bench seat removed from the back of a Studebaker. He saw a young woman crouched over a man's bare, hairy legs with his coveralls and white jockey shorts around his ankles.

She tossed her hair over her shoulder; at that moment, Skid knew who she was.

He watched for a moment, stunned by the naked back and ass. Skid took a ragged breath and tried to speak, but his chest tightened, and his mind froze.

The couple neared the end of the lovemaking session, moving and breathing in rhythm.

"Oh, baby," Skid heard the man say.

"That's, tha-," Skid heard the young woman say.

"Hey," Skid said, this time with enough volume to get their attention.

The surprised couple shuttered and stopped.

Rod looked around Connie's naked torso. "What the fuck?"

The girl looked over her shoulder. There was sweat on her forehead, and her cheeks were flushed. Her mouth and chin trembled.

"No, oh no," she whispered.

"Get off," Rod said, pushing the girl to the side. He was just about to reach down to pull up his underwear and coveralls. But instead, he jumped to his feet and stood naked in front of Connie as she tugged on her shirt and underwear.

"What the fuck, Rod?" Skid said.

He moved toward the mechanic with his hands balled into fists, and his eyes lowered.

"Kid, come on," Rod said. He jerked his underwear and clothes into place, then let his hands hang loosely at the end of his sleeves. He moved his feet apart to better balance himself.

Skid threw the first punch. It missed and whizzed by Rod's head. The boy almost fell over the man's outstretched leg and into Connie as she struggled to put on her blouse.

"Let me explain," Connie said, looking up at Skid. Her eyes were wide, and her mouth was a tight slit.

"It was nothin'," Rod said just as Skid backhanded him across the face. He touched the corner of his mouth and found blood on his hand. "She don't care nothin' about you, boy."

"No, stop, Rod! Please, Clarence, that's just not true. Please stop!" Connie screamed. She stood and straightened her blouse and skirt. Her shoes sat at the end of the seat.

The men circled each other with eyes and jaws tight.

"She's my girl," Skid said as he lunged at Rod.

"Look, kid, shit happens," Rod said as he slapped the boy on the back of the head as he swept by him. "She's leavin' town anyway. You'll get over it."

Skid rubbed the back of his head and turned. "I'm gonna kill you."

Rod said, "I've been in enough bar fights to know that the next likely step…"

"I don't care," Skid said as he punched the older man on the chin.

Connie had her shoes on by now and was tugging at Skid's sleeve.

"Don't, Skid. Just stop. Please," Connie pleaded. "He'll kill you!"

"Look, she wanted a man and not a boy. Women's got needs. What's wrong with that?" Rod asked. He stepped around Skid's feeble right cross and peppered the boy's face with two jabs.

Skid stepped back and glared at Rod. "This ends today," he said as he threw a right haymaker. Unfortunately, the punch missed Rod's face, and the opening was all the mechanic needed to throw an uppercut.

Skid fell on the concrete floor with a thud. His feet flew up in the air, and he heard his shoulder crack before he lost consciousness.

The sound of the Jaguar's engine woke him up. Skid shook his head and leaned on his right elbow. His shoulder felt out of place, and he winced as he pushed himself to his feet.

"Son of a bitch," he muttered through clenched teeth.

As his head cleared, he debated whether to let them go or chase him. Revenge for Rod's slights of the last year flashed through his mind. He was angry with Connie, too. He had to know why she would do this. He had questions for them both. What would a real man do?

Skid stepped through the sliding door as the Jaguar slipped into gear. He saw Rod in the driver's seat and Connie next to him. The top was down, and the rear wheels threw gravel at the shed as they sped through the back door.

"Son of a bitch," Skid said as he searched his pockets for the keys to his mother's car. Finally, he opened the door, dropped the keys on the floor next to the gas pedal, picked them up with a grunt, and shoved them into the ignition. "Owwww, shit," he muttered. His shoulder really hurt. The Chevy engine roared to life, and he jammed the gear shift into reverse.

Skid heard the Jaguar's wheels rattle the cattle grid and the tires bite into the two-lane asphalt in front of the farm. He turned the Nomad's steering wheel, backed onto the gravel driveway, and raced after them.

A light rain added a sheen of silver to the blacktop in front of the farm. Skid gunned the engine and spun the back tires, shifting through the gears as best he could with his injured shoulder.

"Oww, shit, oww, shit, son of a bitch," Skid said, his lips tight and forehead furrowed. He glanced in the rearview mirror and saw his right eye swelling. He could still see, but the first question about what he might do if he caught them entered his mind. He was no physical match for Rod, and he'd already embarrassed himself in front of Connie. How could he win her back by getting beat up even more?

He'd call the police and have Rod arrested. Connie must have resisted him. Sex with him couldn't have been her idea. And then he remembered Monte's encounter and how the girl had pursued him, kind of attacked him. But Connie wasn't like that? Skid flushed the thought from his mind. She couldn't have been willing to hurt him like that.

He stepped on the gas and spun the passenger side back wheel into the ditch. Skid twisted the steering wheel left and gained control as the mailman's car topped the ridge.

He stepped on the brakes as he passed a farmhouse on the right. "Son of a bitch, you're not goin' to get away with this."

The rain peppered the now steaming hood of the Chevrolet. Skid twisted the knob that controlled the windshield wipers. It dawned on him how fast he was going and how Rod was driving even faster. The old man's racing experience would give him the edge, but Skid knew he would never stop, and eventually, one of them would run out of gas.

He looked down at the speedometer and remembered the night he and Connie had fought at the drive-in. Then, Skid acted out and frightened her with his reckless driving. He tried to imagine how terrified she was now with Rod at the wheel.

Skid gave the old car more gas and passed a tractor with a hay baler attached to the back just as a van approached. Typically, a friendly greeting would have occurred, but not this time, not today. "Son of a bitch," he repeated himself.

The boy knew he had a tire iron in the trunk. It was the only weapon he could think of that might be in the car. So he'd pull them over, somehow, open the lid, and get that twisted hunk of metal. He'd seen dozens of heroes in movies and TV do something like that, and it had evened the score between physically mismatched characters.

"Yeah, that's a great idea," Skid said as he gripped the steering wheel until his knuckles grew white. Rain drenched the windshield, and he had to wipe the window with his hand to see through the condensation. "Damn it," he muttered.

Over the hill, he saw a puff of smoke and heard a loud bang. Skid had never heard anything like it before and was confused about its origin and location.

As he drove down the hill, he could see the top limbs of the old oak tree at the right of the hairpin curve move as if struck by a high wind. The rain pounded the car, and the wipers had a hard time clearing Skid's view.

He tapped the Nomad's brakes as the rear bumper of the Jaguar came into view. The car sat at an odd angle near the tree. "Oh, no," he whispered. "No, no, no, no," he muttered.

Steam came from the crumpled front end of the car. Skid could see the driver's side wheel still spinning and how the shattered windshield rested on the ground near the passenger side door.

Skid pulled the Nomad off the road and jerked the door open. He ran to the wreck, stumbling over the rocks and divots of grass in a ditch leading to the tree.

He first saw Connie. A bleeding gash ran across her forehead. He picked up her hand and squeezed it, but it was limp. "Connie, no," he whispered as she stared at him with lifeless eyes.

He circled the back of the Jaguar and saw Rod hanging halfway out the driver's side door. His chest had a deep impression from the steering wheel, and he wasn't breathing. Skid pulled him from the car and laid him on the ground next to the front wheel.

Skid knelt next to the body and touched the man's forehead. He heard a truck slow and park in the ditch. He didn't turn to see who it was. Instead, his gaze fell on Rod's placid and unmoving face. Skid felt a hand on his shoulder.

"We need to call the sheriff and an ambulance."

"Right," Skid said. "I'll stay here."

Chapter 59

Preacher Jake turned the page in his Bible and looked out over the crowd in the small chapel. The pews in the funeral home sanctuary were filled, and a few people sat in folding chairs in the back.

Skid knew the rituals around death were designed to comfort and ease the loss of loved ones. He didn't believe he was one of those people but knew how it would be seen if he boycotted either of the funerals. Death was a frequent companion of his. If asked, he'd say his soul was numb to loss. So, he sat dutifully through both funerals and tried to control his thoughts and emotions.

"Come to me, all you who are weary and burdened, and I will give you rest," Preacher Jake read. "Take my yoke upon you and learn from me, for I am gentle and humble in heart, and you will find rest for your souls. For my yoke is easy, and my burden is light."

Several people coughed as the minister paused.

"One life affects so many others," Jake began. His white shirt and black tie matched his black suit. Skid had seen the outfit many times and assumed Jake only wore it to funerals.

Most of the mourners were acquaintances of Skid and his mother. Before she got sick, she was the best friend anyone could have, and when she died, there was such an outpouring of grief that Rod and Skid were overwhelmed. They sat, slump-shouldered, together, both wearing sunglasses and black suits.

It had been different at Connie's service. Skid had sat in the back, again with sunglasses, and found himself weeping softly. Dee Dee took some tissues from her purse and handed them to Skid.

"Just let it go," she whispered. She wore black, just like Skid, and later she stood next to him as the crowd approached the casket.

"I know," Skid said. But he couldn't help but feel the mix of emotions brought on by the service.

The ambulance drivers had pronounced Connie dead at the scene. Skid watched as attendants placed Rod's body on the stretcher and hustled him into the vehicle. Rod died during transport to the hospital.

The story reported in the newspaper and circulated and believed by the townsfolk was that Rod was repairing Connie's car and giving her a ride to work when the accident happened. He was driving too fast and recklessly and lost control, slamming into the tree at a high rate of speed. The inspection of the Jaguar revealed a worn tie rod on the driver's side wheel that might have broken loose before the accident, but the evidence was inconclusive. There would be no definitive explanation of why the accident happened.

Skid knew the truth behind the innocent lie that would save Connie's reputation. A part of him felt he owed some respect to Rod since, at the beginning of their relationship, he tried to be a good stepfather. But, after Donna died, Rod seemed lost. Skid couldn't blame him for that. But the head and the heart don't always agree.

Connie wore a black dress, and her hands were folded across her stomach. She looked like she was sleeping. The funeral director had masked the effects of the accident. Skid fought the urge to reach out and shake her awake.

Skid sat on the front row at Rod's service and barely acknowledged the well-wishers who passed by him. He sat motionless in the same clothes he had worn to Connie's funeral two days before. He pushed his sunglasses up on his nose and wiped a line of drool from the corner of his mouth. His jaw was so tight that he felt he might break a tooth or even several.

Dee Dee sat behind Skid this time and tried to touch his shoulder, but he pulled away. She could see the muscles tensing on the side of his neck, and his ears glowed red.

"Knock it off," she whispered. "You're goin' to hurt yourself."

Skid sat motionless and took a deep breath. Then, through clenched teeth said, "I don't care."

Preacher Jake paused for a second and looked at Skid. He'd changed much of his talk with new Bible verses and a story of how Rod had repaired the church van free of charge one hot summer day.

Jake could see the boy was in deep distress but couldn't stop the service. He felt the urge to leave the podium and sit next to Skid. But, any counseling would have to take place after the service.

The funeral ended, and the pallbearers slid the closed casket into the hearse. Dee Dee tried to talk with Skid on the ride to the cemetery, but he didn't respond.

After the "ashes to ashes" speech at Rod's grave, Skid took a clump of earth and crushed it in the palm of his hand. Dee Dee stood next to him as he stared into the black hole. Finally, he nodded to the gravediggers, and they started shoveling the rich, black earth into the grave.

A stream of well-wishers passed by Skid, offering assistance if needed and a pat on the shoulder expressing sympathy. Skid's sprained shoulder still hurt, but he couldn't acknowledge it. If he sought treatment for it, he'd have to come up with another lie, and he was just too tired to make an effort.

A large man wearing an Army uniform hovered around the back of the small tent beside the grave. Skid tried to place the stranger and wondered why he attended the service.

Skid guessed he was a Captain, made his way through the crowd, and offered his hand to Skid. The boy shook it just as Rod had taught him.

"I'm sorry for your loss, Son," the man said.

"Thanks," Skid said, glancing at the man over his sunglasses.

"We never met. Your dad was fixing my Mercedes. No doubt, he was a wizard with a welding rod," the Captain said. "I'm Larry Cox."

"Oh, right, I recognize your name. I keep the, or, kept the books at the shop. I'm not sure what to do about your car now. I don't think..."

The gravediggers continued their work. They tamped dirt in the hole with a long pole, ensuring the ground wouldn't settle after a few rain showers. Unfortunately, it was something Skid had seen too often now.

Larry adjusted his belt and smiled down at the boy. "You don't never mind about that. I'll come get it, and I'll figure out somethin'."

"I'm sorry. Rod left behind so many projects. I'm not sure how I'm gonna get everythin' together."

"I was in import/export before I retired. Maybe I can help. I owe your father that much," Larry said.

"You knew him?"

"You could say I ruined his life. At least, that's what Rod thought at the time. He'd just landed in Vietnam and was about to be sent into a hot zone. I caught him with his friend, Joseph, in a, what should I say, a compromising position."

"I don't understand," Skid said. He felt a bead of sweat run down the side of his cheek. He brushed it away with the back of his hand, wincing as the shoulder rotated against his bruise.

"I caught them in bed together one night. They could've denied it, but they owned up to it. They said they *loved* each other. That was against regulations, and I could have had them discharged, but I saw somethin' in the both of them. So I had Rod transferred to the motor pool, and eventually, he ended up in Europe. Joseph learned Vietnamese and became a translator for me. He was my right hand, I guess you could say."

Skid felt the corner of his mouth twitch and reached up to try to stop it. "Oww," he said as he touched his face.

"Anyway, I thought you should hear about that. Rod was a hard man to figure out."

Skid thought, *you got that right*, but said instead, "This puts a lot of pieces of the puzzle together."

"I hope it's okay that I said what I said here. I've learned over the years that keeping stuff like that secret can kill your soul," Larry said. "I'll see you at the shop." He turned and walked down the slope that led to the parking lot.

Skid watched the gravediggers finish filling Rod's grave and covering the dirt with bright green sod. Then, after they left, Skid looked up at the sky and said, "What the actual fuck."

Chapter 60

Graduation day represented years of study and maturation. It was an event that changed a person's identity forever.

Skid stood in the hallway leading to the gym floor. His graduation gown hung loose on his thin frame, and he held his mortarboard hat. Dee Dee stood next to him.

"I can't see them," Dee Dee said as she scanned the crowd.

"Why would they even come?" Skid asked.

"They're going to award her diploma posthumously," Dee Dee said. Her hair was chopped off into a pixie cut that accentuated her cheekbones and large eyes. She wore bright red lipstick and high heels, something Skid had never seen on her before. "They'll stand there on the stage, and people will applaud. I've seen it happen."

"Right," Dee Dee said. She adjusted her short skirt under her gown.

Skid wore his black suit pants, black shoes, and white shirt. He couldn't find a tie he liked, so he just went without.

"Why do you think Mom married Rod?" Skid asked Dee Dee.

"You want to talk about that here?"

"Seems as good a place as any."

Friends and families filled the basketball gym that now doubled as an auditorium. It was where Skid and Connie had seen the Joe Walsh concert just months before. It was where he'd played basketball with Leon.

"The heart wants what the heart wants," Dee Dee said. She knew it was a cliché and that explaining human attraction was a question that poets and philosophers had pondered for years.

"The usual bullshit," he said through clenched teeth.

"Yeah, pretty much."

Streams of people moved in front of them. Families of every kind, shape, and ethnicity found places on the pull-out benches and folding chairs behind the reserved section.

"What would he have said if he found out my mother was part Black?"

Dee Dee adjusted the collar of the graduation gown. Her breasts had gotten larger over the past few months, and she had difficulty adjusting.

"I can't imagine he'd have liked that news."

"But would that have been enough to keep him from marryin' her?"

"Given his experience in the Army and workin' with all kinds of men there, he would have been okay with it."

"And like you say, the heart wants what the heart wants."

Graduates would soon file into the room to the pre-recorded strains of "Pomp and Circumstance." An air of optimism and sadness accompanied the most significant life changes.

Monte's posse filed past Skid with all looking down and unable to make eye contact. They had attended the funerals but couldn't find words to console Skid. Monte had stopped by at the graveside and struck Skid three times very hard on the shoulder. His face at this friend in his sorrowful time somehow displayed horrible and hopeful. As they passed by at graduation, their faces held similar expressions.

Dee Dee straightened her gown and adjusted her mortarboard. Like most young women, she'd used Bobby pins to ensure the hat would stay in place.

"What are you gonna do?" Skid asked. He glanced at her as a family of four circled and found their seats behind them.

"Workin' this summer at the restaurant," Dee Dee said. "I'm gonna save some money and apply for college somewhere."

Skid nodded. He had had the same plan at one time. However, the death of his stepfather complicated the decision-making process. He'd talked with the family lawyer and said it would take months to file the will and life insurance policy payoff. After that, Skid would have money in the bank. When that was settled, he'd decide about college.

He fingered his black hat. "You know, Rod knew the name for this. It's a mortarboard." Skid looked at Dee Dee. "What have I done?"

"You didn't do anything," she said, taking his hand. "They were the ones who did somethin' wrong. You were just mad."

"I don't know what I would have done if I'd caught them."

She squeezed his hand. "Nothin' would have happened, and there's nothin' you need to worry about. So, pick up your diploma and move on."

Skid bowed his head. A single tear crept down the side of his cheek. "I thought I'd already cried enough."

Dee Dee swept the back of her hand across his face. "Do what you gotta do. Cry if you need to cry. Get mad if you need to get mad."

"That's just it," he said, "I don't know what to do."

The class filed into the back of the gym and was lined up alphabetically by Miss Black. She wore a summer dress with multicolored flowers on a white background. Skid noticed she had on black, patent leather shoes that caught the light as she checked students off the list on her clipboard.

"Don't forget who's in front of you. And don't switch around, or you'll get the wrong diploma." She spoke louder than at any other time Skid had been around her. She was emphatic, and there was a no-nonsense tone to her instructions.

"Clarence," she said, not looking up from the clipboard.

The boy shuffled to his place in line. But, of course, everyone had heard of his stepfather's and his girlfriend's tragic deaths. And, except for Dee Dee, he was the only one who knew what led up to the crash and would never tell anyone else the truth.

"I'm here, Miss Black," Skid said. He tugged on his mortarboard and brushed the hair on his forehead.

"Right," the counselor said and checked off his name. She looked at him, forcing him to match her gaze. She nodded. He waggled his head up and down.

"You're gonna be alright," Miss Black assured him.

Skid nodded at her and pasted on a smile, but he didn't believe it. Her face told the story that neither did she.

The graduation speaker was Gloria Gaiter, who once led the lunch counter sit-ins in Nashville. She adjusted the microphone down so she could be heard. She was tiny and needed a box to stand on. She wore a graduation gown, a black Tam o'shanter, and a gold tassel.

"There will be times when you are forever changed," she began. She spoke with a deliberately slow pace and with perfect elocution. "Your decisions will be challenged, but you have a rock-solid basis to begin making those choices. America's public education system gives children a beginning, but it's up to you to find your own path."

She told them her story and how the graduates would change the world someday. Her giving the speech was part of the agreement following the student walkout. After reading her address a few months later, Skid found the narrative and ideas inspirational. On graduation day, though, his mind was a thousand miles away and filled with a jumble of barbed wire and gelatin.

She'd talked about how graduation ceremonies were called a 'commencement' for a reason. It was a celebration of completing an essential phase of one's life and the beginning or commencing of another. "This is one of those days in life where you'll never be able to go back," she said. "Like getting married or becoming a parent, this event is forever."

Skid looked down his row and saw Leon sitting with his hands folded in his lap. Clearly, he was listening intently and internalizing every word. Skid tried to imagine how the words might inspire him to continue his efforts to bring more equality to the world.

Gloria ended her speech with a passage from President Theodore Roosevelt's address entitled "Citizenship in a Republic" at the Sorbonne in Paris on April 23rd, 1910. The speech is commonly called "The Man in the Arena."

"It is not the critic who counts; not the man who points out how the strong man stumbles or where the doer of deeds could have done them better."

Gloria adjusted her reading glasses and continued. "The credit belongs to the man who is actually in the arena, whose face is marred by dust and sweat and blood; who strives valiantly; who errs, who comes short again and again, because there is no effort without error and shortcoming; but who does actually strive to do the deeds; who knows the great enthusiasms, the great devotions; who spends himself in a worthy cause; who at the best knows in the end the triumph of high achievement, and who at the worst, if he fails, at least fails while daring greatly, so that his place shall never be with those cold and timid souls who neither know victory nor defeat."

Gloria finished to applause and received a hearty handshake from the principal. He wore his graduation gown and a mortarboard. What looked like a stack of black plastic notebooks sat on a table behind him. He told Miss Gaiter how much he appreciated her talk and turned to adjust the microphone. He pulled a stack of cards from his pocket and handed them to the Vice-Principal.

Skid realized how many important events had occurred in this facility. He heard the story years later singer/songwriter Jackson Browne would headline a concert in the newly finished ten-thousand-seat gymnasium next to the current one. Skid had heard Browne asked to see the Special Events director before going on stage. Students and stagehands backstage believed Browne would take the opportunity to confront the director who'd forced him back on stage during that disastrous first concert. Instead, when the man arrived, Browne shook his hand and thanked him for making him retake the stage and finish the show. He said he needed to grow up, and this incident, though it stuck in his memory for a long time, was a turning point in his maturing as an artist.

Skid didn't fully comprehend the story when he'd heard it. Still, months later, he realized the importance of taking responsibility and doing the right thing. It took him a while, but he visited Connie's parents a few weeks after graduation and shared his sorrow and loss. They sat in the living room, held hands, remembering Connie, and hugged Skid as he left.

Skid watched as Connie's parents shuffled across the stage and accepted her diploma. They both walked stoop-shouldered, and he could see their red-rimmed eyes. When Connie's father took the certificate, he shook hands with the school principal and held the folder up to the crowd. The students leaped to their feet and applauded. Connie's father smiled. He continued across the stage, but now he held his shoulders back and looked over the gathering.

That afternoon, Skid returned the rented cap and gown to Mr. Goldstein's store. Unfortunately, the owner wasn't there, but a new girl stood behind the counter. She was younger than Connie but was personable and helpful when he handed her the costume.

"I'm sorry about what happened to your dad and Connie," she said as she folded the black cloth across the counter.

"Stepfather," he corrected her.

"Right, sorry," she said. "So, where do you go from here?"

"That's a good question," he answered and turned to leave.

"Congratulations on graduating. That's a big thing."

Skid smiled at the clerk and touched one of the cashmere sweaters on a table near the cash registers.

"Those are really nice," the clerk said.

"Maybe next time," Skid said.

He walked through the store, taking in all the smells of cotton, wool, starch, and Mr. Goldstein's cologne.

Skid opened the glass and aluminum front door. He stepped out on the sidewalk and looked left and right. He put on his sunglasses and fished in his front pocket for the car keys.

He was a high school graduate with all the world at his feet and couldn't decide which direction to go.

Chapter 61

The graduation night dance featured a rock and roll cover band of Skid's fellow students. They called themselves "Freddie and the Four Barrels" and played album hits of the day.

Skid had planned to attend the festivities at once but was too tired after all that had happened. So instead, he drove around the downtown area for an hour, hoping to see other lost souls in the same state of mind as his.

There weren't any.

So, he drove to the cave and sat in the parking area where he and Connie had first made love. The full moon illuminated the location, and the temperature hovered around the seventies that night. Skid kept the windows down as he sat behind the driver's wheel.

The farmer who owned the adjacent property had put in a cattle gate and had mowed a large portion of the field. It was far from where Skid sat, but he could see the white Camaro rattling across the red iron rods.

After the Camaro found a secluded spot, Skid saw the car's body move up and down on its springs, but the doors stayed closed. *Ah,* he thought, *lovers.*

He considered exiting the car and walking around the cave, hoping to clear his head. But, instead, he opened the door, leaned against the fender, and gazed at the stars.

"Wish I may wish I might have the wish, I wish tonight," he recited the childhood saying his mother had taught him. "And what would that wish be?"

Would he want Connie and Rod to be alive? Would he wish his mother was still with him? Would he want to go to college?

The sound of another car on the gravel road caught his ear. He waved at the police cruiser across the car's shiny hood. It looked like the same officer rousted him and Connie that night so long ago.

Did he know what had happened to her?

Skid was sure the cops were current on everything in the town.

He was surprised when he saw the cruiser cross the cattle gate and cut its lights. The officer rolled up next to the Camaro and opened his door. He pulled his flashlight and shone the cone of white light into the open window. Even though it was over fifty yards away, Skid could see what was happening. He knew the officer's routine.

The driver's side door opened, and Leon emerged. His shirt was unbuttoned, and his pants hung low on his hips. The cop held the door. Another young man got out of the back seat and unbuttoned his shirt. Who was that? Skid recognized Jacob French from his Biology class.

"Holy shit," Skid said. He ducked into the window of the passenger side of the Nomad and popped open the glove box. He put the camera strap around his neck and walked toward the scene.

He didn't know what to say or do, but he felt drawn to the confrontation. It was just then the cop punched Jacob in the jaw.

Leon stepped up and began to wrestle with the cop. The cop pushed him back and was about to draw his weapon when Skid walked up.

"Leon," Skid asked, "are you okay?"

"Step back, Kid," the cop said. He turned and recognized Skid. "What the... What the fuck are you doin' here?"

"Just hangin' out," Skid said as he fingered the focus on his camera. He'd already fixed a flash bulb into the socket. "Maybe takin' a few pictures. There's deer around here."

"Get lost, Kid. It's none of your business," the cop said, smashing his flashlight into Leon's head. The ball player fell against the car fender. Jacob took a step forward but stopped when the cop turned to him.

"Hey, I know you. How's that girl of yours?"

Skid took a deep breath and felt his jaw tighten. Maybe the cops didn't know everything that went on in the town. Or, perhaps they did.

"Why are you bein' an asshole?" Skid asked.

The cop backhanded Skid and stepped back.

"Get outta here, or I'll take the lot of you in," the cop said.

"No," Skid said.

"Look, just get outta here. This is none of your business."

Skid rubbed his jaw and glared at the cop. "I'm makin' it my business."

"I'll give *you* some, too," the cop warned. And swung the flashlight at Skid. The battery-filled pipe hit him on the shoulder. It was the same one he'd bruised in his fight with Rod. The leftover pain and anger bubbled inside him, and he threw himself at the cop.

Skid swung his right hand and missed. His left arm hung uselessly by his side. The smiling cop popped him once in the eye and again in the mouth before the young man could make a serious move. "Back off," the officer commanded.

Leon stepped up and shoved Jacob into the back seat. He opened the driver's side door and was about to get in when the cop said, "Don't you move. Nobody moves. You're all under arrest."

Skid's camera shutter opened, and the flash bulb illuminated the area. The picture would show the cop with his flashlight raised and a wild, out-of-control look on his face. That is if Skid had ever had a chance to get the film developed.

"Gimme that," The cop said. His eyes were still adjusting from the flash, but Skid could see he meant business.

"All right," Skid said as the shutter opened again. This picture wouldn't be as good, given only the full moon would be the light source.

"I said, give me that now," He'd put his flashlight in his belt holder and held out his hand. His other hand rested on the butt of his pistol. "I'm not goin' to say that again."

The words and threat stopped Skid, and he stepped back, rubbing his shoulder. He felt good standing up for his friends but didn't want to die for them.

Leon launched himself at the cop but missed and ended up between Skid and the officer. The policeman pulled his gun and aimed at Leon's chest.

"No, stop," Skid said. He pulled Leon to his side. "Stop."

"Please, Sir," Jacob said. "You don't have to do this." The young man stood by the car with his hands folded. He'd closed his eyes and appeared to be praying.

Skid watched as the cop took a deep breath and slowly put his gun back in the holster. "I don't need this shit. Turn around," the cop said to Leon. He was clearly the most significant threat because of his size and musculature. The big man complied.

"You're next," the cop said to Skid. "Put your hands on your head."

Skid interlaced his fingers on top of his head. The movement made him wince in pain, but he did what he was told.

The cop's radio crackled, "10-82, 10-82 at the high school. All officers reply."

"Shit," the office said. He leaned into the cruiser's passenger side window and picked up the radio microphone. "This is car 52. On the way."

The cop unlocked Leon's handcuffs and motioned for Skid to lower his hands. "You got lucky," he said, putting the cuffs back on his belt.

"Yeah, that's me, Mr. Lucky," Skid smarted off.

"And give me that film," the cop said, holding his hand.

Skid opened the back of the camera and yanked the brown plastic strip from the reels. The cop snorted and threw the film in the front seat of the squad car.

The cop huffed and clamored under the cruiser's steering wheel. Then, finally, he turned over the engine and cut a donut on the soft ground.

"If you hadn't been here," Leon said. His left eye was almost swollen shut, and there was a split in his bottom lip. Blood dripped onto his clean, white T-shirt. "There's no tellin' what he'd have done."

"We're just lucky Jacob got through to him," Skid said and looked across the Camaro's hood at Jacob.

"Yep, he's a good man," Leon said.

"It's okay. I get it." Skid said, "I'm Black, too."

Leon studied Skid's face. Black, straight hair topped Skid's head. His smooth, white forehead led to soft, pink cheeks and a pale chin. Dark, brown eyes stared back at him. "Sure you are."

"Yes, I am. I talked with a researcher at the state archives, and she looked up my family. We go back to before the Civil War; one of my ancestors was Mulatto. So that means somewhere back in time, my great, great, great, great, grandfather or mother was Black."

Leon smiled and started laughing. "Hey, Jacob," he yelled to the young man who had returned to the seat behind the passenger seat in the back of the Camaro. "We got a brother up in here."

"Really," Jacob said. "He don't look Black at all."

"Naw," Leon said as he eyed Skid from head to toe, "I see it. He's one of us." Then, he offered his hand to Skid and said, "Welcome to the revolution."

Skid smiled. The big man's hand wrapped around his, and the long fingers almost touched.

"Thanks," Skid said. He shook Leon's hand just as Rod had taught him what seemed a lifetime ago.

Leon and Jacob laughed, and Skid joined in.

"Yeah, we showed that cop, didn't we?" Skid said.

"Yep, we bad to the bone," Leon said, still laughing and trying to catch his breath.

Chapter 62

"Where do you think you're goin'?" Dee Dee asked.

Skid stood next to the Nomad. He glanced at his face in the distorted mirror image in the chrome fins as he circled to the passenger side. He stopped to check the black eye and small cut on his chin the cop had gifted him. Both were still healing. He smiled and winced in pain. His jaw felt loose, and he was glad he still had all his teeth.

"I'm not sure. Just drive." He said as he closed the car's rear hatch.

"Aren't you scared?" She asked. She wore her McDonald's uniform top and black pants. She was on her way to her four to midnight shift.

"No, not really. Whatever it is that I need ain't here."

He searched his pocket for the keys and looked at the dashboard. The keyring dangled from the ignition. *When did he put that there?* He asked himself.

"I wanna go with you," Dee Dee said. "I mean, I've been thinkin' about it, and it's time for me to go too."

"You've got college, and your dorm room is set up. So, no, you stay here. But, hey, I'll send you postcards from along the way."

"You need to stay here." Dee Dee was emphatic.

"I'll be careful," he assured her. Then, he flashed a roll of cash at her. "And I'm goin' to have fun."

"You can't flash that at people," she said with a motherly tone. "They'll..."

"I'm joking. I'll be careful. No more than twenty dollars in my pocket at any given time."

Satisfied that she'd imparted as much wisdom as possible, Dee Dee said, "Well, okay then. So where are you goin'?"

Skid took a quarter from his pocket and flipped it into the air. "Heads it's West, and tails is East." He caught the coin in the palm of his hand. "Looks like it's West."

He threw his bag on the back seat. It was a canvas overnighter his mother had bought him for his fifteenth birthday. It was the last present she'd given him. Next to the bag was a copy of his script for "The Waltons" and his diploma. He didn't know why he felt it was necessary to carry them with him on his trip, but something in his mind told him it would be a good idea.

Skid opened the door and turned over the engine. "Could you check on the place from time to time?" He asked Dee Dee. "Mr. Cox is almost finished boxing up his stuff. There may be some other car owners coming around. I left a note pinned to the shed door for them to give you a call."

From where the car was parked, the edge of Captain Cox's Airstream peeked around the edge of the shed. He was a late sleeper, so he was several hours away from getting back to organizing the workshop.

She dangled her key ring in front of him. "I've got it. When will you be back?"

"I'm not sure," he said as he checked his rearview mirror. "When it feels right."

Skid looked at her as Dee Dee leaned against the passenger side door. She had a quizzical look, and for a moment, he thought she might go with him.

"Be good," Dee Dee said as she moved her hand from the handle and patted the top of the car door.

"And if you can't be good, don't get caught," Skid said with a smile.

He turned on the radio and heard Rockin' Rudy say, "The third album from the young man from New Jersey that has the rock world on its ear. So, I'll let Bruce Springsteen's new 'Born to Run' track just because I can. I'll be back with you in about forty minutes."

A plaintive harmonica trickled from the speakers behind the back seat, followed by a poignant piano. Bruce's voice sent chills up Skid's back as he described a young man escaping with his girl from a small town with too many memories to a better time and place.

Skid looked in the rearview mirror and thought he saw Connie as she walked past the porch swing. He didn't believe in ghosts but knew the power of magical thinking and how he felt then. He blinked, and his girlfriend sat next to him. She'd hung her arm out the open window as she always did.

It was too perfect. The song's lyrics mimicked his fantasy that Connie was still with him and their lives together would be long and prosperous. But was all this really happening?

And then he knew he'd think of Connie every time he heard that song. She would be with him forever, and he had Bruce to thank for that. So he set a new goal. He'd write something that would affect someone the way that song touched him.

He felt the weight of his loss in his left shoulder blade. He would stretch his arm and twist it at the elbow, but there was no relief. Skid raised his shoulder and could feel the bones crack and slide against each other. He held so much tension in his shoulder and neck. He pulled his shoulder up again, and it popped.

He glanced in the mirror and saw Dee Dee standing near the porch. She'd leaned her bike against the post. She smiled and waved, but Skid saw lines creasing on her forehead. Was she worried about him? Did she think he might never come back?

Skid's thoughts returned to Connie's specter. Would she ride with him all the way? Memory fades, and people, no matter how consequential, may be lost in the fog of daily life. Skid hoped that wouldn't be the case with Connie. She had been a good friend, his first love, and his first sex. They would be bonded forever.

And then he considered how the song had created the scene in his mind's eye, probably just as it had for Springsteen. The words and emotions of the song resonated in Skid's imagination, and he filled in the blanks with his own characters and experiences. Connie had skipped past the place on the porch where Joseph had hung himself, bringing more depth and pathos into the song than Springsteen had portrayed. This is how artists reshape the world and make sense of it all to them. That's how art strikes a chord with another person. In that case, the art could create something that could only happen to them in the listener's or reader's imagination.

Skid realized at that moment just how powerful human creativity might be and how he wanted to reshape and better understand his world by expressing his talent.

The young man gunned the engine and popped the clutch. Gravel sprayed from the back tires, and Skid let out a "whoop" as he laughed. The cattle gate clanged together as they always did as he crossed it. He hit the gas and left snake-like skid marks on the two lanes in front of the farm.

Chapter 63

The coin toss would always send him West, even if it took two out of three flips.

First, Skid had to drive northwest, knowing he'd soon connect with Route 66. He'd heard of the legendary highway and understood you could follow it to the Santa Monica Pier and the Pacific Ocean. In addition, he'd read an article about how the route was a ribbon of hope for victims of the Dust Bowl and the Depression in the 1930s. The travelers expected their journey would provide them with an opportunity for work and prosperity in California.

And he knew the old song, *Get Your Kicks on Route 66* by Nat King Cole. That song was nothing like Springsteen's stories about leaving for hope and freedom. Instead, this jaunty tune made it sound like Route 66 was a kicky, hip place that only exists in a musician's imagination.

The trip would take days, so he stopped at the Music Shop, a small business next to Goldstein's. He may have *wanted* the Nat King Cole song for the journey but *needed* the Springsteen album. He peeled off seven ones from his "travelin' money" roll and purchased a copy of *Born to Run*. The cellophane wrap required slashing the end with the car key, but soon he'd freed the tape. He pushed the white plastic cassette into the machine and raised the volume.

Skid played the tape repeatedly. From the opening song *Thunder Road* to *Tenth Avenue Freeze-Out* to *Night* to *Backstreets*, to side two opening with *Born to Run* to *She's the One* to *Meeting Across the River* and ending with the cinematic *Jungleland*, the songs spoke to him like nothing ever had before.

And after hearing the album for the tenth time, he found his eyes welling up and his chest tightening. Skid whispered along with the song lyrics to *Born to Run* and had to pull over. He was near a stand of trees whose branches seemed to reach out toward the road. Tears flowed, and he knew if he did become a writer someday, he'd want readers to feel just like he felt that moment.

Skid crossed the Tennessee/Missouri state line on Highway 60, eventually joining 66 in Springfield. A light rain ended, and he pulled over at a gas station to fill up and check the oil. He'd recently driven across the Mississippi River. He remembered how Siddhartha's journey on a similar tributary helped him learn and accept life's challenges. He acknowledged the teacher's beliefs that the self is continually transforming and that, most importantly, no one is broken, merely human.

Springsteen's music and Skid's replaying of the novel's events helped him find shape and the depth of his emotions. The abstract images allowed him the distance he needed to sort through all that had happened. His mother and father had died, and his stepfather and girlfriend had betrayed him. And now they were dead, too. He had never felt so alone yet connected to life as he did right then. Could he ever write something that could move people's emotions like Hesse and Springsteen?

The ribbon of asphalt, split with a single dotted line, seemed to move under the wheels of his mother's car. And yet, he sat motionless and serene under the driver's wheel. He glanced in the rearview mirror and only saw his reflection. His sunglasses rode high on his nose, and when he took them off, he could see how clear and focused his eyes were.

He came upon a truck carrying a tractor on a flatbed trailer. He imagined how that machine would soon be repaired and deliver years of service for some hardworking farmer. How much easier would this farmer's life be with the wonder of modern machinery?

Skid again considered Rod's suggestion that maybe his best path was to work in the shop, and for a moment, he slowed and turned the steering wheel toward the ditch. He'd do a U-turn, return home, and continue Rod's business. It was the logical choice, and he knew that, after a short time, he'd be able to provide a good life for himself.

And then he imagined a conversation with his mother about studying to become a mechanic. Of course, she would be supportive and say she just wanted Clarence to be happy with whatever he chose to do with his life. But was this his best path?

He checked the road behind him and tapped the gas pedal. The setting sun shone red as it set over the mountains.

His time on the road made Skid think about how people always worry about the future when we already know our lot. It's the amount of time we have on earth that we don't know. He finally concluded that, for most people, the fear of death is deadened by the fear of living. He recalled how he'd faced death on his trip down the side of Tiger Hill on his bicycle. He'd survived and vowed now that he wouldn't be one of those people afraid of living.

Chapter 64

As the hours passed, he noticed how the green foliage of the mid-west gave way to a tan and dry desert. The highway stretched to a vanishing point. The hills and valleys of home were lush and undulating, but this flat and desolate land seemed from another world. It felt like he might never reach the end and would drive forever.

And the towns along the way were so different. Brick and siding houses gave way to adobe-clad homes. The walls appeared thick and sturdy compared to the buildings back home.

Skid stopped at Clanton's Café in Oklahoma and had lunch at the bar next to a man who looked as old as the hills. His dusty overalls smelled like oil. He told Skid how he'd worked on the rigs for decades. The aroma reminded him of Rod's coveralls and how they were part of his expertise.

Customers filled the booths and bar for the noon-time lunch. Skid knew what it was like working in a hamburger place at that hour and found the staff there courteous and efficient. It was a pleasure watching them work.

Skid caught a whiff of the old man's body order as he lifted his arm to take a bite. The man didn't seem to care.

"Plenty of money and not enough time," the old man said as he sopped up Ketchup with his French fries.

"Too much time and not enough money for most of us," Skid said.

The old man chuckled and took a sip of his iced tea. "Where you headed?"

"I've never seen the ocean," Skid said. "I've never seen the Grand Canyon."

"Sounds like you've never seen much of anything," the old man said.

Skid glanced at the old man and ate his club sandwich.

"It's time I looked at that big, old hole in the ground."

The wildcatter turned and stopped chewing. His eyes sparkled, and he smiled as he said, "It'll change your life."

Skid remembered in Siddhartha how the old man who operated the ferry dispensed wisdom and welcomed the young man into the fold of seekers of truth. The oilman would be a stand-in for Skid.

Back on the road, Skid thought about how often his life changed. Now, he was a high school graduate. No one could take that away from him. But he was an orphan now, and that will never change. He'd had a first love and made love for the first time, which would never change.

Chapter 65

While the Grand Canyon wasn't on Route 66, Skid studied his map on the motel room bed and decided the South rim would be the best choice for him to detour and visit. But, as he approached, the immensity of the location overcame him. Finally, he pulled into an observation point parking lot and turned off the engine.

Skid sat for a moment and wished Connie was there with him. He knew she'd never seen this wonder of the world, and she would be just as awed by the sight as he was.

He opened the door and stepped on the brown river rock. He felt it crunch under his sneakers. He smelled the pine trees planted alongside the parking lot. Skid couldn't hear the water rushing through the canyon below him, but he knew it was there. He walked toward a wood rail fence and a marker.

The panel featured information about the depth and width of this part of the canyon and the animals that frequented the area. Skid looked up from the board and stared at the vast gash in the Earth. He had read that scientists didn't know how the chasm was formed. He knew it wasn't a miracle and that a working theory would be proposed to explain what happened someday.

Skid stared at the multicolored layers of rock leading down to the canyon floor. The height and slope reminded him of riding his bike down Tiger Hill. He remembered how he could feel his breath leaving his body for a moment and, for a second, believed he could see something. A glimpse of the edge of consciousness between breaths. A realization life and death are parted by a slender shadow veil.

Skid wondered if Rod's cousin Joseph shared that feeling as he took his last breath on the front porch. Would his body relax, and his mind finally find peace? Would Skid feel that same release?

He found himself on the other side of the fence. He didn't remember stepping over the railing and was surprised when he looked down at his feet inches from the edge. *What would it feel like to just let go*, he thought? How long would it take, and would he feel any pain? He remembered flying down Tiger Hill and how this feeling of being so close to the edge made him feel most alive. He inched forward and then heard something behind him. He turned and saw a fawn grazing near a clump of bushes. He could see the doe just beyond her baby, watching over it but still giving the offspring its freedom.

Skid took a step back, choosing the path of most resistance.

At that moment, he felt safe, loved, and fully alive.

He didn't understand that bike ride down the hill at the time, but now he did. His next breath was close to the shimmering veil between life and death. He blinked, and it was gone, but now he believed he could see something new in the slant of the setting sun. He turned his head and imagined what his mother might do if she stood beside him.

He remembered how their last conversation ended. "We all know the future," she said. "We die, but we don't know when. If we live a good life, the people who love us will miss us. In them, we live as long as we are remembered."

Skid believed she would explain how Rod had changed, and if he wasn't racked with guilt and pain, he would never have treated Skid the way he did if she were still alive. And he knew that he'd ultimately have to forgive Rod and live the rest of his life knowing he was just a human being, imperfect and impetuous.

And for a split second, he could imagine Connie there, too. He would have to forgive her and learn to move on with his life.

Chapter 66

Highway 66 soon became Los Angeles city streets. Skid had spent six days on the road, and the grind and long hours left him exhausted. But he knew where he had to go; deep down, he wanted to get there as fast as possible.

He entered the crowded parking lot and swung the Nomad into a slot. He scanned the space and watched families with beach towels, picnic baskets, and funny hats racing toward the sound of the water.

Skid walked down the gray planks, hearing the seagulls' " caws " and the waves rushing. There were dozens of the snow, white birds sitting on the top slats of the railing. A few dove from the top rail and swooped down to the beach as he passed. He took a deep breath of the fresh sea air.

He passed a brightly colored hot dog stand and smelled the meat and warm bread. He couldn't remember the last time he'd eaten, but he wasn't hungry.

Skid stopped at the end of the pier and squinted as he watched the orange sun slowly sink into the horizon. He smelled the salt in the air, felt the mist from the crashing waves, and let the dying sun warm his face. He'd come so far.

He grabbed the railing. Then, he followed the waves' approach as they broke on the beach, leaving white foam and smooth sand. And he couldn't keep from smiling.

"How about that?" Skid whispered.

A low rumbling behind him. "A storm?" he murmured. He focused his vision and scanned the sky. No clouds, and yet he heard thunder. But this sound had a metallic echo, and Skid couldn't place where it came from. The sound grew louder, and just as he turned, the skater fell off his board and said, "Dammit."

Skid walked over to the young man and helped him to his feet. "Are you all right?"

"Yeah, sorry," the skater said as he brushed off his clothes.

Skid could smell the aroma of weed as he stepped back. He'd tried the illegal substance a few times but didn't like the effect.

"What up, man?" the young man replied.

"Nothin'."

They watched a pod of dolphins break the surface and slip under. The animals moved with controlled abandon, in sync but wild.

The skater stood next to Skid and stared at the setting sun. "Beautiful, isn't it?"

"Beautiful," Skid said, "doesn't really cover it."

The skateboarder was shorter than Skid. He was thin and wore yellow board shorts. His muscle shirt exposed his tanned arms. He had freckles under his blue eyes, and when he turned to look at Skid, he smiled. Maybe his eyes were glazed because of the light bouncing off the waves, or maybe there was something else.

"Hi," he said. "My name is Kerry," offering his hand to Skid. He glanced down and noticed the young man had painted his nails. He observed that two of the colors of the man's fingernails were Connie's favorites: fire engine red and cotton candy pink. And he shook Kerry's hand just like Rod had taught him, firm but not hard enough to break bones and with three appropriate pumps before you let go.

"I've never seen anything like it," Skid said. His gaze returned to the sunset.

"First time in California?" Kerry asked.

Skid smiled. "First time anywhere."

"Cool, cool, cool," Kerry said. "You picked a good time of the year. The weather's perfect. Where are you from?"

Skid said. "I'm from Tennessee."

"Whoa, man. That's radical."

"How about you?" Skid asked.

"Wyoming."

"Wow," Skid said, genuinely surprised. "I would've never guessed that."

"I've been here awhile. What brings you out here?"

"I've never seen the ocean. It's big." Skid took a deep breath, swallowed, and said, "I feel so small."

"Groovy, man. The ocean puts everything in life in perspective," Kerry said with wonder. "Wait 'til you get up on a board. Then, oh man, surfin', it's like standin' in God's hand." The young man snapped into a pose, mimicking standing on a surfboard and riding a wave.

Skid smiled at the pantomime and said, "I'm sorry. My momma taught me better than that. I'm Clarence," He wore a thin, braided leather headband around his long, brown hair. Skid was sure it was a cultural, possibly even political statement. He thought, *maybe it's time for me to grow out my hair?*

"Clarence," Kerry said. He spun a wheel on his skateboard as it dangled from his hand. "Nice to meet you."

"But everybody calls me," and Skid paused for a moment. Looking at this alien land with so many new sights, smells, and sounds, maybe it was time to make a clean break. In truth, he'd never liked the nickname, and it only changed one letter, so he decided at that moment, "Skip, you can call me Skip."

"So, you're here to see the ocean. Now that you've seen it, what's next?"

"Well," he considered how honest and open he should be with someone he'd met three minutes before, but he decided to trust his gut. "I have a script for the TV show *The Waltons*. I'm gonna drop it off at their office. You never know."

"Ouch, that's a no-go, man," Kerry winced and frowned. "They can't read it."

It hadn't occurred to him that they would reject the script out of hand. He knew from writing letters to the newspaper editor that at least they would take a look at his work. "Why?"

"Oh man, not cool. The producers worry about getting sued by someone who could say the show stole their idea. Ya' gotta have a lawyer or an agent send it in."

"Oh," Skip said. His million-to-one chance at becoming a television writer just dropped to zero. He felt a tightening in his chest, and he swallowed hard. The shit just got real. "I didn't know that."

"How would you, man? Yeah, just part of the business. It's gnarly." Kerry's gaze dipped toward his worn-out Chuck Taylors. A bare big toe peeked through a hole in the shoe's white rubber cap. "I'm a sophomore in the UCLA film program. I could get one of my professors to read a few pages and let you know if you're ready to start pitching agents."

Skip remembered Miss Cardwell's reaction to reading his script. She said she could see the story unfolding just as it might look in an episode of *The Waltons*. She understood the character's conflicts and complimented him on his resolution.

She said it was good. Miss Cardwell reminded him that she was asked to read it and he should always be thankful for people's time and attention. She could have said no. Skip thanked her and nodded in agreement. "I'll remember."

Miss Cardwell noted one more thing about the script. She said she remembered a famous quote about artists. "An audience may forget what you said or did, but people will always remember how you made them feel."

Kerry gripped the pier's top board. He put his foot on the second plank.

"Why would you talk to your professor like that for me?" Skip asked. He was genuinely awed by Kerry offering help to a stranger.

"I'm a good judge of character, and you seem like a righteous dude. And, hey, movie makin' is all about connections and talent," Kerry said, nodding as if he'd got approval from the community. "Have you got talent?"

"I'm not, ahhh," he considered turning down the offer, then said, "Yeah, I do. I'd appreciate whatever you could do. That'd be great."

"About your script. The other day, my professor said in class that what matters more than what your story says is how it makes the reader feel. So how does your script make *you* feel?"

Skip couldn't believe Kerry was paraphrasing Miss Cardwell. "Alive."

Kerry said, "Whoa, so cool. That's good, man. I can't wait to read it."

They looked at the final light beams as the sun slipped below the horizon. The sky glowed red with traces of orange.

"Wow, can you believe it," Kerry said, "that happens every day."

"Wow," Skip said and smiled as a single tear dropped from the corner of his eye. "Beautiful."

"Yeah, man, even with all the bad stuff that can happen," Kerry said as he tucked a lock of hair behind his ear. "Ya know, it's such a righteous world."

Skip realized he loved his life, and given all he'd been through and seen, he had a story to tell about this crazy world. He could write about finding out he had a Black ancestor and how he wondered about what happened when his father left him and why. He could write about loving Connie. He could write about Rod and Joseph and how the war affected them.

Finally, he could find satisfaction in expressing himself, and that was what mattered. It may not mean anything to anybody but him, but he would say it.

He nodded and said, "Yeah, my stepfather used to say I wasn't worth killin'. You believe that?"

"Oh, no, man," Kerry said, "that's not right."

Skip sighed deeply, "No, that's not right."

The sun drew their attention again. Kerry pulled sunglasses from his shirt pocket and put them on. "Gotta ramble," he said, letting the skateboard fall from his hand.

"How hard is it to ride that thing?"

"Not hard," he said, turning and placing his foot on the board. "It takes some practice. And you'll fall down a lot until you get the hang of it."

Skip remembered something Miss Black had said, "Nana korobi ya oki'."

"Whoa, cool," Kerry said, "What does that mean?"

"Fall down seven times and get up eight."

"Nana korobi ya oki'," the skater said as he pushed off. "Let's go get that script."

Skip turned and followed Kerry as the skateboard wheels rumbled down the pier. He took off his shirt and felt the sun's rays on his shoulders. He walked as fast as he could but soon found himself running. He pumped his arms, trying to keep up with Kerry as the skater crouched and extended his arms as if he might take flight.

"Wha whoooooo," Kerry yelled.

Skip ran and laughed, "Wha whoooooo!" Then, he yelled at the top of his lungs, "Wha WHOOOOOOOO!"

END

Leave a Review

I hope you enjoy this novel—if you do, I'd appreciate it if you could write a short review. Your ratings make a difference for authors; you're helping other readers find books they might enjoy.

You can rate this book or leave a review at:

Amazon

www.amazon.com

Goodreads

https://www.goodreads.com/#_=_

Barnes and Noble

https://www.barnesandnoble.com/

Or your preferred retailer.

And check out https://www.randyobrienwriter.com/

For more information.

Thanks.

Other fine books available from Histria Fiction:

 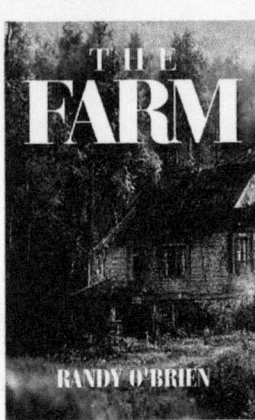 

 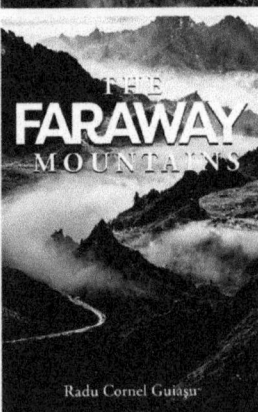 

For these and many other great books visit

HistriaBooks.com